COMING HOME SERIES - BOOK TWO

Coming Home to Truth

MICHELLE DE BRUIN

Published by Scrivenings Press LLC
15 Lucky Lane
Morrilton, Arkansas 72110
https://ScriveningsPress.com

Printed in the United States of America

Paperback ISBN 978-1-64917-208-2

eBook ISBN 978-1-64917-209-9

Editors: Erin R. Howard, Linda Fulkerson

Cover by Linda Fulkerson, bookmarketinggraphics.com

All characters are fictional, and any resemblance to real people, either factual or historical, is purely coincidental.

All scriptures are taken from the KING JAMES VERSION (KJV): KING JAMES VERSION, public domain.

To young women on the adventure of discovering who they really are.

My soul magnifies the Lord,
And my spirit has rejoiced in God my Savior.
For He has regarded the lowly state of His maidservant;
For behold, henceforth all generations will call me blessed.
For He who is mighty has done great things for me,
And holy is His name.
Luke 1:47-49

LIST OF CHARACTERS

The Jones Family from Silver Grove

- Lacy—Lacy Jones
- Roy—Roy Jones, Lacy's father
- Maria—Maria Jones, Lacy's mother
- Cal—Cal Jones, Lacy's brother

The Citizens of Oswell City

- Agnes Rose Harper—Lacy's best friend
- Conrad Van Drunen, Markus and Betje—The town carpenter and his children
- Logan De Witt—the local pastor
- Karen De Witt—Logan's wife and Lacy's former teacher
- Matthew and Margaret Kaldenberg—the doctor and his wife
- Dan and Ruth Van Drunen—Conrad's brother and his wife

- Nick and Hannah Van Drunen—Conrad's brother and his wife
- Eva Synderhof—Seamstress and owner of the dress shop

1

Silver Grove, Iowa
July, 1917

"Ready to celebrate?" Lacy Jones's brother, Cal, wrapped an arm around her shoulders. "Grandpa and Grandma have arrived."

"Almost. I need a few more minutes to myself. So many memories of my senior year of high school are here. I have this feeling that everything is about to change." Lacy glanced at the pennant on her bedroom wall proudly displaying the name of the Bridgewater Springs High School. "Look at this." She pointed to a cluster of flowers. Dried and faded, the corsage she'd worn to the senior banquet hung nearby. The tassel from her graduation cap dangled from another pin.

"It's the photos that impress me." Cal gestured to the pictures that covered the top of the dresser. "I can't believe you took all of these. You are quite talented." In one of the photos, Mama and Dad stood in front of the house, dressed in their best on her graduation day. Another photo displayed friends from her graduating class. More photos captured the landscape.

She sighed. "If only I had frames to put them in. But frames are expensive." She'd seen the prices on the various frames available for sale at Carter's General Store in Silver Grove. They had a particularly lovely line that Lacy adored. Tillie Carter had explained to her that they were a brand known as Angel Frames. Made of smooth dark wood with a little ornament in the shape of an angel situated in one corner. Lacy wanted one in every size.

Her shoulders slumped as she studied the pictures. As a farm girl, she had no way to put her hard-won education to use making enough money to buy such an extravagance.

"Lacy? Cal? Are you coming? We're waiting." Maria Jones's call rang down the hallway to Lacy's bedroom.

Cal released his hold on her shoulders. "Mama's looking for us."

She'd better heed Mama and stop dallying in her room. But today, the day she turned eighteen, marked the end of all she'd ever known. Childhood was behind her. High school was behind her. Most of these summer months since graduation were behind her. The time of her life had come to discover a direction and decide what she should do.

"Happy birthday!" Shouts from her cousins filled the farmhouse's large kitchen.

Grandma Jones came forward and placed a kiss on Lacy's cheek. "You've grown into a lovely young lady."

"Thank you, Grandma." Heat warmed Lacy's face, but she managed a smile.

"Here's a seat for you." Cal pulled out the chair next to his.

Agnes Harper, Lacy's best friend from high school, prompted from across the table. "It's time to blow out your candles."

Lacy glanced up in time to watch Mama set the birthday

cake before her. Eighteen reminders of her age blazed on top. The group sang while she inhaled. With one breath, she extinguished every flame. Her guests cheered.

Mama reached for the knife and cut the white cake into even slices. Dad produced a cooler of homemade ice cream and added a scoop to each plate.

"It's so nice of you to come for my party." Lacy smiled at the group as they ate. Plain country people. Every one of them.

"We're happy to help you celebrate. Eighteen is a turning point in a young lady's life." Grandma smiled back.

Her grandparents lived on a nearby farm. So did her aunts and uncles. Even Agnes and her family lived in a simple little house on the edge of a tiny town. Her father worked at a mill instead of farming like Lacy's father did. But Agnes's family didn't have much more than Lacy's.

Maybe that's why the two girls discovered a friendship in high school. Few of their country school classmates had gone on to town to pursue a high school education. Lacy had been relieved to find a friend who understood scarcity.

"Tell us about Bible College. What are you studying?" One of Lacy's uncles directed his question to Cal.

He laid down his fork and answered with fancy words Lacy couldn't begin to comprehend. "I have one more year left."

Serving a church had been Cal's dream ever since his eighth-grade year. Tillie Carter's brother had lived in Silver Grove during that time and had influenced Cal. Tillie's brother had also married the best teacher Lacy had ever known.

Miss Karen Millerson had tutored Lacy through sickness and given her extra instruction so that she could keep up with her classes. Lacy would never have gotten to high school without her help.

"Time to open gifts." Mama worked to clear Lacy's plate away and then set a stack of presents in front of her while her cousins cheered.

"I'll start with this one." Lacy picked up a small square package.

"It's from us," one of the little girls said.

Lacy unwrapped it and found a pretty pin with blue, pink, and green rhinestones on it. "Thank you," she said to her small cousin, and the girl beamed.

Lacy continued to open her gifts. Grandparents gave her clothes. The girls gave her handkerchiefs. Agnes gave her a lace dresser scarf.

Cal's gift came next. She opened it to discover a brown box inside. It looked much like the one she'd bought used. "A new camera!" Her voice rose as weightlessness filled her chest. "How did you ever afford it?"

He laughed. "That's a secret. But the one you have now is starting to look worn out. With so many flowers in bloom and green leaves on the trees, I'm sure you will find plenty of uses for a new one."

"I will. Thank you." Flowers and leaves. Clouds and birds. Friends and family. Lacy would certainly find uses for her brand-new treasure.

She reached for the last package and unwrapped it. Her breath froze in her lungs as she held the contents up and studied it.

After several quiet moments, Mama spoke. "What's wrong? Don't you like it?"

Lacy glanced at Mama. "Like it?" Her words came in a whisper. "I love it. I've always wanted one. It's beautiful."

"Mrs. Carter over at the store calls it an Angel Frame. She said they're made right here in Iowa. With all your picture takin', your dad and I figured you could find somethin' to put in it."

Lacy traced her finger along the edges of the shiny angel in the corner. Tiny wings etched with a lace design shimmered in the light from the windows.

Her stomach tightened as she looked around the room. Repurposed flour sacks made into curtains hung at the windows. Furniture older than Lacy filled the rooms. Worn rugs covered the floors near the sink and the doorways. Mama's dress, and Lacy's, too, were faded and washed thin in places. The new, sparkly Angel Frame was a luxury far out of place in these surroundings.

Lacy pushed the frame away. "I'm not sure I should keep it. Maybe I should return it and use the money for other things." She gulped at the thought of parting with the beautiful creation.

Mama and Dad exchanged a meaningful glance with each other before Dad cleared his throat. "Lacy, we want the best for you that we can possibly give. Keep the frame and enjoy it as a special gift from us on our daughter's eighteenth birthday."

She blinked back tears and nodded.

Tears glistened in Mama's eyes, too, but she stood and wiped them away. "Now that Lacy has opened her gifts, let's move this party outside so the kids can play."

Others around the table followed Mama's lead. Soon plates were stacked on the counter and silverware was soaking in the sink. Lacy carefully lifted her new camera out of its wrappings and ran outside.

"Let me take your picture," she said to aunts chatting with Mama on the porch. Then she asked the same from cousins playing games in the yard. She worked her way over to Agnes who lounged in the shade of a tree.

"I suppose you'll want me to pose for you." Agnes sat straighter.

"No. Stay right there. I want a picture of you just as you are." Lacy held her camera to her eye and clicked a photo.

"Don't show that to my mother. She'll get upset with me for not looking like the proper lady she raised me to be." Agnes gave Lacy a teasing glare.

Lacy laughed. "I won't. But this picture captures you. Agnes Harper from Meadow Creek. Confident. Relaxed. Happy."

Agnes chuckled. "I'd be happier if people would remember to call me by my middle name."

Lacy frowned. "What do you mean?"

"My full name is Agnes Rose Harper. I'm named after two great-grandmas with old-fashioned Victorian names. Why a mother would do that to a person I don't know. Who names their little girl Agnes?" she said the name like it was a disease.

"I think it is a pretty name." Lacy shrugged.

"It makes me sound old. I like Rose better. Now that I'm out of high school and all grown up, I'm going by my middle name. People may call me Rose." Agnes, or rather, Rose, sat up with a straight back and lifted chin as if to defy anyone who dared to default to her first name.

"I'll try my best to remember." Lacy lowered herself to the grass and leaned against the tree trunk.

Rose pulled a folded paper from her pocket. "A letter came from my aunt Helen today."

"What did she say?" Lacy asked.

"Do you know that I've been accepted to the college at Clear Brook to study to become a teacher?"

Lacy nodded.

"Well, my parents couldn't afford the full tuition. If the school was close enough for me to live at home, I could hold a job and still attend school. Aunt Helen learned of my predicament somehow. She and Uncle Lester live in Oswell City, the nearest town to Clear Brook."

"I remember you telling me they moved away from here a few years ago." Lacy polished the lens on her camera before setting it down on the grass.

"In her letter, Aunt Helen invited me to live with them during the school year." Rose smiled.

Lacy frowned. "How will you get to the college if it is in another town?"

"Aunt Helen says several other young people from Oswell City travel together to the college. I can ride along with them." Rose's smile grew wider.

"That sounds like a wonderful plan." Lacy fought the slump that wanted to dominate her. If she was smart enough, she would train to become a skilled seamstress, or a writer, or maybe even a journalist for a newspaper. She stifled a sigh. So many possibilities, but she had so many limitations.

"Maybe I'll meet Miss Millerson again. She moved to Oswell City, too, didn't she? It's because of her that I want to become a teacher. She helped Mama save my life one night when I was sick with a fever. The trouble is, I don't remember her married name. Maybe I won't be able to find her again." Rose picked at the grass near her skirt.

"De Witt." The name burst from Lacy's mouth.

"What?" Rose glanced at her.

"Miss Millerson's married name is De Witt. She married a preacher. His sister is Mrs. Tillie Carter at the store in Silver Grove."

"Oh, yeah. I remember now. He was friends with my dad. Helped him quit drinking. It worked. Well, most of the time." Rose lowered her head and went back to picking at the grass.

Lacy watched her friend with an ache in her heart. She'd been the only other girl in the high school who knew Rose's painful secret. Their classmates could boast of fathers who were businessmen, lawyers, and leaders. Rose's father was a struggling drunk. He'd do well for weeks and months at a time, not even looking at a bottle. But then he'd go home and surprise Rose, her mother, and her two brothers with the smell of whiskey on his breath.

Rose had always appeared perfectly groomed with no

evidence of bruises or battering. Lacy never could bring herself to ask Rose if her father ever physically harmed her.

Lacy shuddered. Her family might be poor, but at least her father didn't drink. She couldn't imagine what life must be like with a father who did.

"Hey, you know what?" Rose leaned closer.

Lacy shook her head.

"You should come with me."

Lacy blinked. "What, me?"

Rose nodded. "Yes, of course, you. We both want to see Miss Millerson again, don't we?"

"Well ... yes ... sure."

"Here's your chance." Rose lounged again, propping herself up on one arm.

"Rose ... I ... I don't know. This scheme would be too much of a surprise to Mama. And well, my family doesn't have the money to send me anywhere. They can barely scrape enough together to keep Cal in school."

Rose shrugged. "Then get a job when you get there. You've always hoped to be independent and make your own way."

"Yes, I have. But I ... I mean ... you know I'm not smart enough to do anything very important." She glanced at her camera. Too bad picture taking didn't count. "I'm just an ordinary girl from a poor farm family. I struggled so much with schoolwork that decent grades were almost impossible. As much as I want to, I don't see how I can break out of ... out of ... this." At a loss for a better explanation, Lacy gestured at the scene before her.

Her mother wore a patched apron, even on this special occasion. The barns and small house were all weather beaten and in desperate need of fresh coats of paint. Poverty and the limited opportunities that went along with it—those were her destiny.

Rose sat up again and held both of Lacy's hands. "It's the

same for me. But this invitation from Aunt Helen is my one chance. It might be yours too. Let's do it."

Lacy glanced away from her friend and looked at the farmstead she'd always known. Going along with Rose meant leaving home. Is that what she wanted? What awaited her on the other end? Did Oswell City have any opportunities for a girl like her, someone weak in academics? What work could she do?

"Where would I stay?" She turned her attention back to her friend.

"Aunt Helen would give you a room. She works at some large house where people live until they find a home of their own. It would be perfect for you."

"Well, I guess. If I have a place to stay it might work." Lacy lowered her gaze to the ground. If she didn't have to shell out the money for a hotel, she could see her parents cooperating a little better with this plan.

"Say you'll come with me." Rose squeezed both of Lacy's hands.

"Let's talk to my parents first." Lacy stood and led her friend across the yard. "Mama, could I please talk to you and Dad?" Lacy tugged on her sleeve to interrupt the conversation with the other women.

"I suppose. Where is he?" Mama shifted her attention to the cluster of men.

"He's getting ready to go to the barn with the others." Lacy shielded her eyes from the sun and waved to her father with her other hand.

"Roy!" Mama called.

He lifted his head to look in their direction.

"Come here!" She joined Lacy in waving at him.

Dad tipped his hat to one of the other men and left the group. His long strides carried him to the place where Lacy stood with Mama and Rose.

"Lacy says she wants to talk to us." Mama looked at her.

She licked her lips and dove in, unable to meet the gazes of her parents. "Agnes, I mean Rose. She wants to go by her middle name now. Anyway, she got a letter from her aunt in Oswell City inviting her to stay with them so that she can go to college. Oswell City is where Miss Millerson lives. You remember her, don't you, Mama? Rose and I both want to see her again, so Rose asked me to go with her. May I?"

Dad leaned away from her and looked to the sky.

Mama's hand fluttered to her chest. "Oh, my. I never thought that plans to leave us would be part of your birthday party." She looked at her husband. "What do you say?"

Dad sucked in a deep breath. "I don't know. Is this what you want, Lacy?"

Her insides tingled. "I never really thought of it before Rose mentioned the idea. But I can see that it might be fun."

"Where would you stay?" Mama asked.

"Aunt Helen would give her a room." Rose shrugged.

"Have you checked with your aunt?" Mama gave Rose a stern look.

"No, not yet. But I will. I'm sure it won't be any problem." Rose waved her hand around as if to dismiss any difficulties.

"How will you travel?" Dad's gaze bore into Rose.

"On the train."

Dad's attention shifted to Lacy. "Where will you get the money for your ticket? You know all of our extra funds are tied up in Cal's schooling."

"She'll get a job when she gets there and pay you back." Rose's announcement carried a high level of assurance.

"A job!" Mama's eyes grew round as she looked at Dad.

Lacy held up a hand to silence her friend. "I got some money for my birthday. I could use that. It would cover most of the cost. Maybe you could make up the difference."

Dad folded his arms across his chest. "Now, Lacy. You heard what I said. We have to pay for Cal's school."

"I know." Lacy hung her head.

"What's this I hear about Lacy needing money?" Grandma asked from her place on the swing.

"It's nothing, Ma. We'll take care of it." Dad's eyes narrowed.

"How much do you need?" Grandma turned around and pushed her glasses up.

"Two dollars," Lacy ventured to answer in spite of Dad's frown.

"Grandpa could help you with that. What are you buying?" Grandma's brows rose.

"Lacy wants a train ticket so that she can travel with her friend to visit a former teacher." Mama's tone declared the idea as risky.

"That sounds like fun. Let me talk with Grandpa and see if he can't loan you two dollars." Grandma patted Dad's arm as she passed him.

He blew out an exasperated breath.

"Does this mean she can go?" Mama looked at him.

He ran his hand through his hair. "I suppose. She's eighteen now. If she has the money and a traveling companion, I don't have the right to hold her back."

Rose squealed.

"Thank you, Dad." Lacy gave him a hug, but he remained stiff in her embrace.

Grandma returned and placed two bills in Lacy's hand. "Two dollars straight from Grandpa's wallet."

"Ma, really. You didn't have to do that." Dad growled. A softness in his eyes undermined his words. He might be angry with Grandma, but his love for Lacy shone through. His words from earlier that day came back to her. *We want the best for you that we can possibly give.*

Lacy's heart constricted. Mama and Dad sacrificed so much for her to have nice things.

"Nonsense. Consider it part of your birthday gift. Now go and have a good time." Grandma patted her shoulder.

"Don't stay away too long. Only take enough time for a good visit with your teacher." Mama shook her finger. "Then come home."

Lacy nodded.

Rose tugged on her arm. "Come on. Let's go take a look at your dresses. You have the perfect hat for traveling that will look nice with the jacket you wear on Sundays."

Dread threatened to twist her stomach, but she willed it away and followed Rose to her room. She was eighteen now. Grown up. She should look forward to this first venture into the wide and waiting world.

2

Des Moines, Iowa
August, 1917

Conrad Van Drunen's chest filled with warmth as he listened to the kind words coming from Mr. Gresham. He pushed away from the table and stood up to receive the other man's handshake. "Thank you for negotiating a new contract with me this afternoon. The items you asked for will be delivered by the end of the month."

"Fine. I'll be watching for them. The furniture and household goods from your woodworking shop are selling well. Our department store is happy to work with talented young men like yourself." Mr. Gresham poked his cigar into his mouth.

"We'll be in touch. Thanks for coming in today." Mr. Blaine, the other partner in Gresham, Blaine, and Company, shook Conrad's hand as well.

Conrad offered the men a smile and tipped his hat to them as he left the building. He stepped onto the street and walked to his car. Dropping his briefcase onto the seat, Conrad blew out a breath. He'd actually secured another contract with one of the largest department stores in the country. His skills at building furniture and items of household décor were becoming known.

If the terms of the negotiation he'd signed today developed the way he expected, Conrad would become a very wealthy man. Several moments of silence passed as he leaned against the car hood absorbing the facts. He'd never been in want of funds, thanks to his handyman job, but now he could offer his children, Markus and Betje, luxuries belonging to a whole new standard of living.

Thoughts of his son and daughter spurred him to action. He must drive home tonight and resume care for them as soon as possible. His sister-in-law had agreed to take the children home with her after school and to feed them their supper, but Conrad missed Markus and Betje. He wanted to be on hand to hear the stories from their school day and tuck them into bed.

He gave his car a crank, slid behind the driver's seat, and started the engine. Then he pulled into the street and guided his Ford through the busy intersections of downtown Des Moines. Smells of meat cooking wafted on the summer air. His stomach rumbled as he scanned signs on the restaurants lining the street. He should stop for something to eat before heading out into the countryside for his trip home.

But staying in town for a meal would delay his arrival in Oswell City by at least another hour. He didn't want to wait that long to see his family. Maybe his brother's wife would take pity on him and heat some leftovers when he came to pick up his children.

Conrad kept driving and turned onto the street that ran along the back of the train station. Porters scurried in all directions. Carts and wagons occupied the parking spaces near the depot. People milled around the vehicles carrying satchels and pieces of luggage. A train must have recently arrived. If only his meeting had lasted fifteen more minutes. Then he could have avoided this congestion. But then the extra time would've put him even farther behind in getting home to his children.

He shifted his attention to the scene through his windshield. Two young women stepped off the curb, and one of them tripped and fell into the street—right in his lane.

Conrad's eyes bugged. A jerk of the steering wheel swerved him into the other lane. Oncoming cars honked. A man shouted.

A turn of the wheel brought him back into the right lane. He slowed and glanced behind him as his car drove over an uneven patch in the street. The young lady still lay face down. Her companion knelt beside her. Conrad parked and looked out his back window. He'd better get out and see if he could help.

All kinds of fears assaulted him. What if she was injured? Maybe she'd need to go to the hospital. He'd never called an ambulance in the city before. What should he do if she had broken bones or was knocked unconscious? A policeman would know what to do. He scanned the sidewalk in search of one, but he approached the two women before spotting any police.

"Are you all right?" Conrad knelt next to the companion. "May I help you?"

"Lacy tripped on the curb. I don't think she's hurt too bad. She's been talking to me." The friend looked at him. Her brow smoothed and her eyes lit up with an emotion Conrad couldn't quite name. Was it admiration? Interest?

He shifted his attention off her face as relief flowed over him. At least the girl in the street hadn't been knocked unconscious. Talking was a good sign. He settled a hand on her shoulder as she rolled onto her side. But he'd need to stay alert where her friend was concerned. She continued to watch him as though he was someone she'd like to know better.

"Rose? Where are you?" Lacy's voice trembled.

"Right here. Do you think you can get up?" Rose tore her gaze from Conrad and spoke to her friend.

"I'll try." Lacy closed her eyes as if concentrating on how to accomplish the effort. Then she pushed away from the asphalt. Her skirts twisted around her legs. She wouldn't be able to return to a standing position without assistance.

"Let me help you." Conrad wrapped his arm around her waist and lifted her to her feet. She leaned on him, blinking and shaking her head.

"Did you hit your head?" Rose asked.

She raised her hand to her forehead. "No, I don't think so. I have a bit of a headache, but it isn't from a bump on the pavement."

"You should sit down." Conrad led the girls to a park bench near the entrance to the train station.

Lacy gasped. "Where is my satchel?"

Rose glanced at the street. "I'll find it."

Conrad settled Lacy on the bench and sat next to her. "I wish I had a cool drink to offer you."

"I'm sure I'll be fine in a few minutes. I don't feel pain anywhere. That means neither of my ankles are twisted for which I'm very relieved." She glanced down at her ankles. A frown wrinkled her forehead. "Oh! I'm so ... dirty." She looked at him with a hint of shame in her eyes.

Conrad swallowed and looked away. If he could offer her a quiet, private place to change her clothes, he would. But out here in the sun on a busy street gave her nowhere to hide.

Rose hastened in their direction. "Found it!" She handed the crumpled bag to her friend. "He ran over it. I had to tug it out from under his rear wheel. That's why the handle is broken."

Conrad raised his brows. So that was the uneven patch of street he'd hit as he came to a stop. Surely nothing valuable had been in that bag.

Lacy accepted it with a moan and looked inside. Tears filled her blue eyes. "Oh, no." She pulled out a portrait of a cluster of people in a frame that had come apart at the corner. The wood splintered where a crack ran the length of one side.

"That's the Angel Frame you got for your birthday. I'm so sorry. I know how much that frame means to you." Rose patted Lacy's shoulder.

"This is the picture I had you take of me with my family." She wiped her eyes and then glared at Conrad. "How could you?"

"I'll help you replace it." He looked into her eyes for a long moment. She had a softness and graciousness about her even if she was mad at him.

"No, you don't understand. This frame was a gift from my parents. I'd wanted one so badly. They bought it for me even though they can't afford it. That can never be replaced." She sat slumped over as if defeated.

"I'm sorry." Conrad laid his hand on top of hers, but she flinched away from him.

"Lacy, I know you're upset, but we have less than an hour before we must catch our next train. If we want to get to that café across the street for supper we need to hurry." Rose shifted her weight from one foot to the other and pointed across the street.

Lacy straightened. "Oh, yes. You're right. We won't have another chance to eat if we don't get something now."

"Can you stand?" Rose asked.

"I think so." Lacy pushed off the bench.

Conrad shot to his feet ready to offer her support.

She swayed a bit as she smoothed her skirts.

Conrad held his hand to her back, but she soon steadied. "Please allow me to buy you ladies your supper. It's the least I can do."

The girls looked at each other before Lacy turned to him.

"That's very kind but not necessary. Rose and I were going to catch only a quick bite. You don't need to stick around to take care of us."

"I'd be happy to." The faces of Betje and Markus came to mind. If one of them was in this situation, he'd want a kind stranger to look out for them too. Seeing these girls through the next hour until they were safely on their train was worth the delay. "Lead the way." He gestured to Rose.

A smile tugged at her mouth and the glow of interest entered her eyes, but she cast a quick glance at her friend as if she didn't dare accept Conrad's invitation without Lacy's approval. Taking Lacy's hand, she guided her through the thinning crowd, leaving Conrad behind. He jogged to catch up. After they crossed the street, he held the door to the café open for them.

Lacy glared at him, but her friend's smile peeked out. They passed in front of Conrad, met a waiter, and followed him to a table.

A second waiter came along. "May I help you, sir?" he asked Conrad.

"I'm with them." He pointed to Rose and Lacy.

The man walked him to their table.

"I thought we told you we don't need anyone to take care of us by paying for our meal." Lacy's eyes rolled as Conrad sat in the chair across from her.

"Consider it a gift." Conrad removed his hat. He intended to stay right here at this table until the last bite had been eaten.

Lacy sighed as she shifted her attention to the menu.

"Where are you ladies headed?" He asked after making his choice from the list of sandwiches.

Rose slipped her gloves from her hands. "Oswell City."

"You don't say. That's where I'm from." A smile tugged at his mouth.

Rose glanced at Lacy but received no indication of her feelings. She turned back to Conrad as if she'd decided to take the matter into her own hands. Elbows on the table and a smirk playing about her lips, she asked, "So, who do I have to thank for picking my friend up off the street?"

Conrad's brows rose. He wanted to form an acquaintance with these two girls since they were going the same direction he was, but he didn't want to give this young lady too much encouragement to become familiar with him.

"You may call me Mr. Van Drunen." He settled back in his chair since the waiter had come to take their orders. "Why are you going to Oswell City?" Conrad asked when the waiter left.

Lacy busied herself wiping the smudges on her skirt.

"I'll be starting classes at the college in Clear Book and staying with my aunt and uncle. Perhaps you know them, Helen and Lester Brinks." Rose sipped water from her glass.

"Your aunt Helen and I work together at the orchard. I'm the handyman." Conrad said.

"Oh!" Over the top of her glass, Rose gave him a look that would've encouraged a weaker man to acknowledge this unbreakable bond she believed her aunt had forged between them.

Conrad cleared his throat.

"You should tell him why you came along." Rose whispered as she nudged Lacy. "He probably knows Miss Millerson's husband."

The waiter came with their sandwiches. Rose may have met with success in getting Lacy to talk, or the delicious smell of food might have broken her silence. Whatever it was, Lacy heeded her friend's suggestion with a quick glance at Conrad.

"I came with Rose to see my teacher from country school. She lives in Oswell City now. Married to a preacher." She picked up her napkin and dabbed at the black smear on her jacket sleeve, but the strokes made little difference.

"She could be none other than Mrs. Karen De Witt."

Conrad smiled as he said the name of the woman who had been a close friend to his late wife. He didn't know what he would have done without the De Witts in those dark days following Angelien's death.

"Yes, I believe that's her name." Lacy gave up trying to clean her jacket and ate her sandwich.

"Lovely people." If another Karen De Witt existed somewhere in the world, Conrad would search for her and bring her home as a mother for his children.

He coughed, which led to a fit of choking. Reaching for his glass, he took a sip of water. Maybe it would help soothe his throat. A mother for Markus and Betje meant a wife for him. Not sure he was ready for that sort of thing. His son and daughter might benefit from the addition of a woman to their home, but Conrad would not. His heart lay in the grave with no prospect of a resurrection.

The first sip of water didn't make much difference, so he took a second one. Still choking, he pounded on his chest.

"Mr. Van Drunen, are you all right?" Lacy's brow wrinkled as she watched him.

"Fine." He croaked. The choking eventually died away, allowing him to settle in and enjoy his sandwich.

After several moments of silence while everyone ate, Rose shoved the last bite of food in her mouth. "We must go."

"I'll pay the waiter." Lacy reached for her rumpled satchel.

"Let me cover it. Please," Conrad said.

"No, Mr. Van Drunen." Lacy held up a hand. "You've already done enough."

"I'm sure two young women traveling alone have plenty of expenses. Let me help you with this one." Conrad flipped his billfold open and handed some cash to Rose.

"Rose, you shouldn't take his money." Lacy frowned at her friend.

"There's enough here to cover his meal too. We don't have

time to argue with him if we want to catch our train." Rose slid out of her seat.

Lacy directed her frown at Conrad and followed her friend. Conrad replaced his hat and went to the door to wait for them. He followed the girls across the street to the depot. As soon as they went inside, Rose turned white.

"I can't find my ticket." She reached in the pockets of her skirt and checked her handbag. "It isn't here anywhere."

"But you had it when we got off the train. I saw it." Lacy's brow creased with concern.

"You don't suppose I lost it in the street." Rose glanced out the window.

"If you did, it's long gone by now." Lacy reached for Rose's bag and conducted her own search.

"Our train arrives in five minutes. What do I do?" Fear froze Rose's features.

"I don't know. It's too late to buy a ticket for tonight's train. But they'll never let you on without it." Lacy handed Rose's bag back to her.

"What if I have to stay behind in the city? Alone. Oh, Lacy!" Rose's hand fluttered to her chest and rested there.

"I'll give you a ride. I was on my way home when I stopped to help you." Conrad pointed out the window to his car still parked along the curb.

"Mr. Van Drunen, we couldn't possibly expect you to do that. You've already done so much for us." Lacy shook her head.

"I'm uncomfortable with the thought of a young woman staying in the city overnight alone. There is no reason why your friend shouldn't come with me. I have plenty of room."

Rose sent Lacy a helpless, questioning gaze.

"I want to take the train. Grandma helped me buy my ticket and I don't want to waste it." Lacy held the valuable slip of paper in the air.

"Well then. Your friend can come with me, and we will meet

you and all of the luggage in Oswell City." Conrad held his hands out with the palms up. He'd do what he could to improve the situation, but a great deal of it was out of the control of any of them.

A whistle pierced the air as the faint chug of an engine grew nearer.

"There's the train." Lacy gave her friend a hug and whispered in her ear. "Be careful. He's a stranger. I wish there was another way."

"I'll be fine." When she pulled away, Rose gave Lacy a shaky smile.

"Watch for me in Oswell City. I'll meet you there." Lacy called as she walked away.

Conrad turned to Rose and took her bag. "You might as well come with me."

Rose still looked frantic as she followed him to his car. As he drove out of the city and into open country, she stayed quiet. The sun hovered on the horizon casting orange rays across the lush fields. Puffy clouds glowed with a golden light as they reflected the sunset. A warm breeze blew in the open window.

Straight along the unbending highway they cruised. When they stopped for fuel at the first little town on their route, Rose got out and stretched. The activity must have loosened her tongue because she dove into a one-sided conversation while Conrad drove. An outgoing and lively girl, that's all she was. He didn't need to worry about her wanting something from him he couldn't give. He leaned back in his seat and set a relaxed pace for the rest of the drive home.

"You'll like Lacy, and she'll like you once she gets to know you. She's not very outgoing so it takes her a while to warm up to people, especially strangers. It's probably the broken picture frame that has her upset." Rose hung her arm out the open window.

"You know I couldn't have avoided running over her bag. I

was more concerned that I didn't run over her." Conrad spoke while keeping his eyes on the road.

"Oh, sure, I understand," Rose said with a wave of her hand. "Lacy will, too, after a good night's sleep. She's not one to hold grudges. We're good friends, her and me. We got to know each other in high school. We'd gone to two different country schools near our homes but attended the same high school. We both graduated in May."

"Interesting. You're both older than I thought." Conrad slowed as he came up behind a truck and then took advantage of the open road to go around it.

"I'm eighteen. So is Lacy. That's not so young." Rose's voice carried an air of offense. "I'll be going to college."

"Oh, I see." A woman out on her own and ready to experience the world. That's who she wanted to be. Conrad stood corrected.

"Lacy just came along for fun. She wants to see Miss Millerson again. Well, Mrs. De Witt she is now." Rose lifted the arm that had been hanging out the window and waved to the young men in the truck he passed.

Rose shifted in her seat so that her one leg was tucked under the other and her arm was slung over the back. "You know what I'd like to see for Lacy?"

Conrad shook his head.

"I want her to get a job. Have lots of good friends besides me. Make her own way. We're both poor girls, you see. This trip to Oswell City is our one big chance. I want Lacy to make the most of it. Have fun and start out on her own life. Do you think she could do that in Oswell City? I've never been there before, you know. That's why I'm asking you." Rose stared at him much like the citizens of Oswell City stared at the mayor ready to make an important speech.

"Well ... I ... I couldn't say." Conrad shrugged. "I came to

Oswell City from Holland with my family. My situation is a little different from that of your friend."

Rose sucked in a breath and shifted back to a normal seated position, facing forward. "I figured you'd say something like that."

"But that doesn't mean your friend couldn't be quite happy in our small town." He risked taking his eyes off the road for a moment to glance at her.

"Yeah. I'm going to do the best I can to get her to stay instead of going back home. There's nothing for her on the farm in Silver Grove. But maybe there is in Oswell City." Her thoughts faded away.

Conrad didn't try to follow them. The trip continued in silence for a while. Then Rose turned to him again.

"Hey, thanks for helping Lacy and for supper and this ride in your car. I really appreciate it." She gave him a look full of admiration.

Conrad nodded. He'd enjoyed himself. He had to admit how nice it felt to be a young lady's hero again. Too many years had passed since he'd last had the pleasure.

3

Oswell City, Iowa

Stars studded the sky and a ribbon of crimson glowed on the western horizon. Activity around the Oswell City train depot waned as people met up with relatives and business associates. Thumps from inside the building indicated the shutting down of a busy terminal for the night. A drawer closed. Heavy items—crates maybe—thudded to the floor. Men's voices droned through the walls. Lights switched off. A door opened then closed. The premises fell silent except for the rasping of locusts in a nearby tree.

Lacy left the bench she'd been sitting on as she waited for Rose and Mr. Van Drunen. Surely they'd think to come to the train depot to find her. Mr. Van Drunen had mentioned the luggage. It would have to get collected and brought along to the home of Rose's aunt. What if they'd already arrived in town and forgotten about her? Maybe Rose was at her aunt's this very minute enjoying a comfortable chair and a good visit.

Lacy should go there and meet Rose. But she didn't know Rose's aunt and uncle. Neither did she know how to find their home. If the large house in the orchard Rose spoke of was anywhere around, she'd go there. But from her friend's description, it was way out in the country, too far for a young lady to walk at this time of night.

A lamp glowed in a window of the hotel. She had no money to stay there, but maybe someone could give her directions. With a sigh, Lacy picked up her damaged satchel. Heat flushed through her. Who did he think he was? Mr. Van Drunen might have picked her up off the street and bought her supper, but he drove his car right over her Angel Frame!

Her parents should be told that their special gift to her had been destroyed. Except she couldn't bear the thought of doing so. Her tragic news would surely hurt them as much as it hurt her.

Lacy's feet dragged as she walked down the street. If only she hadn't tripped on that curb. Then her satchel wouldn't have flown into the line of traffic. The damage Mr. Van Drunen had done that day was unfair, not only to her but to her family who sacrificed so much. And now he was on the loose somewhere in this dark night with her best friend. He might harm Rose in some way if he got in a wreck or stopped for a drink or went off course and never drove her to this town at all.

Why, oh why, did Lacy allow Rose to travel with a stranger? She should have insisted that Rose take the train, even if she would have had to wait until morning. But Mr. Van Drunen would have known her plans and probably demanded to pay for her hotel and another train ticket just as he'd done with the bill for their supper.

Lacy gritted her teeth. Now she disliked him not only for the damage he'd done with his car, but for the indebtedness she and Rose owed him. Frustrating man!

Few times in her young life had she grown so angry with anyone. At least her disgust with him would keep her out of trouble. Dad's prayers were working. If only he'd pray for Rose too. She might be in trouble if she was still in Mr. Van Drunen's company.

Lamps in the hotel's window cast a shaft of light over her traveling suit. Grime streaked her jacket and skirt. She was in no condition to walk into the lobby of a hotel. Halting, she turned around. Where could she go in this town at this time of night?

The church steeple caught her attention. Maybe she dared to search for Miss Millerson. If she'd married a preacher, then she would live in a house close to the church. Lacy trudged down the street in that direction. If only her clothes were clean. She'd prefer not to meet her teacher looking as if she really had been run over.

At the intersection, she crossed the street and strolled past the dark church building on the corner. The brick house next door had a light glowing in one of its windows. Lacy ventured across the lawn. Maybe this was where Miss Millerson lived. Or if it wasn't her house, maybe the people living there would be nice enough to tell her where to find her teacher.

Lacy held her breath and knocked on the door. A tall, blond-haired man opened it. He held an adorable baby girl at his shoulder.

Recognition flowed through her like warm sunlight. Mr. De Witt. It had to be him. Memories of a party the Silver Grove students held at their school so many years ago came rushing back to her. He'd been there, and he'd taught her how to play croquet. He'd also visited with her brother Cal over the following winter helping him understand the call to preach the gospel. A smile broke out on Lacy's face.

"Logan, who's at the door?" A voice Lacy knew and loved floated from the room beyond.

Then she appeared. Her golden hair glowed in the lamplight. Deep blue eyes full of compassion stared at Lacy. Her mouth dropped open as recognition dawned on her too.

"Why, it's Lacy Jones. It has to be you." Miss Millerson's hands flew to her cheeks. "What are you doing in Oswell City? Oh, my goodness! What a surprise!"

"Then I have the right house?" Lacy gestured to the couple in the doorway.

"Yes. Oh, it's so good to see you. Come in. Come in." Mrs. De Witt backed away as her husband stepped to the side for Lacy to enter.

She stepped into the hall. A dining room and kitchen were visible off to the left. A stairway rose a short distance away to the right. The home appeared cheery and comfortable with its elegant furniture, rugs, and children's toys scattered about.

"You look as though you've been in an accident. Are you hurt?" Mrs. De Witt studied her jacket and skirt.

"I tripped and fell before boarding the train in Des Moines. I look much worse than I feel." Lacy made an attempt at a smile.

Mrs. De Witt's expression relaxed a bit. "Well, come right this way." She took Lacy's hat and satchel before Mr. De Witt led her to the parlor.

"I ... I hope I'm not keeping you up by arriving so late. I didn't want to bother you, but I don't know anyone else in town." Lacy sat in a chair near the fireplace and settled her hands on her skirt, right over one of the worst splotches.

"The boys are in bed, but Logan was rocking Sara, so we weren't ready to go to sleep yet." Mrs. De Witt sat on the sofa and looked at Lacy. "It's so good to see you again. How are you? What brings you to Oswell City?"

"I am well, thank you. I graduated from high school in May."

"You did?" Mrs. De Witt clasped her hands. "What an accomplishment! Congratulations."

"Thanks. I'm traveling with a friend from high school, Rose Harper. She's from Meadow Creek. You might know her. She went by Agnes in school, but now she wants to be called Rose." Lacy glanced over at Mr. De Witt in the rocking chair with his small daughter. Her heavy lids were lowering over her eyes as the gentle sway of the chair lulled her to sleep. She looked content and safe.

A wave of homesickness rolled over Lacy. She gulped. Better not give into that. This visit to a new town was her chance to spend time with her teacher and maybe even find a way to make something of herself.

"Agnes is in town too? I can't wait to see her." Mrs. De Witt clasped her hands over her knee.

Lacy pulled her gaze away from Mr. De Witt. "Agnes, or rather Rose, she's staying with her aunt so that she can attend the college in Clear Brook."

"That's wonderful. What will she be studying?"

"She wants to be a teacher. Like you."

"I'm so honored." Mrs. De Witt glanced over at her husband and received a wink from him. "She wants people to call her Rose, you say?" Mrs. De Witt returned her attention to Lacy.

"Yes."

"I'll try to remember. I knew her as Agnes, so I might slip up from time to time." Mrs. De Witt smiled. "Where is she? Did she come with you?" Mrs. De Witt glanced out the window.

"No ... I mean ... yes. I mean ..." Lacy pushed her hair off her forehead. Where did she begin to explain? She took a deep breath. "Rose and I got separated in Des Moines when we had to switch trains. She lost her ticket so caught a ride with someone."

"Oh, really? I wonder who that would be." Mr. De Witt commented with interest lifting his voice.

"It doesn't matter." The damage done to her picture frame hurt too much, and the separation from her friend left her vulnerable and alone. Talking about the whole episode and Mr. Van Drunen's role in it would add to her agitation.

Starting now, she would do her absolute best to forget all about it. "She'll arrive eventually. She might even be in town now."

A tense silence descended on the room. Mrs. De Witt bit her lip as though she feared she might say the wrong thing.

Lacy straightened and changed the subject. "Could you please tell me where Helen Brinks lives? That is where Rose and I will be staying."

"Helen and Lester? They live two blocks over on Third Street. A white two-story house. Easy to find," Mr. De Witt said.

"Thanks." Lacy stood. "I've so enjoyed seeing you again. I'd really love to visit some more. You see, I came along with Rose for the very reason of finding you. I'm glad my surprise arrival tonight wasn't too disruptive."

"Please don't go, Lacy. It's getting late. Why don't you stay with us tonight? You can look up the Brinks in the morning." Mr. De Witt glanced at his wife.

"Use the guest room. It's down the hall next to the bathroom. Have breakfast with us in the morning. Then you can go find your friend," Mrs. De Witt said.

"I couldn't possibly impose on you." Lacy shook her head.

"You wouldn't be imposing. We'd love to have you." Mrs. De Witt stood and rested her hands on Lacy's shoulders.

Putting an end to this long and painful day sounded nice. And staying here, with so much time to spend with Mrs. De Witt would be luxury.

"Simon and John would love to meet you. If you stayed, you could see them at breakfast." Mr. De Witt's smile was hard to resist.

She'd love to meet Mrs. De Witt's children. They were probably smart and well-behaved with a woman like her as their mother.

"Well, all right. I could use some cleaning up." Lacy fanned out her skirt putting the grime on full display.

"Go and help yourself to the bathroom. I'll give you a nightgown to wear." Mrs. De Witt pointed down the hall.

"Thank you." Lacy rushed away and entered the guest room. A bed with a quilt in shades of blues, a dresser, and a small bookcase furnished the room. Lacy lit the lamp and proceeded to undress. If only Rose could see her now—not just visiting with Mrs. De Witt but staying with her.

Her journey had known its share of struggle, but the welcome she received made up for the disappointments. Well, almost. The sight of the grime on her skirt sent a pang of anger through her. The kindness of the De Witts could not subdue her dislike of Mr. Van Drunen. If that man truly lived here like he said he did, then she had someone to guard against, a man she didn't dare trust.

Lacy finished her preparations for sleep with a strategy for staying out of his way forming in her mind.

"Good morning. We're so glad to have you join us for breakfast." Mrs. De Witt smiled at Lacy. "Here. Take this seat." She gestured to an empty chair at the dining room table.

Lacy slipped onto the chair as two energetic toddlers entered the room with their father. One of them he carried in his arms. The other little boy skipped along at his side.

"We have a visitor today," Mr. De Witt said as he settled the toddler he carried in a chair.

"Who are you?" The little boy standing at his father's side pointed at Lacy.

"Now, John. Give your mother a chance to introduce her." Mr. De Witt pulled a chair out for John and helped him get seated.

"Mama?" Fear entered John's eyes as he looked to his mother.

"Don't worry. This is Miss Lacy Jones from Silver Grove. She was one of my students when I taught school there." Mrs. De Witt poured a small amount of orange juice into John's glass.

"You may call me Lacy." She smiled at the little boy.

"Wacy." The other toddler echoed.

Lacy laughed. "That's right."

John straightened. "I can say it better. It goes like this, Simon." John made a show of sticking his tongue out. "See? L – L – Lacy." He giggled and his brother shared the laugh with him.

"John is already aspiring to be a teacher like his mother." Mr. De Witt tousled his son's hair as he sat next to him.

"Hey!" John smiled and reached up to catch Mr. De Witt's hand.

"Now that you've met the professor of the family, say 'hello' to his unlucky student, his twin brother Simon." Mr. De Witt pointed at the little boy he'd carried into the room.

Lacy waved. "Hello, Simon."

He stuck his tongue out like his brother had done to demonstrate the *L* syllable, grinned and then said, "Wacy."

Everyone laughed. Simon joined in and then stuck his tongue out again.

"Silly boy," Mrs. De Witt said in a voice filled with affection. She glanced at Lacy while she pointed at her husband. "Simon is the one in the family who takes after his father."

"Two of a kind." Mr. De Witt grinned at his son.

Simon giggled and covered his eyes with his hands.

Sara banged a small spoon on the tray of her highchair as if calling an unruly meeting to order.

"Your sister has the right idea. Let's settle down so we can pray." Mr. De Witt bowed his head.

When the meal started, Mrs. De Witt looked at Lacy. "How did you sleep last night?"

"Very well. I appreciate you allowing me the use of your guest room." Lacy cut up her pancake and poured syrup on it.

"I didn't want to send you upstairs. That's where the children's rooms are. We could have put you on the cot in Sara's room, but the guest room all to yourself is so much nicer." Mrs. De Witt fed Sara small bites of a pancake.

Lacy's thoughts wandered to questions about Rose's aunt. She might not have space for two girls to stay with her. Offering the room to Rose made the most sense. Rose was the one staying in town to go to college. She was the girl Helen Brinks had invited. Not Lacy. Her visit to Oswell City might get cut much shorter than she wanted if the Brinks had no room for her.

"Why don't we go with you over to the Brinks'? I'd love to see Agnes again," Mrs. De Witt washed sticky syrup from little hands and faces now that breakfast was finished. She hadn't remembered Agnes's wish to be called by her middle name.

Lacy bit her lip against pointing out the mistake. She had a feeling Agnes Rose Harper should get prepared for much more of that.

"I'd like for you to come. Can I help you get the children ready to go?" Lacy watched the little girl reaching for her mother as a sign she wanted out of her highchair.

"Sara needs her bonnet. Go ahead and put it on while I help the boys with their shoes. It's in her room." Mrs. De Witt pointed to the stairs.

Lacy picked the little girl up and followed Mrs. De Witt's directions. The stairs looked new with highly polished wood gleaming in the morning sunlight. Fresh painted walls and stylish carpet on the floors of the bedrooms matched the new look of the stairway. With the latest addition of the baby girl to the family, it made sense to Lacy that the home had acquired a recent addition to make space for the children.

She found the bonnet on a hook near the crib and tied it

under the little girl's chin. "There we go, Sara. All ready for a walk outside." She was rewarded with a smile.

Lacy and Sara returned downstairs as Mrs. De Witt tied the last shoestring on Simon's shoe. John had both of his shoes on and was hopping around in the hallway eager to get moving. Sara traveled in a buggy. Simon and John ran on ahead. They skipped, threw stones into the street, or waved at the vehicles passing by.

"Good morning," Mrs. De Witt said when Helen Brinks answered her knock.

"Oh! Mrs. De Witt, good morning. I didn't know you'd come calling on me." Helen's eyes widened as she opened the door and let them in.

"I won't stay long. I've brought a friend with me. Her name is Lacy Jones. She's traveling with your niece. Lacy got into town last night. Has Rose arrived yet?" Mrs. De Witt looked down the hall.

"Yes. She got here after dark. Lester is at the train station now fetching the luggage. I'll get her." Helen turned away and called for Rose.

"Hi, Rose. Did your trip go well?" Lacy asked when her friend appeared.

"Couldn't have been better. We looked for you at the train station as soon as we got into town, but we didn't find you, so we came here. I thought maybe you got a room at the hotel." Rose's gaze shifted to Mrs. De Witt and her eyes grew round with pleasure. "Miss Millerson?"

"I stayed with her last night," Lacy said.

"You must be little Agnes Harper from Meadow Creek. My, how you've grown into a pretty young lady. I should probably call you Rose. Lacy said you don't want to be known as Agnes anymore." Mrs. De Witt laid her hand on Rose's shoulder.

"That's right. It's so good to see you again. Did Lacy tell you I want to be a teacher? That's why I'm in town."

"She did. I'm so happy that you are able to attend college. Good for you."

"Are these your children?" Rose glanced around at the small visitors.

"Sara is in the buggy. Simon and John are twins. They are four years old."

"Oh, my goodness. So good to meet you all." Rose smiled at them and then turned to Lacy. "Come on. I'll help you get settled before Uncle Lester comes with your luggage." Rose led the way down the hall.

"Rose?" Her aunt's voice followed them. "Where are you going? I only have one spare room. Surely you know that."

Rose frowned. "But I wrote to you and told you a friend was coming with me."

"I wrote back to let you know that I don't have room for another person to stay here. She could for one night, maybe, but not for as long as you'd requested." Helen settled her hands on her hips.

"Oh, I got that letter," Rose said with a wave of her hand. "But I know you keep house at the orchard. Since you didn't have room here, then I thought starting tomorrow you could give Lacy a room there."

Helen twisted her hands in her apron. "No, I'm afraid I can't. The house at the orchard is full, you see. A new highway is going in south of here, so the church decided to give the rooms to the construction crew. I'm sorry, girls. Lacy can stay tonight but she'll have to make other arrangements for a longer visit. Maybe she can get a room at the hotel. Lester's brother owns it. I could talk to him."

Lacy's jaw dropped. Rose was usually a reliable friend. Why had she made this empty promise to Lacy and her parents guaranteeing a place to stay? "Rose, you knew I don't have the money to afford a hotel room. Not even for one night."

"But Aunt Helen always has room. She wrote Mama about

how large the house in the orchard is." Rose's voice grew louder and faster as she looked from Lacy to Helen.

"Now, settle down. It isn't your fault. I should have thought to explain in the letter about the construction crew. It just never occurred to me that you were considering a room there for your friend." Helen rubbed her forehead.

"She can stay with me," Mrs. De Witt motioned in the direction of her house as she turned to Lacy. "We'd love to have you. Really. Use our guest room."

The invitation sounded like a beautiful piece of music to Lacy's ears. She'd love nothing more than to be in Mrs. De Witt's home watching her, listening to her, and learning from her. But she shouldn't allow it. She'd come with Rose to seek out opportunity and make her own way, not to depend on other people to take care of her.

"I couldn't impose on you like that. You have a family. I fear I would just be in the way."

Mrs. De Witt laid her hand on Lacy's arm. "You would be one of us. I can't imagine quiet, shy Lacy Jones ever getting in anyone's way."

The whole story hadn't yet been told to Mrs. De Witt. She didn't know that Lacy had already gotten in someone's way. A fall into the street had put her in the path of the reckless Mr. Van Drunen. He lived in this town. Maybe Mrs. De Witt's words would act as a sort of shield preventing Lacy from coming near him again.

"Go ahead and stay with the minister and his wife," Helen urged. "They live close by. You'll still be able to see Rose anytime you want."

Lacy looked from her to Mrs. De Witt. Both women smiled at her with their brows raised high in anticipation.

She sighed. "All right. Thank you, Mrs. De Witt. I'll go back home with you."

Mrs. De Witt hugged her.

"I'm sorry about the misunderstanding." Rose's voice pleaded with Lacy not to get upset.

"It worked out." Better than Lacy dared to hope. Rose's lack of planning had led to the best possible arrangement.

"I'll send Lester over with your suitcase." Helen waved at Lacy as she followed Mrs. De Witt out the door.

The children enjoyed the time outdoors running and jumping and playing games on the walk back to the parsonage. Sara kept up a stream of jabber as she pointed to birds and flowers from her place in the buggy.

Lacy's thoughts strayed. She'd decided on a whim to travel with a friend to Oswell City. Now she'd stay in the home of her beloved teacher and husband. She would have to write to Cal and tell him all about it.

4

At four o'clock in the afternoon, Conrad walked into the sixth-grade classroom of the Oswell City grade school. The other members of the Parent Teacher Association sat around the table set up in the middle of the room. Chatter stopped, and everyone turned to watch him slip into his seat.

"Sorry I'm late," he mumbled to Lorraine Koelman at the head of the table and holding a gavel in her hand, seconds away from calling this meeting to order.

"Everything all right?" She asked with a furrowed brow.

"Yeah. It is now. The cow at the orchard got out so I had to chase her out of Fred Akerman's alfalfa before I could come to town." He blew out a breath and ran his hand through his hair.

"We're glad you're here." Lorraine smiled at him and then turned to the woman on her left. "Mary, would you please read the minutes from our last meeting?"

Conrad's thoughts wandered as he scanned the faces of the others in attendance. Women. All of them. Wives and mothers with husbands and with children in school. Not one man present. He stifled a sigh. If his children had a mother, she could attend these school-related meetings. Then he wouldn't have to leave work in the middle of the afternoon and put in an appearance. He only came because this school year was his turn.

Their school was too small to designate people to the committee. Everyone shared the responsibilities. So here he sat. One lone man in a sea of women. He lowered his gaze and studied his hands, still showing traces of dirt from the workday, as he listened to Mary read from the minutes.

When she finished, Lorraine resumed leadership of the meeting. "Thank you, Mary. Any corrections or questions?" She looked at the group. "Let's keep going. Kate, would you explain the plans for the fall carnival?"

Kate Vander Will was a widowed woman in her thirties with four school-aged children. She stood and cleared her throat. "As you all know, our school carnival is scheduled for the second Friday night in September. We will be offering these games for the children to play: sack races, pin the tail on the donkey, horseshoe toss, bobbing for apples, fishing for a prize, and cupcake decorating."

The group murmured and looked at each other with approving expressions on their faces.

"We as parents will supervise the activities by setting up and decorating our own booths. Each booth requires the assistance of two people, so we will need to work as partners. You may choose your spouse, family member, or a friend. I'm passing out the assignments now. You can think it over while we join the teachers for our annual PTA picnic following this meeting. Please make sure to sign your helper up on this form before you leave." Kate waved a paper in the air.

Conrad held his breath as Kate made her way around the table. Maybe she'd give him the fishing pond or the horseshoe toss. Then he'd ask his brother Nicholas to help. Everyone would have a good time that way. He and Nick could work with horseshoes and fishing poles—items they knew something about. The kids could play games to win prizes. Parents and kids alike would all go home happy.

Decorating that kind of a booth would be easy. He'd just round up some props from the barn and scatter them around to add flair. Conrad settled back in his chair as Kate handed a paper to the woman sitting next to him. He had the whole situation settled.

Kate slapped an instruction sheet on the table in front of him. The supplies it listed had nothing to do with the scenario playing out in his imagination. Colored sugar. Tinted frosting. Napkins.

Conrad frowned at the page. Where were the hooks and fishing line, the horseshoes and stakes? His gaze ventured to the heading and his pulse throbbed. These women had assigned him to the cupcake decorating!

He stole a glimpse of the sheet of the person next to him. Pin the Tail on the Donkey. The lady on the other side of him had the instructions for the horseshoe toss. He stroked his jaw. Maybe he could trade. Conrad opened his mouth to ask the question, but Kate started talking.

"The booth assignments have been passed out. Please look them over and make arrangements to provide all supplies."

Conrad bit his lip. He had no experience baking cupcakes or mixing up frosting. Didn't even have the slightest idea of where to start. Whenever Markus or Betje needed a birthday cake, he ordered one from the bakery. Maybe Mildred Zahn would help him out of this pinch too.

"Unfortunately, we cannot allow you to trade booths with another pair. We tried that in the past, but it didn't work because we'd have too many assistants at one booth and no one at another. Too easy to have misunderstandings. You'll have to keep your assignments and do the best you can to fulfill them." Kate stacked some papers in a file and sat down.

Lorraine tapped her gavel on the table. "School starts

tomorrow, so let's spend the rest of our time discussing our roles to help our students find their classrooms. Some of them might need extra help getting to know their teacher and their classmates."

The meeting turned to the subject of the new school year until five o'clock when Lorraine dismissed the group for the picnic. Conrad went with the others to the playground where tables had been set up. He watched the women set out delectable dishes of meatballs, casseroles, and desserts. Yesterday, on his way home from work at the orchard, Conrad had stopped at the bakery for a loaf of bread as his contribution. It wasn't fancy, but for a man who had no interest in cooking and even less time for it, an item someone else had made was the best the group could expect from him.

Teachers joined them. The group soon got organized and crept through a line. Conrad filled his plate with all kinds of good food and found a seat at a table. Carlin Reese, the fifth-grade teacher, sat across from him. She was a single woman. Young, but with no qualities about her appearance to make her stand out.

Conrad wouldn't exactly call her ugly, but the word *beautiful* didn't suit her either. On the other hand, she might make a good partner to help him on the night of the fall carnival. Then again, she wasn't very sociable. Maybe he'd make a mistake asking for her help.

He ventured a question not only to start up a conversation to fill the awkward silence, but also to gather information that might solve his problem.

He tore off a bite of bread from his slice and held it up. "This bread is really good. Do you bake?"

Her cheeks turned red. "No. I never got the hang of it. Cakes and rolls of any kind are beyond me. I'd rather be in the classroom anyway."

Conrad stuck the bread in his mouth. So much for the possibility of Carlin's help.

Kate Vander Will came over with a plate of food and sat next to him. "Hi, Conrad. I haven't seen you in such a long time. You should come to gatherings like this one more often."

He shrugged. "I'm too busy working."

"There are lovely apples on the trees. I see them whenever I drive by to visit my mother. A man must have a lot of skill to maintain such a large, beautiful orchard." Kate gave him a smile that told him she thought he was pretty special.

A knot formed on his insides. The orchard, operated by Oswell City Community Church, had become well known for its cider, pies, and crisp tart apples. But it hadn't become successful by his efforts alone. Helen did the baking, and Logan helped with the cider press. Kate shouldn't pin all the fame on him.

She turned to Carlin and visited about the school. Conrad listened, but thoughts unrelated to their discussion filtered through his mind. Maybe he should ask Kate to help him with the cupcake booth. She obviously liked him, so an invitation for her to spend time with him might solve his problem.

He dismissed the idea. As a member of the PTA, Kate would have her own booth to run. Besides, her family included four children close together in age. She'd never work out. He didn't want Markus and Betje to get lost in a brood.

Blinking, Conrad woke up from the scene playing out in his mind. He'd gone from looking for a partner for the cupcake booth to imagining Kate and her children as part of his family.

He exhaled. Teaming up with someone for one night at a school carnival didn't mean he had the right to evaluate them as potential mother material for his children. If he was serious about finding them a mother, then he'd also need to get serious about finding himself a wife. No. Absolutely no.

He stood. "Good evening, ladies."

"You're leaving so soon?" Kate looked disappointed.

"I must. I haven't been home to see Markus and Betje yet today." Conrad gathered up his plate and silverware.

"That's too bad. Don't forget to sign up a partner on the form." Kate pointed to the food table.

"I won't." Conrad nodded to both women and walked away.

At the food table, he exchanged his dirty dishes for a pen. A few of the other PTA members had already signed up their partners. Joanna had written in her husband Ezra's name. Mary and Lorraine had also signed up their husbands. The space next to Kate's name was still blank. So was the space by Conrad's name.

He'd sure like to work with another man. The faces of his brothers Nick and Dan, and his friends Logan De Witt and Matthew Kaldenberg went through his mind. None of these men knew any more about cupcakes and decorating them than Conrad did.

He was stuck. Just plain stuck. In capital letters, he scrawled the word FRIEND. It wasn't anyone's name, but it did at least communicate the fact that he planned to ask someone. That vague word would have to be good enough. Problem was, he hadn't even the faintest idea who in the world his mystery helper would be.

"This is the last day of summer vacation, so let's do something special, like go to the park," Conrad announced when he arrived at his brother and sister-in-law's home.

"Yay!" Seven-year-old Betje clapped her hands while nine-year-old Markus jumped up and down. "I want to go on the slide."

"How did they do today?" Conrad asked Hannah

"Fine. The cousins get along well. Your kids and mine will

miss each other when school starts." Hannah slipped a stray lock of brown hair behind her ear.

"Thank you for caring for them over the summer. I appreciate it." Conrad smiled.

"Happy to do it." She bent to help Betje put on her shoes.

An idea burst into his mind. Maybe he should ask Hannah to help him with the cupcake booth. But her own children would want to play the games. She'd probably want to go with them. The person he asked would have to be someone who didn't have children in grade school. His friends came to mind again. Matthew didn't have children at all, and Logan's were too young to be in school yet. Too bad neither of those men knew more about cupcakes.

Rose Harper might be a possibility. During their drive to Oswell City, she seemed friendly and outgoing, even if she was a little on the flirty side. Maybe she knew how to bake. But by the time the carnival arrived she'd be a busy college student. She'd probably have a dozen other things to do on a Friday night than help him. Conrad sighed as he ushered his children out the door.

At the park, he helped Betje settle into a swing.

"Push me!" she yelled.

"Watch me, Dad." Markus stood perched at the top of the slide. He waved in the instant before he sailed over the metal to the ground. When Betje complained of hunger, Conrad led them home.

In the kitchen, he opened cupboard doors in his haste to create a meal. An assortment of items grew on the countertop, but he still didn't know what to fix. After four years of single parenting, he shouldn't have this problem anymore. Maybe if he enjoyed cooking, he could eliminate this last-minute indecision.

"What are you making for supper?" Markus asked.

Conrad studied the items on the counter. "What about apple slices, bread and butter, and bacon?"

Markus grimaced. "Aunt Hannah gave us apples for our lunch. Do we have to eat them again?"

Conrad tapped his chin. "No, I suppose not. Mrs. De Witt gave us carrots from her garden. We can eat those."

The expression on Markus's face didn't improve.

"Call your sister, please. I'd like her to set the table."

Markus turned around. "Betje, we're having bacon again," he said in a voice that could have benefited from more enthusiasm. "Dad wants you to set the table."

THE NEXT MORNING, Conrad got up at his usual early time and went to the kitchen to get breakfast started. He'd become pretty good at breakfast food—things like eggs, pancakes, and of course, bacon. Ham wasn't too bad either. Anything requiring a skillet he could handle since he could stand by and keep constant watch. Food that went into the oven he burned. Seldom did his household feast on roast or chicken, pies or cakes, unless Hannah sent her leftovers their way. As much as that practice helped him out, Conrad didn't want to take advantage of her kindness, especially since she provided so much day care for his children.

"Betje. Markus. Time for breakfast," Conrad yelled as he scrambled the eggs. "Come now so we aren't late for school."

Soon two sleepy-eyed children arrived in the kitchen. Although they were dressed, the rest of their appearance needed some work. Conrad had figured out how to braid, so he'd get Betje's hair into nice order. Then she could feel proud to attend her first school day of a new year.

Markus's shirt needed rebuttoned. The buttons were lined up so that one collar sat higher than the other. Conrad would deal with those issues later. First, he must feed them breakfast. Then he would make them look as nice as he possibly could, walk them to school, and help them get settled as had been discussed at the PTA meeting.

The extra time at school would make him late to work, but there was nothing he could do about that. Conrad dished food onto his children's plates with a sigh. At times like this his children could sure use both a father and a mother.

5

Conrad drove to the orchard and parked near the barn. He hastened inside, picked up a pail, and settled onto the stool next to the dairy cow with the question of who he should ask to help him at the carnival still on his mind.

"Sorry to keep you waiting." He patted her side and then worked at filling the pail with rich milk. When the task was finished, he led the cow to the pasture and returned to the barn for the ladder, paint can, and a brush.

During the past week he'd been painting the house, giving the clapboard around the windows and under the eaves a fresh coat of bright white. Water had done damage to one of the sills, so he'd had to replace it. Now that window waited for its protective cover of paint. He wanted to get the job completed on this side of the house before the sun shone on it later in the day to make him hot and uncomfortable.

"Good morning, Helen." He tipped his hat to her when he met her in the yard. "How is your niece?"

"Settling in well. College classes start for her tomorrow. Thank you for bringing her home the other night." Helen set her basket of damp laundry down in the grass.

"Have you met her friend? Lacy, I believe her name is. She took the train to Oswell City instead of coming with us. I haven't heard what happened to her."

"She made it in just fine. Mrs. De Witt brought her over the next morning. She's staying with them."

"Ah. Good for her. Your niece mentioned that both of them wanted to see Mrs. De Witt for a visit."

Helen moved away to the clothesline and Conrad finished his trek to the west side of the house. The image of Rose Harper's blonde friend entered his mind. Maybe she would help him with the booth at the carnival. A young, single girl like her who was new to town wouldn't have any children at the event to monopolize her time.

But she was upset with him. He had no semblance of a relationship with her, so going up to her and asking point blank for her help was unrealistic. If he was in her place, he wouldn't welcome the blunt request.

Conrad sighed as he leaned the ladder against the house. He'd climbed three rungs when an idea struck him. Logan may not know much about cupcakes, but his wife probably did. Conrad should ask Karen to help him. With no children in school, she'd be more available than Hannah. By the time Conrad reached the second-story window, he'd made up his mind to have a chat with her.

At a steady pace, he worked his way along the wall until reaching the next window. Memories from Christmas night four years ago tore through him. They had happened in this room. It was the place where Angelien had lost her life. Conrad had sat at her side throughout the entire terrible ordeal. Her screams still echoed in his ears.

His heart pounding, he dipped his brush into the paint and spread it onto the boards around the window. The room belonged to a highway worker this summer. Angelien and her pain had been removed from it long ago. He must put the memories away and focus on his work.

At noon, Matthew Kaldenberg parked his buggy in the yard. Conrad waved at him and made a careful descent to the ground.

"Hello, Conrad!" Matthew carried his doctor's bag as he approached the house.

"Out making house calls, I see."

"I am. That construction worker is still recovering from his accident, so I came to check on him." Matthew pointed to an upstairs window on the south side of the house where the patient was probably convalescing. "Did the first day of school get off to a good start?" Matthew asked.

"Yes. Betje was happy to see her friends again, but both of the kids will miss the long summer days of playing with their cousins."

"Hanna seems to enjoy taking care of them."

"She does. But I wish ..." Conrad bit his lip. He'd hashed his struggle out with Matthew so much already. No point in forcing his friend to hear it all again.

"You still miss Angelien, don't you?"

Conrad nodded as he swallowed the lump in his throat.

"Have you thought about joining a group or socializing a little more? It might help you get your mind on having fun once in a while. Who knows? You might even meet someone that way." Matthew's eyes twinkled.

Conrad shrugged. "I'm on the PTA committee for the school year."

"But they're all wives and mothers. Find a group with young ladies in it who aren't married, if you know what I mean." Matthew's eyes twinkled some more.

"I don't know. When would I have time? Markus and Betje take most of it. Then there's my job. And now I've signed another contract with Gresham and Blaine."

"Good for you. But don't let your carpentry steal all of your time. The Labor Day picnic for the young people in town is coming up. Logan usually manages to pull together a pretty good crowd for it. Maybe you'd want to go."

"They are all a lot younger than me. You have to remember that I turned thirty this year. Most of that group is barely out of high school."

"Just keep it in mind. I found someone to share my life with after losing my first wife. I'm sure you can too." Matthew slapped Conrad's back and walked to the house.

Conrad watched his fifty-something friend cross the porch and enter the house. Matthew had been given a twenty-year interlude between wives. For as much as Conrad's heart ached some days, he'd need at least twenty years before he'd be ready to marry again.

Matthew had also married Karen De Witt's mother. A more elegant woman he had yet to see. Karen ran a close second to her mother, but she was already taken.

Conrad kicked a tuft of grass as he went to the barn for the lunch he'd brought from home. It wasn't much, only a plain dried beef sandwich and a cookie from a stash he'd bought at the bakery. He sat down on an upturned bucket and took a bite from the sandwich.

His mind turned to Matthew's words. If a woman waited out in the world for him somewhere, she'd have to keep waiting. Maybe for a long time. Matthew might feel confidence in Conrad's ability to find her, but he could very well walk right by without the slightest ability to recognize the girl intended just for him.

~

"I LOVE IT HERE." Lacy rested her head on the back of the lawn chair and breathed in the clean evening air. The boys played with a ball in the yard. Sara sat on a blanket with some brightly colored blocks. The warm breeze lifted strands of Lacy's hair. Sunshine lit the windows of a neighbor's house. Birds chirped. Everything was comfortable and wholesome and safe.

"We've loved having you," Mrs. De Witt said in a soft voice.

Lacy's fingers turned cold as a shiver ran up her back. "The time has come for my visit to end. Mama will be waiting for me to come home again. But I don't want to." Lacy sighed. "I wish there was a way for me to stay in Oswell City, but I shouldn't take advantage of your kindness any longer."

"If you really want to live here, I'm sure you could find a way." Mrs. De Witt laid her hand on Lacy's arm.

"You think so? What is there for someone like me to do?"

"You have a high school education, don't you?"

Lacy nodded.

"Let's see." Mrs. De Witt settled back in her chair and looked at the sky. "I bet you know how to bake."

"Yes."

"The Zahns might have some work for you at the bakery."

"Oh." Lacy hadn't considered that her knowledge of ordinary household tasks could find her a paying job. "I can sew, clean the house, and plant a garden too."

Mrs. De Witt chuckled. "The housecleaning could find you a job at the hotel, and the sewing could give you something to do with Eva at her dress shop. But gardening might be tougher. I can't think of anyone in need of a professional vegetable gardener."

"I like to sew. Who is Eva?" Lacy asked.

"Eva Synderhof. She has lived in town for about five years. She has a dress shop on Main Street."

"Does she make your clothes?" Lacy gave Mrs. De Witt's dress an admiring gaze.

"Yes, she does. Eva does a beautiful job."

"Would it be enough ... the pay ... I mean, could I ... well, live on what she'd pay me?" Lacy's stomach tightened as she asked the question. She hardly dared to believe she might find the avenue out of the poverty that had worn her family down.

Mrs. De Witt gave Lacy her full attention. A light of pleasure, or maybe it was pride, glowed in her eyes. "Yes, Eva would be more than fair."

Lacy gulped. These varied possibilities opened wide to her the door of freedom and independence.

"I need to do some shopping tomorrow. Let's go together to these businesses and see what can be done about finding you a job."

Lacy's insides trembled. Mrs. De Witt made the process of employment sound so easy. Maybe it really was. She'd never tried to become employed. Visions of herself frosting cakes, making beds, and cutting out pattern pieces floated through her mind for the rest of the evening.

THE NEXT MORNING, Lacy held the hands of Simon and John while Mrs. De Witt pushed Sara in the buggy. They entered the bakery where Alex Zahn smiled at them from his place behind the glass counter filled with baked goods.

"Ah, Mrs. De Witt. What can I get for you today?" Mr. Zahn pulled out a pencil ready to list the purchases.

"I'll take a dozen *vet bollen*. Logan likes those." Mrs. De Witt tapped her chin before completing her order. Rolls and breads were added to the growing pile. "Alex, I'd like for you to meet my friend, Lacy Jones. She was one of my students when I taught school in Silver Grove. She has been visiting for a few days and has decided to stay in town. She is looking for work. Do you have any jobs available?"

"None that I'm advertising for, but I'll mention it to

Mildred. She might have a use for someone in the kitchen," he said as he accepted Mrs. De Witt's payment.

She nodded. "Fine. We'll look forward to hearing from you."

Mr. Zahn smiled. "Have a good day."

Lacy smiled back at the man and then followed Mrs. De Witt from the store. He seemed nice enough. As she walked along the street, Lacy imagined what her life would be like working in the bakery.

"Good morning." A woman in a broad gray hat greeted Mrs. De Witt as they passed on the sidewalk.

"Oh, Ethel. I'm so glad we crossed paths. I have a question for you." Mrs. De Witt brought the buggy to a halt.

Lacy paused, too, but kept her firm hold of the boys' hands. She didn't want one of them wandering into the street.

"Yes?" The lady waited expectantly.

Mrs. De Witt gestured to Lacy. "This is my friend, Lacy Jones. She was a student of mine in Silver Grove. She's been in town visiting for a few days and has decided she'd like to stay and look for a job. Do you have any work you need help with at the hotel?"

Mrs. Brinks looked Lacy over from the tip of her shoes to the top of her head. "I assume you know how to do housework."

"Yes, ma'am. My mother taught me. I also have a high school diploma." Lacy remembered Mrs. De Witt's encouragement from the night before. The information may not mean much to a woman looking for a person with housekeeping experience, but she might as well try. She'd worked hard for that diploma, so she'd better mention it in her job search whenever she had the chance.

"Hmm." Mrs. Brinks settled her hand on her hip. "Our room service girls are all new hires, but according to the trend in turnover we've seen this year, they might leave soon too. I'm glad to know you are available, Miss Jones. I'll be sure and call you if something opens up."

Lacy nodded and followed Mrs. De Witt when she moved down the street. The hotel was probably no longer a possibility. Mrs. Brinks said she'd call Lacy if a job came available, but that might not happen for many weeks or even months. Lacy needed a job now.

The next store they visited was the dress shop. Blue curtains draped tastefully over sheers on the front windows. Colorful dresses hung on a rack. A group of comfortable chairs occupied the space near the counter. The whole shop was warm and inviting. Lacy guided the boys to the chairs and pulled a book from the buggy. A women's dress shop didn't feature too many options for entertaining little boys, so Lacy provided her own in the form of a story.

Mrs. De Witt visited with a slim woman at the counter. Bits of conversation reached Lacy's ears while she read. The same introduction Mrs. De Witt had given of Lacy to the other two potential employers was now being given to the woman at the counter.

A moment later she came over the Lacy. She wore a plum-colored dress and a tape measure hung around her neck. Her dark brown hair was swept into an elegant twist.

"Miss Jones?" The lady clasped her hands and smiled at Lacy.

She closed the book. "Yes. Lacy Jones."

"Nice to meet you, Lacy. I'm Eva. Mrs. De Witt tells me you wish to stay in town if you can find a job."

"That's right."

"Can you make buttonholes?" Eva asked.

"I made these." Lacy reached for the neckline of her blouse and held it out away from her skin so that the small cream buttons securely in their holes were displayed.

Eva leaned over for a better look. "Lovely work. You do a nice job. You probably made the blouse you have on."

"I did. Along with the skirt and my petticoat and ... and ... um, the other items underneath." Lacy's cheeks heated. She'd almost gone as far as mentioning drawers and corset covers in her effort to impress this woman.

Eva smiled. "You are quite experienced."

Lacy gazed at her expecting her to go on, but when Eva said nothing more, Lacy dared to ask the question. "Can you use me? Do you have work here for me to do?"

Eva straightened. "I'll have to look around and think it over. I've always handled all of the sewing on my own, but having someone around to do the more tedious jobs like buttonholes and gathers and such would help me out." She turned to Mrs. De Witt. "I'll keep it in mind and let you know what I decide."

The knot in Lacy's stomach tightened even more. This was the last stop on her job search. What if no one had work for her? Maybe she wouldn't be able to stay in Oswell City after all. She'd miss the nearness to Mrs. De Witt and her family. Rose would get to stay, live with her aunt, and attend college. But Lacy would have to go back home.

Nothing plunged her spirits lower than the thought that maybe she really didn't have an escape from the scarcity that had always held her back.

6

"There he is, with that group of people." Rose pointed to a cluster of men and women shaking hands with Pastor Logan. The organ still played as Lacy and her friend inched down the aisle after the morning service.

The music failed to stir Lacy into uplifting thoughts of the week ahead. A sharp spear of pain sliced through her. Rose had just pointed out Mr. Van Drunen. Dressed in a dark suit and immaculately groomed, he looked more like a business professional than the handyman he claimed to be.

Lacy lifted her chin and looked away. He'd driven his car over her Angel Frame. His dapper appearance couldn't hide the facts from her. Underneath it all, he harbored thoughtless contempt for the feelings of others. No amount of food bought for her supper or offers of assistance could undo the damage he'd done.

The frame meant so much more than just a way to display pictures. It was a gift. Proof of her parents' willingness to give when they had nothing. Her heart had expanded with thankfulness for the lovely gift and joy in finally possessing something she'd wanted so much.

Then he'd driven right over it.

"Aunt Helen said he painted the second story of the house at the orchard this week, climbing the ladder all the way to the top and working for hours without scaffolding or anything to keep him from falling." Rose's voice held a note of awe as she recounted the stunt.

"Sounds foolish to me." Lacy crossed her arms.

"And the way he trimmed around the windows. Aunt Helen said there wasn't so much as a speck or a drip anywhere. So neat and precise." Rose watched Mr. Van Drunen walk away with a woman and another man.

"Wonder where he set his paint can and all his brushes." Lacy scowled at the man's back.

"Good point. I don't know. I'll ask Aunt Helen."

Lacy shrugged. She didn't want an answer and she didn't care what impressive hidden talent Mr. Van Drunen might have employed in balancing a full can of paint. What she did want was to see him fail, to mess up and spill the paint. Then he'd know the sorrow she felt over damage done to a beautiful thing.

Shoving thoughts of Mr. Van Drunen from her mind, she turned the conversation to a different subject. "How were classes this week?"

"Fun. In addition to the usual English and Math courses, I'm in one that teaches about the management of a classroom. In other words, I'm learning what I should do with the naughty boys." Rose leaned in and stage whispered.

Lacy laughed.

Rose straightened and grimaced. "But I have Dr. Broekhuizen for history. He's tough. I'll have to work hard in that class."

"But you'll learn a lot too," Lacy prompted.

"Sure I will. If I survive it." Rose put big emphasis on the *if*.

They greeted Pastor Logan and then went to find the Brinks. Lacy was invited to eat dinner with them.

"Have you found a job yet?" Rose asked as they followed the sidewalk.

"No." Lacy sighed. "My visit with Mrs. De Witt is ended. Mama will want me to go home. I'll have to, I suppose. No one has called Mrs. De Witt with an offer."

"I'm sorry to hear that. I'd hoped you could stay." Rose looked at her with a furrowed brow and concern in her eyes. "Hey, maybe Aunt Helen could find something for you to do at the orchard."

"No." The word shot out of her mouth. Mr. Van Drunen worked there. She'd be thrown in his path. Disaster had awaited her when it happened to her the first time. She'd do everything in her power to prevent it from happening again.

"Just an idea." Rose shrugged. "If it means the difference between staying in town or heading back to Silver Grove, you might want to keep it in mind."

They'd reached the Brinks' home, so Lacy was rescued from giving a reply. She stayed and enjoyed a delicious dinner, and then returned to the parsonage.

Everyone was upstairs settling children in for naps. Lacy's feet dragged as they took her to her room. The moment had come. As much as she resisted it, she must pack and prepare to go home. Home to poverty. Home to no opportunity or sense of purpose. She removed dresses from the closet and slipped them from the hangers when the telephone rang.

Lacy jumped. Her home on the farm didn't have a telephone, so the sound had been new to her during her stay in the parsonage. Footsteps raced down the stairs. The fourth ring cut off midway.

"Hello. Oswell City parsonage." Pastor Logan's voice carried through the house. "Oh yes. She's still here. I'll get her. One moment."

The call must be for his wife. Lacy continued filling her

suitcase, but footsteps came down the hall, growing louder as they drew closer.

A tap came on her door. "Lacy?"

"You can come in." She turned around.

Pastor Logan eased the door open. "The telephone call is for you."

Her eyes widened. "Who would call on a telephone for me?"

He grinned at her. "Go find out."

Lacy ventured out of the room and picked up the receiver. "Hello. This is Lacy."

"Miss Jones, I was hoping to catch you. I wasn't sure how much longer you were planning to stay in Oswell City." A woman's voice carried over the line.

"I'm packing now and will probably leave tomorrow," Lacy informed her mystery caller.

"I'm glad I called then. I'd wanted to talk to you at church this morning, but you left before I had a chance." The cheerful voice on the other end puzzled Lacy further.

"I went to the Brinks' to eat with a friend."

"Oh, how nice. I'll get right to the point because I'm sure we will have many more chances to visit later. This is Eva Synderhof. I've thought it over, and I'd like to have you come work for me in the dress shop."

Lacy's head spun. A job! She'd just been offered a job! "Really? You do?" She sputtered into the receiver.

"Yes, and if working for me is still something you'd like to do, you may start tomorrow. Making buttonholes, sewing up hems, and gathers, and anything else I may find for you to do. I'll pay you seventy-five cents an hour. How does that sound?"

A giggle escaped Lacy's mouth. "That's fine! I'll take it."

"Very good. I'll see you in the morning. The shop opens at nine o'clock, so come early. Then I can explain a few matters to you."

"I'll be there. Thank you, Eva."

"Good-bye."

"Good-bye." Lacy hung up the receiver and drew in a deep breath.

At some point during the conversation, Mrs. De Witt and her husband had entered the room. They stood together staring at her.

"I have a job! Eva Synderhof asked me to come work in her shop. I start tomorrow." Lacy laid both of her hands on her chest and inhaled a happy breath.

"I'm so proud of you." Mrs. De Witt have her a hug.

Pastor Logan smiled at her. "Eva is a kind woman. The two of you will get along well together."

His assurance made her happiness surge. But it plummeted when Mrs. De Witt pulled back and looked into her eyes.

"What will your parents say?" Concern furrowed her brow.

Lacy's stomach tightened. If only she knew the answer to that question. But she could guess, though. Mama would be disappointed that she wasn't coming back, and Dad would fail to see any good reason for her to hold a job. She could stay at home until marrying a farm boy in the neighborhood.

Sure, and then she'd spend her life in drudgery and be just as poor as her parents, unable to break the cycle that had held her prisoner for her whole life.

She gulped against the knot in her stomach. Somehow, she'd convince them this job and this move to Oswell City was the very best for her.

"GOOD MORNING, Lacy. Come right over here and I will show you what I'd like you to work on." Eva smiled and led Lacy to a workstation set up near the sewing machine.

"This skirt needs hemmed for Mrs. Ellenbroek. She is

planning to stop in later today and pick it up. Then you may start on this stack of shirts. They need buttonholes as well as the buttons. My business sewing men's shirts is growing. I guess it's because there are no department stores close by. When you finish with that project, start gathering these ruffles for the dress Mrs. Haverkamp wants for her daughter." Eva lifted each item as she talked and then laid them down in a neat pile.

"Oh, dear. I'm afraid that is quite a bit of work. I trust you are an efficient worker. The shirts and the dress must get finished by noon tomorrow." Eva rested her hand on her forehead.

Lacy claimed the chair and picked up a needle.

"While you work here, I'll manage the cash register in between cutting out pattern pieces." Eva hastened to the front of the store and unlocked the door.

Within minutes, customers entered and browsed the racks.

Lacy turned her attention to the hemming and settled in to sewing small, even stitches. She wanted to make the skirt look just right. Mrs. Ellenbroek was a prominent person in this town, and she'd be wearing Lacy's work. Every stitch Lacy made must reflect well on her employer. A loose thread or slipped stitch would cause embarrassment. She must do whatever she could to keep that from happening.

Through the morning hours she worked until Eva left the conversation she'd been holding with a trio of women and came to Lacy. "Mrs. Ellenbroek came in the store just now and wants her skirt. She's earlier than I expected."

Lacy glanced up at her with round eyes. "I won't be finished for at least another twenty minutes."

"You're still working on it?" Eva frowned.

"Yes." Lacy's insides shriveled.

"Oh, dear. What can we do? I hate to make her wait." Eva rested her hand on her forehead.

"I'll work as fast as I can." Lacy thrust her needle through the fabric for another stitch.

Eva hovered around watching over Lacy's shoulder. The close attention to her every move made Lacy's fingers tremble. She lost her grip on the needle. It fell into her lap and required a rethreading.

"How much is this dress?" The question came from the rack near the front of the store where an older woman held up a floral dress. She looked at Eva for an answer.

Eva sighed. "I should go help her, but Lillian needs this skirt."

"Only twenty more minutes." Lacy ventured a glance at the other woman.

"Go as fast as you can." Eva whispered with an edge in her voice and then moved away.

Out of the corner of her eye, Lacy saw Eva stop to speak with Lillian Ellenbroek on her way to the woman at the rack. Lillian lost her smile and exited the store.

The trembles from Lacy's fingers spread to the rest of her body. If Mrs. Ellenbroek left the store in such a hurry, that must mean she was upset about the wait. Maybe she didn't want the skirt anymore. Had Lacy's concern for quality work lost the sale for her employer? If Mrs. Ellenbroek was upset with Eva, then it was Lacy's fault. She blinked back the sting of tears in her eyes and focused on moving her needle as fast as possible.

Eva assisted three more people at the cash register while Lacy worked. They included a woman picking up a man's shirt that Eva had completed last week, along with two other ladies picking up dresses.

As soon as she cut her last thread, Lacy jumped up and took the skirt to Eva. "It's finished."

Eva took the skirt and studied Lacy's stitches.

"Was she upset?" Lacy twisted her hand in her skirt.

"No, not too bad. Just disappointed. She understood she'd

come early when I explained that I hadn't expected her until afternoon. Since her husband's office is in City Hall across the street, she went over there to have lunch with him and then will come back." Eva spoke without taking her attention from the hem Lacy had sewn.

Lunch. Lacy hadn't thought about what she would do for a meal. She had no money to eat at the café down the street. Neither did she have time to walk all the way back to the parsonage. Lacy sighed. She'd just have to skip lunch today.

"Nice work." Eva smiled. "Now go put this skirt in one of those white boxes in the back room along with a tissue paper and put Mrs. Ellenbroek's name on it."

Lacy nodded and followed the instructions before returning to her seat.

Picking up the shirt on the top of the pile, she felt the first rumble of an empty stomach. Ignoring it, she did her best to focus on her work.

An hour later, with two buttonholes to go on the shirt, the doctor's wife entered the shop. Lacy gazed at her as admiration warmed her. If only she could have as beautiful of clothes as those Margaret Kaldenberg wore. But dressing that way took money, something Lacy didn't have. She forced her attention back to the white shirt in her hands. Her secret dream of owning a wardrobe of beautiful and stylish clothing would never come true. Not for plain, slow, poor Lacy Jones.

"I've been to Karen's house. She was concerned about how your first day is going. Packing up the children during their nap time wouldn't have worked very well for her to come check on you, so she sent me. And this." Mrs. Kaldenberg stood before her with a paper bag in her hand. "It's your lunch, my dear. Karen and I fixed it for you."

"Oh, that is so kind. You shouldn't have." Lacy glanced up at her in awe.

Mrs. Kaldenberg smiled. "I think we probably should have.

Karen knew that you hadn't taken any food with you when you left this morning, and she was worried."

Lacy accepted the bag and looked inside. A nice sandwich and a slice of pie rested in the bottom. Lacy couldn't wait to sample them.

"Thank you for making this special trip to deliver my lunch."

"No problem at all. I'm happy to have any excuse to visit the dress shop. Gives me the chance to do a little shopping." Mrs. Kaldenberg raised her brows in teasing.

Lacy chuckled, but as the stylish woman walked away, she sobered. Maybe she'd just learned a secret to maintaining a beautiful appearance. Mrs. Kaldenberg enjoyed shopping. Lacy would learn to enjoy it too. By making the perusal of new clothing a hobby, she'd surround herself with style, always aware of the newest looks. She'd start today, as soon as she got a break, looking over the dresses hanging on the racks.

Mrs. Kaldenberg probably didn't purchase her dresses pre-made from a rack. Eva would custom design her clothes with the closest attention to detail. Maybe if Lacy could keep this job, she'd help with the next dress Mrs. Kaldenberg ordered. The idea lifted her spirits and renewed her energy for the afternoon.

7

Late in the afternoon, Lacy had just put the finishing touches on the last shirt in need of buttonholes when Eva came over once again.

"Are you still working on those shirts?" She asked with a wrinkle in her brow.

"They are all finished as of right now." Lacy clipped a thread with her small scissors and held up the shirt for Eva to inspect.

She traced a finger down the row of buttons. "You do nice work, Lacy. Your mother taught you well."

Lacy's chest expanded and a smile burst across her face.

"But I must ask you to work faster. Customers are used to a thirty-six hour wait time for their orders on simpler items like skirts and underthings. We can't fall behind or we won't have time or work on our larger, more complicated orders."

Lacy nodded. "Today is only my first day, but I'm sure with more practice, I'll get faster."

"Please get right to work on those ruffles. I've collected more projects that will fill our day tomorrow." Eva turned away when the door opened. "There's Lillian. Get her skirt, please." Eva glanced at Lacy and then hurried away.

Lacy brought the skirt to the counter and handed it over to their customer.

An eager look entered Mrs. Ellenbroek's eyes as she reached for the box. The lid flew to the side and the tissue paper rustled as she searched for the new garment. "Oh, yes, this is just what I had in mind." She held the skirt up and looked it over.

"Again, my apologies that we didn't have it finished when you came," Eva said.

"The skirt is sewn to perfection, so I'm not bothered by the wait. Was it sewn by this pretty young lady?" Mrs. Ellenbroek asked.

"She sewed the hem," Eva gestured at Lacy. "Let me introduce you. She's Lacy Jones, a friend of Mrs. De Witt."

"Oh, I see." The expression on Mrs. Ellenbroek's face spoke of deep interest.

"Lacy is helping me in my shop. Today is her first day. She does excellent work. See for yourself on this hem she put in your skirt." Eva directed Mrs. Ellenbroek's attention to the skirt.

"Yes, I knew right away that it is quality work. Very nice, Lacy. I'll look forward to having you sew more articles for me in the future." Mrs. Ellenbroek reached for her handbag while Eva repacked the skirt into the box. "How much do I owe you?"

Eva named the price and completed the transaction.

"Good day, Mrs. Ellenbroek," Lacy said on her way back to her chair.

"It's a pleasure meeting you." Mrs. Ellenbroek waved her gloved hand and left the shop.

Lacy picked up the length of printed fabric intended for a ruffle and ran a loose basting stitch across the top. Pulling on the thread and gathering the fabric, Lacy formed an even ruffle that she pinned to the bodice of a dress.

The door opened again, and Lacy looked up to see Mr. Van Drunen.

Lacy gasped. The pin she thrust through the fabric kept going into her finger. She yelped and held the injured finger to her mouth in time to prevent drops of blood from staining the fabric.

She frowned at the back of the man in conversation with Eva at the counter. What was he doing here? This was a woman's dress shop, not a men's clothing store. Unless he'd ordered one of the shirts she'd sewn buttons on this afternoon. She removed her finger from her mouth and checked it for blood. When none appeared, she quickly wrapped an improvised bandage made from a scrap around her finger.

Eva approached. "Mr. Van Drunen is here to pick up his shirt. I'll see which of these matches the measurement I have here." She laid a slip of paper on the table and slid the tape measure from around her neck.

"Ah. Here it is," she said after measuring the collar and back of two shirts. "I'll take it to him." She picked up the shirt and carried it to the counter.

Lacy moved over to the sewing machine.

Several moments later, a masculine voice said her name. "Hello, Miss Jones."

She paused the treadle with her feet and turned around. Mr. Van Drunen stood there staring at her with a solemn expression on his face.

His hair was a bit ruffled, as though blown about by the wind. He wore a plain shirt, trousers, and suspenders. At this time of the afternoon, he must be stopping by on his way home after work at the orchard.

"Good afternoon." She gave a stiff nod.

"Helen Brinks told me you arrived safely in town on the night of your accident."

"Yes." Her insides stiffened. Why did he have to bring that up? The word *accident* led her mind to the damaged picture frame. She couldn't think of it without remembering this man in front of her. Neither could she look at him without feeling sorrow over the destroyed birthday gift. The two were inseparably linked. The condition of one reflected the other.

And right now, Mr. Van Drunen wasn't improving the situation. But he didn't catch on.

"Are you staying with your friend at her aunt's house?"

Lacy shook her head. "No. The De Witts offered me their guest room."

"Logan and Karen are my good friends." He said the words quietly and with intensity as though they'd gone through great difficulty together.

"Mrs. De Witt was my teacher when I attended country school in Silver Grove. I came along with Rose for a visit that should have lasted only a few days, but I like it here and want to stay. Eva was kind enough to give me a job."

"I wish you the best. I understand you get the credit for this row of buttons down the front of my new shirt."

A smile tugged at the corner of her mouth. "One of my first projects."

"My apologies to you and Mrs. Synderhof for waiting until the end of the day to stop in. I can't come until after work. If I had a wife, she could run these errands, but I do not, so must look out for myself."

No change of expression crossed his face as he spoke, so Lacy couldn't decide if he was sad about this fact or if he teased her.

Her face heated as she turned back to the sewing machine. "Good afternoon, Mr. Van Drunen."

Lacy's insides boiled as he said good-bye to Eva and left the shop. Why had he wanted to talk to her? And worse, why had she given him those answers full of so much personal information?

She huffed to dismiss the unexplainable exchange. These ruffles still waited, so she'd better get busy. Precious minutes had already been lost during her talk with Mr. Van Drunen. Now she'd have to stay late until this dress was complete. Lacy sighed. Browsing among the new dresses hanging on the racks would have to wait for another day.

CONRAD STRODE out of the shop with his shirt box tucked under his arm and his head down. Why had he said anything about his lack of a wife to Miss Jones? He could kick himself. She already didn't like him. The fact was obvious in her stiff posture and measured words. Now she'd think him a selfish heel for wanting to push jobs he viewed as unimportant off on a woman.

But it wasn't like that at all. He didn't want a woman in his life just so he could get out of showing up at PTA meetings and picking up orders for clothing from a feminine dress shop. His children deserved the comfort and stability. Good cooking and displays of affection or nurture were qualities he'd never been good at.

Angelien had been, though. His heart ached as he turned the corner onto Fifth Street. If only she was still here with him. She'd loved their children, and she'd loved him. But the proof of that love in the form of her excellent meals and her careful attention had faded from his life in the days following her death.

He stood on the sidewalk in front of the parsonage and stared. The place overflowed with activity. Horses and buggies were parked in the street along with an assortment of cars.

Through an open window the chatter of women's voices and the clinking of dishes floated on the afternoon air.

Conrad's shoulders slumped. He couldn't go in there. PTA meetings might have toughened his hide against a roomful of women, but he didn't care to test out his bravery with the group gathered at Karen's house. Today was probably her turn to host the Ladies Mission Society. Those ladies would all be dressed in their finest seated in Karen's elegant parlor and sipping from dainty china cups.

Dressed in his work clothes, he'd stand out as a misfit. The curious gazes and listening ears of nearly every woman in Logan's congregation would turn to him. They might discover the question that burdened him. Fighting defeat, Conrad retraced his steps as far as the church. Maybe Logan seated in his quiet study behind a closed door could offer a haven in which to ask his question. Logan may not have an answer, but Conrad would at least get started in the right direction.

Logan was in his study, surrounded by stacks of books and writing on a piece of paper.

Conrad sucked in a breath and knocked lightly on the open door. "Logan?"

His friend glanced up, a thoughtful furrow on his brow. "Hi, Conrad. What can I help you with today?"

Conrad claimed a chair. "I ... um ... well. I have ... this problem."

"Oh, really?" The frown returned. "What has happened?"

"At the PTA meeting this week, we finalized plans for the fall carnival. I'd hoped to get assigned the booth for the fish-pond or the horseshoe toss, but they gave me the cupcake decorating booth instead. I don't know a thing about cupcakes. We're required to work in pairs at our booths, so I thought I'd ask Karen to help me. It looks like she is hosting the Mission Society this afternoon, so I thought I'd stop in and talk to you." His lungs were completely empty of air after his explanation.

The stress of the situation stole his breath more than his request for help did.

"I suppose Karen could help you. I don't know why she couldn't, but I'll mention it to her and have her get back to you with an answer." Logan folded his hands and leaned forward. "But is Karen your only option? Don't you know any other women who might help you?"

"The women on the PTA will be busy with their own booths. I asked one of the teachers, but she doesn't know how to bake. My sister-in-law will go to the carnival with her own family. I could ask Helen Brinks, I suppose, but we work together all day. Somehow it doesn't seem fair to ask her to put more time in at night too."

Logan studied him for a few silent moments. Compassion mingled with a spark of good humor. "Come to the Labor Day picnic I'm organizing."

Conrad frowned. "What does that picnic have to do with anything?"

"You might meet some new people there."

Conrad rolled his eyes. "Now you sound like Matthew. He said the same thing. Told me I should get out and have more fun. But the crowd that attends your picnic is much younger than I am. I'd just stick out like the father with little kids." If he was one of those young women fresh from high school or college, he wouldn't want to get tied down as a parent from risking a relationship with him.

"I could use your help. There's a job that is perfect for you."

"What is it?" Conrad couldn't help asking.

"Karen and I plan to organize a tennis game, and the rackets need repaired. On the day of the picnic, we'll also need a scorekeeper to oversee and referee the game."

"I don't know. What would I do with Markus and Betje? They don't belong at the picnic."

“You wouldn’t have to stay the whole time, just long enough to eat and then watch the tennis match.”

“Well, I’ll think about it.” Markus and Betje might look forward to an afternoon of play with their cousins.

“Fine. Just let me know what you decide.” Logan smiled at him.

Conrad nodded and left the building. If he hurried, he’d stand a chance of getting supper fixed on time.

8

The next morning, after starting the day and taking the children to school, Conrad went to work at the orchard. He'd just finished the repair of some boards on the porch floor when Matthew Kaldenberg drove up the lane.

He parked the car he shared with Logan. Since Matthew had it today instead of his son-in-law, that probably meant Logan didn't have any pastoral visits in the country scheduled.

"Conrad." Matthew held up a slip of paper as he walked.

Conrad rose from his knees and watched Matthew approach.

"A call came in for you on the hotel telephone. Since I was headed out this way, George asked me to deliver it."

"Thanks." Conrad took that paper, unfolded it, and read it.

"What does it say, if I may ask?" Matthew watched him with concern in his eyes.

"The department store firm I'm working with, Gresham and Blaine, want me to come to their office for a meeting." A twist formed in Conrad's stomach. Maybe an immediate request for a meeting meant bad news. He gulped. He'd better go into town as soon as possible and call them back.

"Sounds promising." Matthew smiled at him.

"I hope you're right and that they don't have any concerns to share." Conrad stuffed the note in his pocket, went to the barn for his horse, and headed for town.

Outside the dress shop, he spotted Karen De Witt on the sidewalk. "Good morning," he called to her.

"Hi, Conrad. The fall carnival sounds like fun. I can help you." Karen smiled.

"You can? That's great. I'm so relieved." Karen's words soaked in a little at a time until Conrad grasped what her answer really meant for him. "I don't know how to bake. Can you make the cupcakes?"

"I sure can. My friend Lacy is staying with me. She can help. We'll take care of the frosting too." Karen waved at someone who passed behind him.

"That would really help me out." Conrad exhaled as though the weight of the whole world had been lifted from his shoulders.

"Lacy and I will be glad to do it. All you'll have to do is bring some decorations for the booth, and also some knives to spread frosting."

Conrad shoved his hands in his pockets. "I can handle that."

"Great. See you then." Karen squeezed his shoulder and turned away.

A warm surge flowed through him. Gratitude? Joy? He couldn't tell. But he couldn't let Karen get away without doing or saying something that would accurately express the emotions bursting forth on his insides.

"Karen."

"Yes?" She turned around.

"Tell Logan he can plan on my help at the picnic." The words blurted from his mouth.

A smile lit her face. "He'll be delighted." She turned away again and left him standing there in stunned silence.

What in the world ever made him say that? He hadn't even thought of Logan's invitation. He groaned. Just look where his relief had gotten him. Strapped down to some other volunteer job he didn't want. He could probably go to the picnic long enough to eat and referee a round or two of tennis. But no more. He still wanted time at home with Markus and Betje, as well as a few evening hours for furniture building.

Conrad hastened to the hotel and caught Ethel at the front desk. "Could you please ring the office of Gresham and Blaine for me?"

"Of course." She led him to the room with the telephone, spoke to the operator, and handed the receiver to him.

He waited until a voice came on the other end. A secretary answered. "Yes, I'd like to speak to either Mr. Gresham or Mr. Blaine, please." After a couple of clicking sounds carried over the line, a man's voice came on.

"Good morning. Will Gresham speaking."

"Mr. Gresham, this is Conrad Van Drunen. I understand either you or Mr. Blaine called earlier this morning to request a meeting with me."

"Ah, Conrad! Yes, indeed. We'd like to meet with you on Tuesday morning. The quota of kitchen tables you sent us in July has completely sold out. In our meeting, we'd like to talk about adjusting the numbers we included in your contract." Conrad could picture the sociable man leaned back in his chair, dressed in a three-piece suit, and holding a cigar.

He swallowed. "Yes, of course. Tuesday is fine. I'll plan to meet you in the morning."

"Eight-thirty, please, if that time works for you."

"I'll be there."

"Very good."

Conrad said good-bye and hung up. He'd have to go to Des Moines. But Mr. Gresham wanted a morning meeting which meant Conrad would have to travel the day before and stay overnight. Logan's picnic was scheduled for that day. Conrad could still go to the picnic, but then he wouldn't have any time with Markus and Betje before he left town.

A groan worked itself loose from his lungs as he left the hotel. One man could only be in so many places at the same time. The one place he least wanted to be was at the picnic. He'd have to cancel out on his friend.

Here was a perfect piece of evidence why he didn't try to get out and socialize more. Any effort he made usually got overruled by the demands of his family or his job. His friends were going to have to learn that their attempts to help him meet new people or try to have fun didn't work. He might as well break the news to them as soon as possible by starting with Logan.

Conrad drove to the church, found Logan in his study, and tried not to feel too relieved as he gave Logan his cancellation.

Later in the day, he arrived home in time to fix the evening meal. Hannah walked Markus and Betje back from her house where they spent the two hours between the end of the school day and his return from work. The cousins still got to play together that way, but their games and outdoor ventures were cut much shorter than in the summer.

In his usual way, he fixed the food, listened to stories of the school day during the meal, and helped with the start of homework. Later, he tucked the children into bed and went out to the workshop.

Conrad did what he did every evening. He left the house, crossed the back yard, and entered another world. He'd converted a small barn on his property to his woodworking shop. When he lit the lamp, tools hanging on the pegs reflected the glow. Projects in various stages of progress lined one wall. The smell of wood filled the air.

Conrad put on an apron and went to work. Under his saw and sandpaper, problems melted away. He applied all his concentration to the article of furniture taking shape. More identical to it were promised to Gresham and Blaine by the end of the month. If he dedicated these evening hours to the work, he'd have his business associates quite satisfied with quality pieces to sell in their stores.

~

"THIS IS FOR YOU." Eva handed an envelope to Lacy.

She took it and retreated to her workstation for a peek. Inside, she saw crisp bills in a stack of cash. Her very own money. She'd never earned a salary before. The satisfaction of holding her first payment brought on a sense of light-headedness.

Lacy closed her eyes and sat still for a moment. When the dizziness passed, she slipped the envelope into her handbag and left the shop.

"Mrs. De Witt, look," Lacy said when she arrived at the parsonage. She held the envelope out.

Mrs. De Witt took it and looked inside. "Eva paid you today."

Lacy nodded.

"Congratulations. What are you going to do with it?" A playful light shone in Mrs. De Witt's eyes."

"Maybe buy a pretty dress."

"I think you should."

Lacy took the envelope and carried it to her room. It found a safe home in the top drawer of the dresser where she slipped it under some clothes. That envelope made her happy, but the one lying on the top of the bookshelf made her uneasy. It was from her mother and had come yesterday.

She'd been expecting a note from home, and probably

should have written long ago. But she'd been busy enjoying life in this place and adjusting to a new job. Busyness didn't qualify as her only excuse. She didn't know what to say in a letter to her family. Whatever came to mind to put on paper would only hurt them.

She wanted them to know she missed them, but she also wanted them to understand that she wasn't coming back. The pain that would appear in Mama's eyes as she read the words haunted Lacy's imagination. The truth was cruel. Or maybe Lacy was the heartless one.

Slipping on an apron, she went to the kitchen to help Mrs. De Witt prepare the evening meal. She set the table, chatted with the twins, and settled Sara in her highchair. Mr. De Witt came home, kissed Mrs. De Witt, and claimed his seat. They ate together and then Lacy helped with washing the dishes.

When the job was finished, she went to her room for her mother's letter and her writing supplies. Returning to the dining room, she took a seat at the table and re-read Mama's note.

Dear Lacy:

I hope you are enjoying your visit with your teacher. Did you find her? I hope you arrived safely. Have classes started for your friend? Do you see her very much?

Where are you staying?

Don't you think it's time to come home again? Your visit has lasted two weeks. If it's money you need to make the trip, I'm sure your dad can work something out.

Please write and let us know your plans so we can pick you up at the train station.

Love,
Mama

Lacy dragged in a deep breath. Mama had asked many questions. She should have written sooner and told Mama about traveling and finding Mrs. De Witt. But then she would've had to explain about the damaged picture frame.

That news would have hurt Mama too. There didn't seem to be any way to shield her mother from cold, hard facts. She held her breath as she wrote the greeting across the top of the paper.

Mr. De Witt emerged from the kitchen where he'd been visiting with his wife. "What are you writing?"

"A letter to my parents. I received one from Mama yesterday."

He smiled. "They'll be glad to hear from you."

"I hope so." Lacy fought the urge to squirm. Mr. De Witt didn't know her letter would contain nothing but bad news.

"Can you come to the picnic on Monday? I wanted to make sure I invited you."

Lacy smiled. "I can. It sounds like fun."

"Bring Rose along."

"I'll be sure and tell her about it."

"Dad, come play a game with me." Simon trotted over and tugged on his father's hand.

Mr. De Witt moved in the direction of the parlor with his small son, leaving Lacy to once again face the task of disappointing her family.

While Mr. De Witt engaged both boys in a game and Mrs. De Witt worked some needlepoint, Lacy wrote. The scene beyond the windows darkened, and night arrived before she finished. Sara was fed and dressed in her little nightgown as Lacy read over what she'd written.

Dear Mama and Dad:

I'm sorry I haven't written sooner. To answer your questions, I did arrive safely in Oswell City, but not without a casualty. I'm so sorry to tell you that my Angel Frame was broken. I don't know when I'll ever get another one. You spent so much on my gift but now it is destroyed. I wish I didn't have to tell you. I'm so sorry.

I found Mrs. De Witt and am staying with her. She has an adorable family of two twin sons and one baby daughter. John, Simon, and Sara are their names. College classes have started for Rose. She loves school. I see her on Sundays and frequently during the week. We have fun together.

And now, I must tell you that I don't intend to come back home to Silver Grove. I found a job here working for a lady named Eva in her dress shop. I love this town. It feels like home to me. Rose and her aunt and uncle are here. Mrs. De Witt and her family are also here. I go to church with them and have met many more people through the dress shop.

I know this news is probably shocking to you. Please don't feel bad, Mama. I'm doing well and enjoying myself.

Your daughter,
Lacy

She let out a breath and folded the paper. That was that. She'd said what she needed to say. Mama would cry, and Dad might express frustration, but they'd surely settle down quickly.

Lacy slipped the sheet into its envelope as a knock came on the door. Mr. De Witt went to answer it.

Rose burst into the room. Her eyes were bright and her

speech animated. "Come with us. Some friends of mine from college are going over to Clear Brook to watch a silent picture. One of them has a car and will drive us. I've never seen a movie before. Oh, this will be so much fun. Come on!" Rose grasped Lacy's hand and pulled her out of her chair.

9

Understanding dawned on Lacy as the car sped across the dark countryside. This collection of Rose's friends was made up of couples. Rose sat on the front seat with the man who drove. Another pair shared the back seat with her, and a young man pressed against her side. He had no partner, so he must be the one intended for her.

She crowded closer to the door, looked out the window at the moonlight, and tried her best to enjoy the quiet scenery. It contrasted greatly with the atmosphere inside the car. The young man next to Lacy cracked a joke. Words he used implied lewdness. Her cheeks burned.

The young woman seated on the other side of him gave his arm a playful slap. "Really, Cooper. You're too much!" Hysterical laughter took over her speech.

Rose and the driver joined in with laughter of their own. She glanced at the people in the back seat, her smile stiffening when her eyes met Lacy's.

Lacy inhaled as Rose turned away. She'd probably hear about this later. Rose wanted her to have fun and to meet new people. Any indication that Lacy wasn't going along with this plan would invite criticism.

But how could Rose stand this? And where had she met these people? Surely they didn't all attend the strict private college where Rose was learning to be a teacher.

Lacy's head swam. Why had she allowed Rose to force her out of the house? Her quiet room at the orderly parsonage sounded wonderful right now. She'd been kidnapped. Positively kidnapped. If the walk home would not have to take place in the dark, Lacy would demand to be let out right here along the road.

But no one would pay any attention to her if she were to call out in complaint. Laughter and more silly comments filled the car.

They entered Clear Brook and drove downtown to the theater. Lacy got out and scrambled away from the group, but the young man named Cooper caught up to her.

"Hey, baby. You're my girl for tonight." He offered his arm to her.

Lacy grimaced. She didn't enjoy being called "baby," or the arrogant tone he'd used to say it.

Rose caught her eye, frowned, and cocked her head in Cooper's direction.

Lacy caught the message. Rose wanted her to go with him. An evening such as this one was Rose's way of getting Lacy out of her shell and making friends.

Sighing, she laid her fingers tentatively on Cooper's arm, and walked into the theater. "This is not my idea of fun," she muttered under her breath.

When the ticket booth came in sight, her heart missed a few beats. She had no money except the cash Eva had paid her earlier in the day, and she hadn't brough any of it with her. What should she do? Maybe if she couldn't pay for a ticket, she'd get thrown out. Then she could start that walk home.

Cooper stepped up next to her and gave the clerk enough money for two tickets.

He handed one to her. "Here ya go, baby."

Lacy grimaced again but took the ticket. She could find fun in this portion of the evening. With a growing interest in photography, she wanted to see how a motion picture worked. She settled back in her chair and gave her attention to the black-and-white figures on the screen performing their antics to the sound of comical music coming from somewhere behind her.

"Stop here, Reg." Cooper leaned forward and tapped the driver on the shoulder. With his other hand, he pointed to a building in front of them.

"Who's ready for a drink?" Reg called out.

The couple sharing the back seat with Lacy and Cooper cheered.

A vote of two was enough to sway the driver. He turned the car into the parking lot for Cooper's chosen building and brought it to a stop.

Lacy's eyes grew wide, and her jaw dropped. Cooper had just requested for Reg to take them to a restaurant that served alcohol.

She stole a peek at Rose. Did she know? Her father patronized establishments like this one. Surely she couldn't support the idea of her new friends following the same habits.

But when they sat down, Rose didn't order any drinks. She only had a small portion of food from the menu.

Lacy's faith in her friend recovered, but they were going to have to talk about this at some point. Rose may not choose to drink, but she shouldn't go out with men who did. Rose deserved better.

The concern didn't leave Lacy's heart as they drove back to Oswell City. Even with the late hour, the jovial mood reigned in the car.

"Hey, washn't that a great show?" Cooper asked.

"Loved it. Hadn't seen that one before." Reg had enjoyed a few drinks but apparently not enough to affect his speech or his driving. His words didn't come out slurred, and he managed to keep the car on the road.

"Don't forget, boys. You need to give me a lift home." The third young lady in the party, who Lacy learned went by the name of Brandie, shook her finger as though both of them were in big trouble.

"We'll take the long way. How does that sound?" Reg's suggestion for adventure only served to heighten the level of nonsense.

He slowed at an intersection and instead of going straight for the most direct route into Oswell City, he turned right, revved the engine, and took off speeding into the night.

The group erupted in more hoots and happy cheers. A heavy arm fell across Lacy's shoulders and Cooper's chin rested on the top of her head. He dangled over her in the lazy and inebriated way until they pulled on to the street where Brandie lived. Even her gentle shoves to help him sit upright didn't work.

Reg came to a stop, waved to Brandie when she got out, and then guided the car back onto the street. They'd hardly gone a block when a loud pop reached Lacy's ears. The car lurched and then drove rough.

"Ah, man. I think you've got a flat." Cooper woke up enough to advise his buddy.

Reg parked along the curb and got out. "I'd better check."

Lacy looked out the window. No one had discussed how she would get home. They weren't far away from the church. She could probably sneak out and walk across the yards of the homes between here and there. All of the houses were dark except for the light glowing in the windows of a shop in one of the yards.

Reg came back with his report. "Yep, a flat tire all right. Help me change it."

The other young man opened his door, but Cooper protested. "I gotta take my little lady home. We picked her up somewheres around here." He hiccuped and looked at Lacy.

She had to get away from him. He must not come with her to the parsonage. What would Mrs. De Witt and her minister husband say if Lacy appeared at midnight with a drunk young man? Lacy squeezed her eyes shut. She couldn't even think of it.

Cooper reached across her and opened the door.

Lacy slid out but Cooper kept a firm grasp on her arm.

"I'll walk you home. Don't go off on your own." He staggered to his feet.

"I know the way. I'll be fine." Lacy tugged her arm away, but he maintained his hold.

"I musht help you." He took a step, tripped over the jack Reg had laid in the grass, and fell down pulling Lacy with him.

A yelp escaped her lungs when she landed against his hard chest. Her legs were tangled up in his and her arm was still in his grasp.

"Let go! I must go home!" Lacy wrestled in an effort to get free, but Cooper had passed out. His dead weight kept her legs pinned.

"Allow me." A calm, mannerly voice came from somewhere above her.

She glanced up to find Mr. Van Drunen bending over her. The last time he'd helped her she'd laid face down in a busy street. Now, when he came to her aid a second time, she lay flat on her back with her limbs tangled in those of an inebriated man.

Gentle pressure on each of her ankles extracted her from

the bondage. The loss of consciousness had released Cooper's hold on her, so Lacy pushed herself to her knees. With Mr. Van Drunen's hands on her waist, she rose to a standing position.

"Come on. Let's go." Mr. Van Drunen whispered and led her away from the group.

No one would notice she was gone. Rose and the other man were too distracted assisting Reg with the tire. Lacy drew in a deep breath and flexed her fingers in full enjoyment of her freedom.

"Thank you, Mr. Van Drunen. Where did you come from?" Lacy talked in low tones as they strolled across the neighbor's lawns.

"Your friend's car broke down behind my house."

Lacy gave a cynical laugh. "He isn't my friend, believe me. None of them are. Rose got the terrible idea to invite me along with her friends." She lowered her voice. "I wish I'd never gone."

They walked in silence as they crossed another street. When they were once again in the shadows, Mr. Van Drunen picked up the conversation.

"I'd been working in my shop when I heard your cry. That's when I knew something was wrong. Not every Friday night do I hear voices in my back yard."

Lacy chuckled at his joke. "At least we didn't disturb the neighbors or provoke a call for the police."

He smiled. "It looked to me like one of the men had the situation with the car well under control. They'll soon be on their way again."

They walked in silence until he brought her as far as the pole at the end of Mrs. De Witt's clothesline.

"Well, here you are. Good-night, Miss Jones." A solemn mixture of trust and goodwill lingered in his gaze when his eyes met hers.

"Good night." She nodded and went into the house.

All was dark. Mr. and Mrs. De Witt were surely sleeping. Their children probably were too. Lacy crept to her room, changed out of her dress, and knelt for a quick prayer before crawling into bed. Mr. Van Drunen had actually been quite friendly, and he hadn't damaged any of her property in the act of helping her this time.

She rolled her eyes and groaned. If only she could manage to stay on her feet in his company. He seemed to have a genius for finding her sprawled in the most vulnerable positions. This would probably be the last time she'd speak to him anyway. Then she could forget the mortification and the pain that came with his appearances.

~

"How was the movie last night?" Mr. De Witt asked at breakfast.

"I liked learning more about how motion pictures work, but the rest of the night didn't go at all as I expected." Lacy exchanged a smile with Simon when he laid a section from an orange on her plate.

"What happened?" Mr. De Witt's brow wrinkled.

"I'm concerned about the choices Rose has made in her new friendships." Those were the best words to use in sharing the night's adventures.

"Oh, I'm sorry," Mrs. De Witt whispered as she fed Sara.

"Me too. I won't be going with them again." Lacy picked up her toast and took a bite of it.

Mr. De Witt gave her much the same look as Mr. Van Drunen had last night. Trust and goodwill with the addition of a hint of pride glowed in his eyes.

Lacy ate her breakfast in silent relief when he changed the subject.

After the meal was finished and the dishes were washed,

Rose came over. She sat with Lacy in the rocking chairs in the shaded back yard. Her flat lips and the tightness in her face told Lacy she was angry.

"Where did you go last night when Reg had that flat tire?" She demanded.

Lacy shrugged. "I left and walked home."

"We looked around for you for a long time. Why didn't you tell anyone you were leaving?"

"I'm sorry, Rose. I should have, but it all happened so fast. Cooper passed out, and you were busy helping Reg. Then he came and lifted me up. I had to go where he—"

"Who came?" Rose cut a sharp glance at her.

Pain speared her stomach. "Mr. Van Drunen. Apparently, we were stalled in his back yard. He said he'd been working in some shop he has and came to help when he heard our voices."

Rose started at her with a skeptical air. "Mr. Van Drunen."

Lacy nodded. She couldn't think why Rose would care.

"He appeared out of nowhere and then walked you home in the middle of the night."

"Yes, that's right."

"Are you sure you aren't making this up?"

"Quite sure."

Rose leaned back in her chair with a thoughtful look in her eyes as she gazed into the sky.

"Isn't that what anyone would do for a woman who had to get home in the dark?" Lacy failed to keep the defensive tone from her voice.

"But he could have helped both of us. Instead, he chose to help only you." The pink in Rose's cheeks deepened.

"Oh, Rose. Is that why you are upset? He told me that he thought the situation was under control and you'd get home soon. Besides, you weren't in trouble like I was." Lacy straightened in her chair.

"Still." Rose fingered a corner of the shawl around her shoulders.

Lacy sat in silence unable to think of anything to say. She hadn't wanted Mr. Van Drunen's attention or gone looking for it. Rose could have Lacy's share any time.

"But that's not all." Rose turned a stony gaze on Lacy. "Cooper is a perfectly nice boy. You had no reason to desert him or the rest of us. You didn't have any fun last night. I wish you would have treated Cooper nicer."

Lacy's jaw dropped. "The man was drunk. I refuse to give any attention at all to a young man who makes those kinds of bad choices."

"But he was my friend. And Reggie's, and Brandie's. That's not fair." Rose crossed her arms.

Lacy's blood simmered but she managed to stay calm. "How did you meet them? Do they go to college with you?"

"Only Reggie. He's studying to be a doctor. Cooper and Brandie are people he knows. But I've gone out with them before. That's why I thought I'd invite you. They're nice and we have fun. I thought you would, too, but I guess I was wrong."

Lacy took a deep breath. "Rose, I appreciate your wish to help me make friends, but I don't know that the group we were with last night are people I want for my friends."

"Oh." Rose toyed with her shawl some more.

"In fact, I'm surprised you want them for friends."

Rose glanced up.

"Have you forgotten your father's struggle with drinking? Why do you want to spend your time with people who do that?"

Rose shrugged. "I don't drink. That's what matters."

"Maybe."

"What do you mean?" Rose frowned.

"I just don't want to see you get hurt."

The old carefree Rose peeked through. "I won't. I promise." A hint of a smile pulled at her mouth.

"Pastor Logan invited me to the picnic on Monday. He said a large number of young people from town and the surrounding area usually attends. There's a potluck meal and a tennis match planned. Would you like to come?"

Rose shook her head. "I don't think so. I need to study."

"That's fine. I understand." Lacy's heart sank. After only a few weeks in a new town, she and her best friend were starting to grow apart.

10

"Lacy, I'd like to introduce you to Joy Haverkamp. She works at the library, and to Luke Barnaveldt. He helps his dad and his uncle at the car dealership." Mrs. De Witt gestured to each of her young friends with a smile.

"Pleased to meet you." Lacy smiled at them.

"Were either of you planning to play tennis?" Mrs. De Witt asked.

"We both are on a team." Luke held up his racket.

"Then maybe Lacy would like to play with you." Mrs. De Witt pointed at her.

"If you don't mind, I'd rather just watch. I was hoping to take some pictures." Lacy held up her camera.

"You have a camera?" Joy said with awe. "Take my picture."

"Sure." Lacy smiled, focused her camera, and clicked an image.

"Do you have a dark room and everything?" Joy asked.

"No. I send my camera to the company. They develop my photos and then send my pictures back to me along with my camera, reloaded with a new roll of film. I'll give you a print of this picture when I get it back."

"Thanks."

"Come on. Let's go get ready for the tennis game." Luke beckoned Joy to follow him.

Lacy used the time before the game started to wander around the orchard in search of promising subjects for photos. She caught one of apples ripening on a tree, Mrs. De Witt and a cluster of women visiting in the shade, and a team of men setting up the tennis net.

The rest of the afternoon she spent cheering on her new friends in the tennis match and snapping more pictures.

"I know what you should do with your photos when you get them developed," Mrs. De Witt said after they had arrived home.

"What's that?"

"Show them to Jake at the newspaper office. See if he wants to put them in the *Oswell Journal* along with an article about the picnic. Jake is always looking for news about Logan and the church."

Lacy tucked the suggestion away for consideration.

Mr. De Witt entered the room and settled on the sofa. "It really is too bad that Conrad wasn't able to attend the picnic. I'd hoped he would have the chance to get to know the young people in town a little better, but he had to leave on a business trip this afternoon."

"I agree," Mrs. De Witt said. "I'd love to see him get ... well, you know he asked me to help him with that booth at the school carnival. He needs a special woman in his life. It would be good for him." Mrs. De Witt sighed.

"Conrad and I talked about it again just last week. That's why I gave him a job to do at the picnic, but he canceled. No one can take Angelien's place in his heart, I suppose. I know that's how I would feel if I ever lost you." Mr. De Witt gave his wife a look full of affection.

"Who's Conrad?" The question burst from Lacy's mouth.

Both of the people in the room turned their attention on her.

"You probably haven't had the chance to meet him yet. If he'd come to the picnic today, you would've been introduced," Mrs. De Witt said. "He's a friend of ours. His wife died four years ago, and he has had a bit of a struggle ever since. But Logan and I pray he'll meet the right woman very soon." She reached for her husband's hand and held it.

The conversation tugged at Lacy's heart. How terrible for the young man to have lost his wife. A shudder ran through her. Mrs. De Witt and her husband cared deeply about the situation. Their concern hung on their faces as they talked about their friend.

There was nothing Lacy could do about the circumstances of this stranger, so she forced her thoughts onto the pictures she'd taken. In the morning, on her way to work at the dress shop, she would take her camera to the post office and send it to the factory to get the film inside it developed.

Later that week, Lacy stood at the kitchen table mixing a bowl of frosting. Mrs. De Witt opened the oven door and took out a pan of steaming fragrant cupcakes.

"Those look perfect." Mrs. De Witt touched the top of one. "That makes four dozen. I hope that is enough for the carnival."

"I have this frosting finished. As soon as I tint it with coloring, it will be ready." Lacy set the bowl down, glad for the break from stirring to rest her tired arms.

Mrs. De Witt set her pan on the counter and removed the cupcakes from it.

"Mama." John entered the kitchen.

"Yes, dear. What is it?"

"Sara is sick."

Mrs. De Witt turned to look at him. "What do you mean? She looked fine when she woke up from her nap."

John shrugged. "She threw up."

Mrs. De Witt glanced at Lacy and then raced out of the room.

Lacy followed her upstairs. A thump on the floor and crying greeted them as they entered the boys' room.

Simon sat on the rug surrounded by blocks and train cars. Sara lay on her side. Wails came from her mouth and tears ran down her face.

"What happened to her?" Mrs. De Witt knelt to examine the baby. A small pool of mush dampened the rug near her head.

John pointed to it. "She just threw up."

"Yes, I see that. Do you know why? Did she choke on a toy?" Mrs. De Witt picked Sara up and sat with her on the bed.

"No." John shook his head. Simon mimicked his brother's movements.

"She does feel hot. I wonder if she woke up with a fever." Mrs. De Witt held a hand to Sara's face. "Come, Sara. I'll get you cleaned up." Mrs. De Witt carried her across the hall.

Lacy left for the kitchen, filled a bucket with water, and returned upstairs to clean the rug. John and Simon collected their toys and with arms full, went downstairs to play. Only an occasional thump on the stairs from a dropped toy accompanied the trip. Lacy smiled. Those boys were quite determined to get away from the scene of their sister's vomit.

Soon everyone was gathered in the parlor. The boys with their blocks and train set, and Sara in her mother's arms.

Mrs. De Witt continued to check her over. "Lacy, could you please run across to the church and ask Logan to get the doctor?"

"Of course." She left her chair and hastened to the church.

Mr. De Witt stood in the hallway talking with two other

men. Lacy slowed her steps as she approached. They might be carrying on an important conversation that she shouldn't interrupt. But Mr. De Witt held his hand out to her as though to welcome her. She ventured closer.

"We can talk this over some more at the next meeting." One of the men tipped his hat as they left.

Mr. De Witt turned his attention to Lacy. "Hi, Lacy. What can I help you with?"

"Mrs. De Witt sent me. Sara is sick. She wants you to go for the doctor."

His easy demeanor turned stiff and tense. "I'll go right now."

Lacy nodded and ran out.

~

"Will Sara be all right?" Simon watched his sister crying and writhing on her mother's lap. She looked very uncomfortable.

"The doctor is coming soon. That will help her." Mrs. De Witt forced a smile.

Lacy answered the door when the doctor arrived. He strode into the house and began an immediate examination on the small patient.

"She has symptoms of influenza. Not too serious, but enough that you should keep an eye on the rest of the family. I expect it should clear up quickly, but she'll have a rough night. This strain has been around town recently, and this is how it has affected most of my patients. Only feed her liquids overnight and bathe her face and neck to keep her fever down. I'll check on her in the morning." Dr. Kaldenberg put his hat back on and left.

Mr. De Witt rested his hand on his wife's shoulder. "He didn't sound too worried, but she does look sick."

Mrs. De Witt stood and held Sara. "I should stay home with her tonight instead of helping Conrad at the carnival. I wish I didn't have to cancel, but I can't leave Sara."

"I'll keep the boys occupied and help you with supper if you like." Mr. De Witt offered.

"Thanks, Logan. I wonder if Lacy could go in my place." Mrs. De Witt and her husband both looked at Lacy.

"I guess I could. If Mr. De Witt is staying home to care for the twins, then I'm the only one available. Sure, yes. I can go." A sense of heroism crept over Lacy. She'd change her evening plans to go out among strangers and help Conrad, the De Witts' lonely, grieving friend.

Mrs. De Witt smiled. "Collect the cupcakes in a basket and cover your bowls of frosting. Logan can drive you."

While Mr. De Witt set to work frying food in a skillet, Lacy divided her frosting, tinted it in a variety of pastel colors, and prepared her supplies for travel. At the last minute, she sneaked into her room for a camera. Her new camera, the one Cal had given her for her birthday, was on its way to have the film developed, but her old camera still worked. It was worn on the edges and had a small scratch on the lens but could capture scenes just fine. She slipped it into her basket. The night ahead might offer intriguing opportunities to snap a photo.

After supper, Mr. De Witt drove her to the school. Cars, horses, and buggies filled the parking lot. People milled about, entering and exiting the building. Light spilled from the windows. Children ran around laughing and playing games.

"I'll take you inside so that I can introduce you to Conrad and explain Karen's absence." Mr. De Witt steered his car into an empty gap between two other cars, shut off the motor, and escorted her into the school.

They wove through the congested hallway until reaching the gymnasium. Past the fishpond, the pin-the-tail-on-the-donkey, a horseshoe toss, sack race, and bobbing for apples,

Lacy spotted the cupcake decorating booth. A table with chairs were set up in the center. Knives and plates filled the middle of the table.

A man stepped out from behind a shelf. His dark hair, brown eyes, and solemn expression belonged to someone she'd never forget.

A gasp escaped her lungs as the basket she carried thumped onto the table.

"Hi, Conrad. Karen can't come this evening since Sara isn't feeling well. Her friend has come in her place. I'd like for you to meet Miss Lacy Jones, a former student of Karen's from Silver Grove." Mr. De Witt gestured to Lacy and then to Conrad. "Lacy, this our friend, Conrad Van Drunen."

Her knees went weak. The carnival swirled around her. Voices buzzed in her ears. Children ran past. Noise and energy and motion were everywhere. But where Lacy stood, the world came to a halt and went silent. All she could do was stare.

Conrad offered her a tiny smile before turning to Mr. De Witt. "Miss Jones and I have already met."

"You're ... you're ..." Lacy's limp hand pointed a weak finger at him.

"Mr. Van Drunen." A grin tugged at the corner of his mouth as though he enjoyed the memory of their first meeting. "But please, call me Conrad."

Lacy covered her hand with her mouth. Her heart pounded and her eyes smarted. Something was terribly out of place. This man, the villain who destroyed her precious gift, shouldn't be standing here as Mr. And Mrs. De Witt's good friend. How did Mr. Van Drunen come to be Mrs. De Witt's partner at a children's carnival, and decorating cupcakes of all things?

"How did the two of you meet?" Mr. De Witt asked.

"In Des Moines when I was on a business trip." Conrad spoke quietly while keeping his attention on Lacy.

She closed her eyes for a moment. He'd better not say any more. The details were better left in the past.

"I'd love to know more, but I see that a line is forming for your booth. Time for me to get out of the way." He nodded to Conrad and left.

"Come on over, everyone. Take a seat. Here's a cupcake for you." Conrad unpacked the basket she'd brought. As soon as each child at the table had a cupcake, he left the parents to assist with the spreading of frosting. "Miss Jones? Are you all right?" He bent and whispered in her ear.

She didn't know. All she could do was catch her breath and fight dizziness.

He grasped her upper arm and led her to the corner, partially hidden by the shelf. "What's wrong?"

Lacy shook her head to clear it. "I didn't know. I mean ... I'd promised to help Mrs. De Witt at the last minute. She said Conrad needed a partner to help him at the carnival, but I didn't know I'd get paired with ... with ... you." Her chest tightened. This man had destroyed her cherished gift. But he had such expressive brown eyes. Warmth and understanding glowed in them as he looked into hers.

His attention flicked away from her face as he glanced at her arms and skirt as though searching for a clue to her distress. Then he looked into her eyes again. "Come on. This booth is busy. The kids need our help."

Lacy let him guide her to the table.

11

Conrad released his hold on Miss Jones's arm and bent over a boy at the table with a frosted cupcake in his hand.

"Now sprinkle on some of this." Conrad took a pinch of colored sugar from a bowl and rained it over the cupcake.

"Look, Mom!" The grade-schooler smiled and held his finished cupcake out to his mother.

"That looks really nice. It'll probably taste good too. We need to go find your sister. Come on, now, and let someone else have your seat."

The boy left with his mother and a girl of the same age bounced into his chair. She claimed a cupcake and reached for a knife. Miss Jones appeared on the scene to help the girl choose a color of frosting.

Conrad moved on to assist another child. He gave enough attention to the tasks before him to satisfy his young customers, but his gaze returned again and again to his partner.

She moved among the children and their parents with grace. A quiet comment for an adult, or a word of encouragement for a child flowed naturally. When one of the girls dropped her cupcake on her plate, leaving frosting behind, Miss Jones soothed her and showed her how to redecorate it. Soon the little girl was happy again.

Another time, Miss Jones knelt beside a young boy and helped him hold his knife. They worked together smoothing blue frosting over the surface of his cupcake. When he laid the knife down and took a generous bite of his finished product, Miss Jones laughed.

Enjoying the scene, Conrad crossed his arms and leaned against the wall. *Nurture* was the word that came to mind as he watched her. Kindness swirled around her, touching everyone.

From her place at the end of the table, she reached into her basket and drew out a small brown box. "Will you let me take your picture?"

Several children raised their heads from the cupcakes they'd been concentrating on and looked at Miss Jones.

"Sure!"

"Yeah."

"Wow, a real camera!"

The enthusiastic response made her laugh again. "All right, then. On the count of three." She counted and then snapped a photo.

Strolling around the table, she clicked more photos of the children, of their cupcakes, and even of him.

Conrad grunted and straightened away from the wall. He'd gotten caught noticing a pretty blonde. Time to get back to work. Shoving his hands in his pockets, he sauntered over to a newcomer and helped him find a place to sit.

Miss Jones worked her way around the table assisting the children until stopping at the one next to him. "These kids are doing a really good job. Look how much fun they're having." She picked up a decorated cupcake. "Doesn't this look nice?"

He took a step closer for a better look. His hand rested on her arm as he admired a grade-schooler's creativity. "It sure does. You and Karen did a great job baking all of these cupcakes."

Miss Jones flushed as she set the cupcake back in front of the little girl she'd borrowed it from.

A deep, sweet pang shot through Conrad. In that moment, he caught a vision of what his homelife could look like again. Children seated at the table. A kind and attractive young woman at his side nudging him to appreciate the beautiful and the creative. His soul longed for it. Beyond delicious cooking and care for his home, Conrad desired a person in his life who would do this very thing for him.

He created beautiful pieces of furniture every day. The interest in making art was present in his character, but Angelien hadn't fully understood that. She'd chafed at his woodworking endeavors. The handyman job had been enough for her.

But what if he could find a woman who shared his enjoyment of crafting something meaningful out of nothing? That's the fun he had in his workshop every night.

Miss Jones sewed dresses with Eva. She took photographs, and she decorated cupcakes. A fellow artist had come to help him this evening.

She turned to look at him. A smile lingered on lips inches away from his. He wrestled with the ache deep inside him to love again. Did he dare to listen to those thoughts that maybe a woman meant just for him existed in the world? Was she standing here in front of him? Conrad looked into her eyes in a search for answers.

"Conrad!"

The moment shattered. He turned in the direction of the call.

Carlin Reese, the fifth-grade teacher, waved at him so he went over to her. "We thought you and your partner might like something to eat." She pointed to another one of the teachers who carried a stack of sandwiches.

"Fresh from the concession stand," she said.

"Very thoughtful. I'll ask Miss Jones if she would like one." Conrad got her answer and returned to the teachers. "Two sandwiches, please."

"Coming right up." Carlin handed them over to him. "Would you like anything to drink? Coffee?"

"I'll take some. Bring a cup for Miss Jones too." Conrad took a sandwich to her while Carlin and her assistant hurried away. "For you," he said as he gave a sandwich to her.

They ate in silence while another batch of children left with their frosted cupcakes. Activity at the carnival had started to wind down so fewer children came to their booth.

"Thanks for being willing to come in Karen's place tonight. You really helped me out." Conrad glanced at Miss Jones before taking another bite of his sandwich.

"The children had a good time," she said in a soft voice as she watched the dwindling activity around them.

"I did too." Conrad's voice was just as quiet as hers.

She turned her attention on him. A hint of a question hung in her eyes.

"You aren't still mad, are you? About your damaged picture frame, I mean." Until he'd spoken the question out loud, his feelings on the subject had lain dormant. Now they surged to the surface. Only one answer would calm them.

She sighed. "No, I guess not. Just sad."

Sorrow was much better than anger. Her reply soothed him enough that his emotions settled down.

"Maybe you can get a replacement." He took a sip from his coffee cup.

She shook her head. "No, I don't think so."

Logan approached their booth and looked at Miss Jones. "Are you ready to go?"

She put the last bite of her sandwich in her mouth and nodded.

"How did it go?" Logan asked as Miss Jones gathered her belongings.

"Really well. Everyone had a good time." Conrad drew in a breath.

"Even you?" Logan's brow rose.

Conrad nodded. "Even me."

"Good." Logan grinned.

Miss Jones returned to his side. "Good night, Conrad." A hesitant smile tugged at her mouth.

"Good night. Thanks again." He puffed out some air. The thoughts and emotions churning inside him all evening had worn him out. A fishpond or the horseshoe toss would have been much easier. Cupcakes opened up to him a world he wanted but feared he would never find.

MONDAY AFTERNOON, Lacy tidied her work area while Eva helped a customer. She glanced at the clock. The workday had ended, and the shop was quiet. Lacy wandered over to the racks of dresses. They were on her way to the door, so she'd take a few minutes to browse.

Ever since Eva had paid her, Lacy had her eye on a pretty dress. Secretly, she'd picked it out as hers. But if a customer came to the shop and wanted it, the dress must go to them instead. Her first paycheck shouldn't be spent all on one garment. She must wait until after Eva paid her again so she could save a little more money. But she could admire the dress in the meantime.

She lifted the skirt out so it fell in attractive folds. The cream-colored fabric rippled in the sunlight. The delicate lace overlay on the bodice gave a touch of elegance. It looked like the kind of outfit Mrs. De Witt or her mother would wear. If she timed her purchase right, she'd have some extra money to spend on a matching hat.

The vision of herself in the stylish gown filled her imagination and stole her breath. How grown-up and sophisticated she'd feel wearing it. But then a heated wave of nausea rolled over her. A fancy dress couldn't cover the facts. She'd still be poor little Lacy Jones, the girl who'd been sickly as a child. The girl the boys in her country school tormented with pranks and teasing because of her difficulty comprehending her schoolwork. Poor, sickly, and stupid. Yes, those words summed up her experience.

Head hung low, Lacy turned away from the dress. Who was she to ever desire wearing such a creation?

"See you tomorrow," Eva said as Lacy sauntered toward the door.

She raised her hand for a wave, but her usual cheery response wouldn't come. The walk to the post office made her feel better. She'd sent the camera away to get the film developed. Enough time had passed for her pictures to return, so she went inside to check the De Witt mailbox.

A box filled it. The return address belonged to the company that made her camera. Lacy held her breath as she opened the package. Mrs. De Witt had planted the idea in her head to show her photos of the picnic and of the carnival to the editor of the newspaper.

A stack of black and white prints slid into her hand. A quick glimpse at the ones on top assured her that the rolls of film she'd received had come from her camera.

She bent for a look in the box to check for more mail. Three envelopes lay in it. Two were addressed to Pastor Logan, but the third one had Lacy's name on it. The letter had come from Silver Grove. Dad's name along with Mama's filled the first line of the return address.

A knot formed in Lacy's stomach. This letter must contain the response to her news of a job and decision to stay. She longed to know what Mama said, but she dreaded the discovery. Reading the note was an activity she must save for later instead of indulging her curiosity here in the lobby of the post office. Tucking the envelope in a pocket, she returned outdoors and followed the sidewalk to the office of the *Oswell Journal.*

Rose stood outside the bank smiling at a man as she talked. The light in her eyes and the pleasure on her face told Lacy that her friend thought highly of him. Lacy narrowed her eyes and studied the back of the person in conversation with Rose. Something about him struck her as familiar.

"Hi, Rose. Nice afternoon, isn't it? I'm so glad to see you back in town already today. Are your classes finished for the week?" Lacy stopped and gave her attention to her friend.

"Yes, classes are done. Conrad was just telling me of his assistance to my aunt Helen. He helped her get started making apple cider today." Rose cast an adoring glance at her subject.

Lacy's jaw dropped as her attention strayed to him.

He smiled. "Good afternoon, Miss Jones. What a pleasant surprise."

"Conrad offered to take me to the orchard sometime to help with the cider. Doesn't that sound like fun?" Rose's voice cut through Lacy's haze.

She glanced at her friend. "Yes, it does."

"It isn't quite like that." Conrad chuckled. "You can come along, too, if you like."

A frown wrinkled Rose's brow. "You're probably busy working, aren't you, Lacy?"

"Not any more than you are in school." Lacy shrugged.

"Maybe a Saturday will work out. Have your aunt bring both of you girls when she comes to work." Conrad's offer deepened Rose's frown.

"I'll check with Mrs. De Witt." Lacy spoke softly. Maybe her peaceful answer would make Rose's frown go away.

"What do you have there?" Conrad pointed to the package in her hand.

"These are the photos I took of the Labor Day picnic and of the school carnival. Mrs. De Witt suggested that I submit them to the newspaper."

"That's a great idea." Conrad's enthusiastic comment brought the frown back to Rose's face.

Rose's scowl made Lacy uncomfortable. She backed away and held her packet of photos closer. "I'd better keep going. Nice to see both of you."

Her stomach quivered as she passed the stores along Main Street. Rose's attention to Conrad shouldn't bother her, but Lacy kept recalling the pleasure on Rose's face as she stood on the street with him. The scene played over and over in Lacy's mind until a startling truth dawned on her. Rose had been flirting with Conrad. Lacy's arrival had been an interruption.

But Conrad had invited her to the orchard along with Rose. Surely Rose hadn't developed an interest in him. If she had, then she wouldn't want any interference.

Lacy lifted her chin. Rose didn't need to worry about her. She had no designs on Mr. Van Drunen. She'd helped him out as a favor to Mrs. De Witt. No further reason existed for her to spend any more time with him. If the trip to the orchard transpired, she'd go only as Rose's friend.

Entering the newspaper office, she found Jake Harmsen, the editor, seated at a large wooden desk.

"Good afternoon, Miss. What can I help you with?" He pushed a pencil behind his ear and looked at her.

"I'm Lacy Jones. I'm new to town, but I work at the dress shop and stay with the De Witts. I enjoy photography, so I took pictures of the Labor Day picnic and of the carnival at the school. I wondered if you might be able to use them."

"I'll certainly take a look at them. Adding a photo or two to an article makes the paper more interesting."

Lacy laid her pile of photos on the desk. "Here is the entire collection. You may choose the best ones."

"Fine. Return in a couple of days to pick them up. We'll make a decision by then."

Lacy nodded and returned to the street. Her chest swelled. She'd just submitted her first photos to the newspaper. No decision had been made yet, but the editor was positive. She'd taken a step in the right direction.

But maybe he'd decide not to use any of her photos. They might not be good enough. She'd used her old, cheap camera to take the pictures. The editor would probably notice.

She drew in a breath. She'd just have to wait for him to decide. At least she'd tried. Mrs. De Witt had given her a suggestion, and she'd listened.

Now that she'd arrived home, the time had come to find the courage to read Mama's letter. It probably didn't contain any more good news than Lacy's had. After greeting Mrs. De Witt and handing her the mail for her husband, Lacy went to her room, slit the envelope, and began to read.

12

"You look troubled, Lacy. What's wrong?" Mr. De Witt studied her as he sat across from her at the dining room table.

Lacy roused from her thoughts and pushed the food around on her plate with her fork. "I received a letter from Mama this afternoon."

"What did she say?" Concern wrinkled his brow.

"She and Dad want me to come back home. They insist on it. In fact, my brother Cal is coming to get me over his mid-term break." Her forlorn voice didn't do very well disguising her tears. They stung the corners of her eyes. "But I don't want to go. I want to stay in Oswell City. My job is here, and so are all of you." She wiped her eyes with her hand, but too late to prevent a trickle of tears from running over her cheek.

"What are you going to do when your brother comes? He'll expect you to go home to Silver Grove with him." Mrs. De Witt paused in feeding Sara.

"I have to prove to him that I can make a way here on my own. With my salary from Eva's shop, I should be able to do that." Lacy scooped some vegetables onto her spoon and raised it to her mouth. She must try to eat something even though her stomach felt tight.

"What do you have in mind?" Mr. De Witt's brow rose.

"An apartment of my own to rent. There must be somewhere in town for a girl like me to live." She sat straighter in her chair as she dared to take another bite.

"But is that really necessary? We love having you here. You are welcome to stay as long as you like." Mrs. De Witt's voice held disappointment.

"I know, and I enjoy staying with you. But don't you see? If Cal finds me living with a family, he'll think I might as well go home and live in Silver Grove. But if I am living in my own place, he'll believe me when I say that I don't have to return to the farm. He'll just want to take care of me, like Mama and Dad. That's how it's always been. But I'm healthier now, and stronger too. And I turned eighteen this summer. I don't need big brother Cal looking out for me anymore."

Mrs. De Witt exchanged a look with her husband.

"Sounds like we better start finding a place for you to live." Mr. De Witt broke eye contact with his wife and shifted in his chair.

"Do you have any ideas, Logan?" Mrs. De Witt asked.

"I'll check with Paul. He usually has the best information on the housing available in town."

"But she doesn't want a house, just an apartment."

"Maybe two or three rooms. Nothing fancy." Lacy ate the food on her plate as the conversation turned to other topics.

If Mr. De Witt could help her find a place to live, she'd surely have the proof of her independence to convince her brother to let her stay.

The next afternoon, while Lacy fitted a collar to the neckline of a dress, Mr. De Witt came in the dress shop. He pulled a chair up next to her and spoke in a low tone. "I think I've found a place for you."

"Really? So soon?"

"Yes. Artie Goud has two rooms available on the second floor."

"You mean the building next door?" Lacy pointed to the wall separating the dress shop from the Goud family's jewelry store.

Mr. De Witt's smile answered her question.

"I can't believe it. I never thought I'd get to live so close, right downtown. When would it be available?"

"The rooms are empty now. His wife wants to clean them, and then they are yours."

"Did he say how much they would cost?"

"He did, and you can easily afford it."

"What about furniture? Does he have any? I would need furniture since I don't have any of my own."

"I'll check with Karen. Her mother might have some. The doctor's house is large for only two people. I'm sure they could spare a dresser or a table. Helen might know of some extra pieces at the orchard as well."

Lacy gulped. "I don't know what to say. This has come about so suddenly."

Mr. De Witt gave her one of his trademark smiles. "We want to help you, Lacy. You were special to my wife when she had you as a student in Silver Grove."

A warm feeling of belonging flooded through her. This was why she wanted to stay here. Mrs. De Witt and her husband were here and so was a larger community of people who welcomed her and offered to support her.

"Thank you. This is all very kind."

He laid his hand on her shoulder. "I'll go home and let Karen know. She'll start collecting furniture for you."

"Tell Mrs. Goud I want to help her with the cleaning."

He nodded and left the shop.

Lacy drew in a deep breath. In the course of one conversation, her life had completely changed. She was moving into her own apartment as her way of stating to her brother and everyone else that she could take care of herself. The days of poor health and poverty were behind her. A steady job that paid well and a place to live were hers. She had friends and the love that came with them. Lacy couldn't think of one more thing a girl could possibly want.

MRS. GOUD ACCEPTED Lacy's offer to help clean the apartment. The two of them finished the job on Saturday morning. Mrs. De Witt and her mother provided her with basic pieces of furniture.

"We'll miss you. But you are nice and close. Come over to see us as often as you can." Mrs. De Witt hugged her.

"I will. I promise."

"Bring your brother for supper tomorrow night. Logan and I will look forward to seeing him again." Mrs. De Witt pulled away and kept her hold on Lacy's upper arms.

She nodded. "He'll enjoy that. We both will."

Mrs. De Witt looked around as though she searched for one more task that might delay her departure. When she couldn't find one, she turned to Lacy. "You have a nice comfortable home here. I'm sure you'll enjoy it very much."

"Come, Karen." Mr. De Witt rested his hand on her back and guided her to the door.

When they left, Lacy took a tour of her nest. A table and two chairs sat beneath the window that looked out onto the street. A small stove stood on one wall with the sink on the opposite one. The other half of the room held a loveseat and a well-used wingback chair the doctor's wife had pulled out of her attic. The second small room held a bed, a dresser, and Lacy's suitcases.

She was all moved in except for a supply of groceries. The cupboard on the wall near the stove was empty. Lacy must get down to the store and buy a few items before it closed.

But first she must count her money. She was on her own now, with no one to look out for her. Spending must happen carefully and only on important purchases. Her childhood on the farm in Silver Grove had taught her well about frugal living.

Lacy sat at her table with a pencil and paper. She must pay Mr. Goud rent every month. That would take over half of her income. And then there was that cream dress hanging on the rack in the dress shop. If she set aside some money from each of her paychecks, she could save gradually until the big day when she might claim the dress as hers.

A few scratches of her pencil as she subtracted another amount left her with a number smaller than she expected. Lacy frowned at the page. Could she really live on that? But oh, how she wanted that dress. Surely she'd get by on simple meals until she bought it.

Sighing, Lacy stood, gathered some cash, and went to the store.

Jake Harmsen from the newspaper met her in an aisle. "Good evening, Miss Jones. I'm glad to see you because I wanted to tell you that I've used three of your pictures in next week's paper. You can stop by the office on Monday and pick up your photos."

A smile broke out on Lacy's face. "I'll do that."

He nodded and moved to the cash register. She walked the aisle in a daze of pleasure. Mr. Harmsen had used her photos. They were good enough to put in the paper. Maybe he would accept more of her work in the future. If he did, then Lacy may have finally found a way to use her interest in photography.

More than just hanging photos on her wall that only she would see, she could publish pictures in the paper to help tell stories, sharing beauty and memories with others. Weightlessness accompanied her motions as she collected food items from the shelves and took them home. This new arrangement with the newspaper was yet another reason why she wanted to stay in town. She couldn't let her brother or anyone else steal it away from her.

~

SUNDAY AFTERNOON, Lacy stood on the platform of the Oswell City train station and watched passengers get off the train. One young man caught her attention. He wore a suit and a trim haircut.

"Cal!" She waved at him.

He shifted his focus onto her and smiled. Dropping his bag, he gathered her into a hug. "Hi, little sis. How are you?"

"Fine." She chuckled.

He pulled away and glanced at her. "You look well. Enjoying your time here?"

"Yes, very much. Come on. I'll take you to my apartment." She picked up his bag.

"You have an apartment?" The disbelief raised his voice.

"I do. You'll like it. Mrs. De Witt invited us for supper, so we'll only stop long enough to show you around." Lacy threaded through the crowd to the street.

Cal followed. "It'll be nice to see Pastor Logan again. I want to tell him about my classes. But first, I want to check in at the hotel. Do you mind?" He tilted his head in the direction of the Oswell City hotel when they passed it.

"No, not at all." Lacy came to a stop.

"Great. I'll just be a minute." Cal went inside.

Lacy stayed on the sidewalk while she waited for him. Her stomach trembled. Now that Cal was in town, they'd have a conversation. A serious one about Lacy's situation. She must stand her ground. Her family didn't see her life in the same way she did. She must make Cal understand.

He emerged from the hotel and fell in step at her side. "This is a nice little town. I bet you like it here."

"I do." Her voice shook. "Here's the door to my apartment," she said when they reached the jewelry store. She produced her key, unlocked the door, and led her brother upstairs.

"So, this is where you live." Cal settled his hands on his waist and looked around the room. "How do you afford it?"

"I have a job."

"A job?" He sounded more astounded than he did over the news of her apartment.

"Yes. I work at the dress shop next door." Lacy couldn't keep the defensiveness out of her voice.

Cal whooshed out a breath and ran his hand through his hair. "Dad and Mama wouldn't approve." He looked at her. "You know why I'm here, don't you?"

"Yes. Mama wrote to me and said she and Dad had asked you to come get me and take me back home." She folded her arms over her chest.

"Right. I have to be back to school by Wednesday, so, if you'll just get packed up, we'll catch the morning train for Silver Grove."

Lacy shook her head. "No, Cal. I can't do that."

"Why not?"

"Well, like I said, I have a job."

He shrugged. "Quit."

"I also pay rent on this apartment." Her veins heated at his nonchalance.

He shrugged again. "Move out."

Her temperature rose. He wasn't catching on. What else could she do to make him see? "Cal, leaving isn't as easy as you think. My friends are here. Rose, Eva, and the De Witts."

He leaned forward. "You have friends in Silver Grove.

Family too. What about Dad and Mama, Grandpa and Grandma, and all of the cousins? How do you think they feel about you refusing to come back?"

Lacy settled her hands on her hips. "They weren't enough to hold you in Silver Grove. You left. Why can't I?"

Cal stood. "But that's different. I hope to go back when my education is complete. You ... well, you took off on a whim with that Agnes Harper girl, never to be seen again."

"How do you know you'll have anything to do in Silver Grove when you graduate from seminary? Maybe you'll end up at a big church in the city."

Cal shook his head. "No, it's the country for me. If Peter Betten is still at the church in Silver Grove when I graduate, then I'll ... I'll settle in a town nearby. There are plenty, you know. I won't desert Mama and Dad like you have."

His words sliced, but she must still keep standing. "I'm not deserting them. My choice to stay here is about me. For my whole life, I've had you or Mama fussing over me, watching me, and taking care of me. I was glad to have your attention when I was a child. But I'm not a sickly little girl anymore. I need to know that I can take care of myself, that I'm like other young women my age, and that I have something to offer that makes a difference."

Cal frowned for a long time. "I don't know, Lacy. You could live with Mama and Dad on the farm and do everything you want to do."

"No, I couldn't."

"Why not?"

She gazed out the window. "There are things I want to find out about me ... about the world."

Cal whooshed out another breath. "You sure are a stubborn one."

"The De Witts are expecting us for supper. Come on. We

can talk more about this later." Lacy led the way to the door and walked ahead of him down the street.

She and Cal hadn't been at odds before. He'd always been her champion, the strong one rescuing her from threatening situations. Love for him nearly burst her heart. But she no longer needed his solicitation. Respect was now all she asked.

Mr. De Witt threw the door open wide as he welcomed them inside. The tension faded into the background for the evening but heightened when Cal came to her apartment from the hotel the next morning.

Lacy had finished pinning up her hair and went to the door on her way to work at the dress shop. Cal stood there tall and unmoving, an obstacle planted squarely in her way.

"Where are you off to?" He frowned at her.

"I must be at work in ten minutes."

His eyes rolled. "Enough fooling around, Lacy. Our train leaves in an hour. You have to get ready to come with me."

"I'm not going." She glanced into his eyes, squeezed past him, and descended the stairs to the street.

He followed her. "Lacy, come on. This is silly. You have to come home. Now."

How dare he order her around like a preschooler. Hot tears slid down her face as she turned to him. "Don't talk that way out here. I don't want to make a scene."

Businessmen she knew along with shoppers and other citizens walked past them. A few glanced at her. Others raised their brows. She didn't want anything to happen with Cal that would send questions her direction later. Or that would intensify her embarrassment. If they had to have an argument, why couldn't he have waited until they were off the street and out of the public eye?

"Then come with me."

"No. I'm going to work."

Cal huffed. "Then what am I supposed to do?"

Lacy gritted her teeth. "Catch the train by yourself. I'm staying." She spun around, walked to the door of the dress shop, and went inside.

Her brother didn't follow, so she didn't see him again. She pictured him checking out of the hotel, riding the train to the farm, and confessing to Mama and Dad that his mission had failed.

Would he try again? Probably not. Travel was expensive and he likely didn't have much more money than she did.

Lacy settled in at her workstation and tried to focus on the stack of pattern pieces, but Cal's visit had rattled her. She'd sent him off alone, but inside she wasn't as strong as she wanted him to think. Shaken was the best word to describe her frame of mind. She was still the ordinary and struggling girl she'd always been. Her life here in Oswell City was an experiment, after all, and it was a project that could very easily fail and come crashing down around her.

13

"Hold that side," Conrad said to Helen as they worked together at the cider press.

"Got it." She leaned in with both hands on the frame.

Conrad made some turns with the large screw that ran down through the middle of the press. Soon a stream of honey-colored liquid flowed into the bucket.

"Looks good." Helen glanced at the cider and then at him.

"Sure does. How many more bushels do we have?" Conrad asked as he turned the press.

"The supply is endless this year. Seems to me we are just getting started."

He nodded. Ever since they'd begun to harvest the orchard's apples, he'd thought the same. The crop was abundant, overflowing into baskets and wagon boxes. He'd be at this task for a long time. But the surplus was good. Since the orchard ran on funds generated by the apple harvest, the large crop meant stability.

"I think that does it." Conrad made one more turn of the press, but no more apple juice trickled out.

"I'll pour." Helen lifted the full bucket and took it to the table where empty glass jars waited.

A Ford Model T puttered up the lane and parked in front of the house. Two men got out and walked over.

"Hello, Conrad!" Matthew Kaldenberg waved. Logan came with him.

Conrad straightened from cleaning apple peelings out of the cider press.

"How is the cider coming along?" Logan asked.

"Great. Helen and I were just commenting on the large apple crop." Conrad pointed to the wagon parked under a tree containing his day's work.

"Matthew and I came out to help. Mind if we lend a hand?" Logan asked.

"Please," Conrad invited. The orchard belonged to the church. Logan, as the pastor, and Matthew, as a member of the church board, would want to get involved in turning a profit.

"We brought the mail out for you." Matthew handed a stack of newspaper and envelopes to Helen. "We know how busy you are right now, so we thought it would help if we saved you a trip to town."

"It does. Thanks." Helen smiled at him, opened the paper, and began to read.

Matthew and Logan rolled up their sleeves and set to work grinding a batch of apples in the mill. Conrad finished clearing the press of peelings so that it was ready for another batch.

Helen came over and patted his cheek. "Congratulations, Conrad."

"About what?" He frowned.

"Your girlfriend. I'm so glad you found someone to court. She looks like a nice young lady." Helen smiled at him.

"What?" Had she gone crazy? He was courting no one, and he certainly did not have a girlfriend. "Where did you get an idea like that?" He placed his hands on his hips and peered at her.

Logan and Matthew quit working and joined the group.

"Why, it's right here in the newspaper. You can't miss it." Helen pointed to the front page of the *Oswell Journal*. "Folks will be so happy for you."

Conrad whipped the newspaper out of her hand. The photo on the front page threatened to relieve his stomach of his breakfast. There in plain black and white for all the world to see blared a photo of him and Miss Jones. His hand rested on her arm, and he stood only inches away from her smiling into her eyes. The moment in which this photo had been taken would remain etched in his memory forever. It was an evening he'd never forget. And now that this picture had appeared in the paper, it would stay in everyone else's memory too.

A description of the school carnival surrounded the photo, but he didn't have the wits about him to read it. Heat washed over him and seared his cheeks.

"What's wrong?" Logan's brow wrinkled as he took a turn with the newspaper. A grin tugged at his mouth but didn't get the chance to spread across his face.

Logan tried his best not to laugh, for which Conrad thanked him. But the fact that he wanted to made the heat in Conrad's cheeks flare again.

Matthew looked at the paper. After a moment of silence, he turned to Conrad. "That's Miss Jones, isn't it?"

Conrad nodded.

"She stayed with Karen and me until last week when she moved into the apartment above Artie's store." Logan read as he talked.

"I'd asked your wife to help me with the carnival, but she sent Miss Jones in her place. I should have just gone against the rules and managed the cupcake booth on my own." Conrad kept his focus on the toes of his shoes.

"You look quite well acquainted," Matthew said.

Conrad dared to glance at him. "Not very much."

He'd scooped her out of a busy city street and helped her find her way home in the middle of the night, but neither occasion gave him the right to think of her in relation to him at all, or to look so pleased with himself as the paper suggested.

He slammed his hand on the table. "Now the rumors will spread that she's my girl. But she isn't. I don't have one. I don't even—" He'd planned to say that he didn't want a girl for his own. But after spending the night of the carnival with Lacy, that was no longer true. He did want someone in his life that he could look at just like he was looking at Lacy in the picture.

But to see it plastered all over this week's newspaper exposed him. The truth of his lonely, love-starved life hovered too close to the surface. So did the pain of Angelien's death. With the photo of him and another woman came the deep sorrow of his loss. His heart still belonged to his wife. The pursuit of anyone else would be disloyal and too full of pain to make the endeavor worthwhile.

Matthew and Logan exchanged a look. In it, Conrad read concern and the tiniest bit of amusement.

A second automobile puttered up the driveway and parked. Lester Brinks, Helen's husband, emerged from the car. Another door opened. Miss Jones and her friend Rose got out.

Conrad lurched for the newspaper and tore it out of Matthew's grasp. "Put that thing away." He folded it but his haste only produced a crumpled mass.

He kicked it under the table. A chuckle rumbled in Logan's throat, so Conrad glared at him. Would he show that photo to Miss Jones? She couldn't be prevented from ever reading another newspaper, but if the moment she discovered the photo arrived at a time when he didn't have to witness it, he could get a handle on his emotions.

"Hi, Conrad." Miss Harper waved at him. "Thanks for

inviting us out to help with the cider." She flashed him a brilliant smile.

He stifled a groan. Sometimes this girl acted too friendly. At least she wasn't the one pictured with him on the front page of the newspaper. Miss Jones would never get the wrong idea, but Miss Harper might. He'd better be careful in his response to her.

"Good morning. I'm glad you could come." He motioned in Helen's direction. "Your aunt could use help carrying the jars to the kitchen."

Giving these girls an errand would occupy Miss Harper and remove Miss Jones far away from that humiliating newspaper.

"Of course." Miss Jones smiled at him, but disappointment replaced Miss Harper's bright smile. She probably expected to spend all of her time outdoors with him and the other men.

"Come here, girls. Load the jars in a pan and follow me." Helen led the way to the house.

When the coast was clear, Logan reached for the crumpled paper, smoothed it out, and folded it properly. He tucked it under his arm and then helped Matthew fill the mill in preparation for another batch.

Conrad didn't see that newspaper again until the noon hour when he followed the other men to the house for the meal. Miss Jones stood alone on the porch reading from it. Matthew and Logan went inside but Conrad stayed behind watching her. Heat radiated in his cheeks all over again.

Her jaw dropped open as her gaze swung over to him. "Conrad!"

"Where did you get that?" He pointed to the paper.

"It was laying here on the swing. I don't know where it came from."

"You saw the front page."

She nodded.

"Who took that picture? How did it get in the paper?" He frowned at her.

Her lip trembled. "I don't know. Obviously, I didn't take it because I'm in it. Maybe one of the kids got a hold of my camera and snapped the photo."

Conrad gave a caustic laugh. "Then that kid was pretty smart to know how to use a camera. It's a good picture."

"It probably went to the editor with the rest of my photos. I told him to make his own choice about the ones he wanted in the paper. He must have thought it was good too." Her gaze left the newspaper and settled on his face.

He couldn't stay mad at the vulnerability standing before him. She'd done nothing wrong. An innocent mistake had been made. But the removal of guilt wouldn't change the impression this photo made.

"You know we have a problem." His brow rose.

Her forehead wrinkled.

"This picture makes us look ... well, it makes us look ..." He gulped, unable to say what had to be said.

"Like we're a couple?" She finished the thought for him.

"Yeah." The word escaped cracked and hoarse.

"But we're not." A hint of determination strengthened her voice.

"Not in any way. No." Determination edged his voice too.

"But you think our friends will draw a different conclusion after reading the paper." She crossed her arms.

"Right."

She huffed out a breath. "What do you suggest that we do?"

Conrad ran his hand through his hair and turned his attention to the sky. "We start by telling the same story." He shifted his focus to her. "Karen was the person I'd asked to help me. Sara got sick, so you came in her place at the last minute. How does that sound?"

"It's true, isn't it?" She leveled him with a solemn look.

"As far as I can tell. Can you come up with anything better?" The question sounded like a dare, but all he wanted was to learn her thoughts.

"No. I don't want this to get out of hand any more than you do."

"Good. Hopefully that story will smash any rumors before they start."

Her brow quivered above her left eye giving her the slightest mischievous expression. In her gaze he read amusement as though she found him comical and foolish. He couldn't blame her. On the night of the carnival, he had been foolish. Never should he have noticed her good qualities and her attractiveness. For sure he shouldn't have hung on her every word, enamored by her as the photo so blatantly displayed.

Miss Jones's eyes also held a hint of defiance. Maybe she wouldn't cooperate with his plan. She might come up with her own version of the story, abandoning him to face the rumors alone.

He sighed. If she undermined him, he'd know to keep his distance. And if his friends refused to believe him instead of her, he'd know the time had come to leave town.

"I must go find Rose." Miss Jones slipped past him, maneuvering through the narrow space between him and the railing, and went inside.

He stood on the porch watching the activity beyond the windows. Helen hustled between the kitchen and the long dining room table arranging jars of apple cider in rows. Miss Jones tied an apron around her slim waist as she laughed with Miss Harper. The girls would return outside to help with the next batch of pressed apples, but for now Conrad had a span of time in which he could work with his friends alone.

He shuffled off the porch and returned to the press. Logan dumped a bucketful of chopped apples into the press as Conrad grasped the large screw.

"It's full. Ready to go." Logan announced.

Conrad drew in a deep breath. Nothing in Logan's tone hinted at his thoughts about the newspaper. Maybe he'd already forgotten.

Conrad set to work with all his energy as though he could reverse the happenings of the morning by sheer force. If only he could. Then he wouldn't have to remember even one word of the story intended as a barrier between himself and the onslaught of misunderstanding he had to face.

14

With his children in school and Helen busy preserving cider in her kitchen at the orchard, Conrad stayed home. Instead of reporting to work, he'd use the day to ship his supply of furniture to Mr. Blaine. If Conrad got an early start putting his items on the train this morning, they would easily arrive mid-afternoon, giving the department store owners plenty of time to unload.

The wagon he'd brought home with him the night before was parked in his yard, backed up to the wide doorway of his workshop. His brother Nick lifted the end of a table. On the opposite end, Conrad lifted his side and helped maneuver the item into the wagon.

"You've got some room in that corner. Do you want to load one more piece?" Nick pointed to an empty space.

"There's a cupboard that should fit." Conrad led the way into the workshop and helped Nick carry the article of furniture.

"I'll help you unload at the station." Nick climbed onto the seat next to Conrad.

He tapped the horses with the reins. When they pulled the wagon onto the street, Conrad guided the team to the station.

A cluster of station attendants watched him pull in. As soon as he brought his wagon near the tracks, one of the men directed him until the wagon was positioned to unload onto a car.

"The next train is due to arrive in twenty minutes, so you've got a bit of a wait," the attendant said.

Conrad nodded. He'd rather be early and wait on the train than come late and miss it. The train stopped for only a few minutes, so Conrad and the crew would have to work fast to get everything loaded onto the car and secured before the train left again.

Nick went inside and bought a newspaper, but Conrad stayed outdoors and watched for the train.

Eventually, Nick emerged from the building and strode in Conrad's direction. A grin stretched across his face.

"Have you seen this?" Nick thrust the newspaper's front page under his nose.

"Yesterday." Conrad groaned.

"I didn't know you were courting anyone. Good for you! Markus and Betje will enjoy having a mother again." Nick smiled at him.

"We're not courting." Conrad returned the smile with a frown.

"What? Not courting?" Nick studied the paper.

"Never mind what's in the paper. Miss Jones is a friend. I mean, she's a friend of a friend. The friend of the wife of a friend. That's who she is." He stifled another groan. So much for that pretty speech he'd planned to give in moments like these. Miss Jones surely would do a better job than him at telling their agreed-upon story.

"Oh, I see." Nick still looked confused. "But, Conrad, it

would be a good idea for you to consider courting a young woman. Your children need a mother. Hannah thinks—"

"I don't care what Hannah thinks. The young lady in the paper isn't my girl because we're not courting." Conrad turned for a glance at the rails when a whistle pierced the air. "Come on, the train is almost here." He hopped into the wagon and worked to unlatch the gate.

Men scurried around, preparing to move Conrad's load onto the train. As soon as it stopped, everyone worked with haste.

When the whistle blew announcing departure, Conrad wiped his forehead. "Did we make it?"

"Sure did," a crewman answered. "Everything is secure and ready for travel."

"Good." Conrad smiled. This shipment of his custom-made furniture would earn him quite a comfortable income.

The train sped away while Conrad guided his horses onto the street. At Nick's house, they parked and went in for lunch. Hannah met him with a sorrowful expression in her eyes.

"What's wrong?" He asked.

"Oh, Conrad. It's Markus."

"Markus? What happened to him?" Conrad's heart thudded in his chest.

"The principal sent a note here. You'll want to go to the school right away." Hannah clutched his arm in her effort to comfort him.

"Right." He headed back out the door.

"We'll save food for you," Hannah called after him.

Conrad jogged down the street and over three blocks to the school. What had happened to his son? Was he sick? Hurt? In danger? He couldn't imagine. When the principal is the one asking for a meeting, the situation had grown serious. He entered the building and stared at the woman behind the desk. His chest heaved, delaying his questions.

"He's in there." She pointed to an open door. A sign with the word *principal* hung on it.

Conrad raced through the door. Markus sat on a chair crying. His trousers were torn at the knee. Blood stained the ripped fabric. Smaller rips and dirt stains decorated the boy's shirt.

His heart lurched. "Markus, what happened?"

The boy sobbed, so the principal, seated in his chair behind the desk, cut in. "Fighting at recess, Mr. Van Drunen. Markus was caught hitting another boy and wrestling him to the ground. You must take him home. He is not allowed at school for two days."

The demand punched Conrad in the gut. Suspended. His own son was suspended from school for fighting. A model of behavior and a good student, Markus had hit the bottom.

Conrad went down on one knee. "Markus? Care to talk about it?"

The boy threw a glare at the principal. "No." He crossed his arms, but the angry tears coursed down his cheeks.

"Take him home. He is welcome back on Thursday." The principal stood and left the room.

Conrad exhaled a deep breath as he rose to his feet. "Come on, Markus, Let's go home." He held out his hand to his belligerent offspring, but Markus shoved past it. "Tell me what happened," Conrad prompted as they walked.

"I gave Bert Vander Will a full knuckle sandwich. He deserved it." Markus glared at the street where vehicles passed and horses trotted.

"Why did he deserve it?"

"He was makin' fun of me." Markus's voice turned peevish.

"What did he say?"

"He said that since I didn't have a mama, I couldn't take a turn with the sleepover the boys have planned." Markus kicked at a rock.

"Why should that matter? Your friends are always welcome, and there's plenty of space in your room for them to spread out."

"But they want food, Dad." Markus glanced at him with pleading in his eyes. "The whole town knows you can't cook."

Those words would slice him if said to him by anyone else but this ragged, defeated fellow. Conrad sucked in a breath. "I'll get what you need from the bakery."

"It's not the same. None of the other boys do that. Their mothers all know how to cook special things for us when we come over. Bert's mom makes these gooey, yummy cinnamon rolls. Chris's mom makes coffeecake. Len's mom makes quiche. It's so good. But when they come to my house, they don't get nothin'. Just dry stuff out of a box from the bakery. That's no fun. Chris and Len took Burt's side. It got so bad that now I'm not even allowed to go." Markus crossed his arms and scowled.

Conrad's throat ached. Their situation as a family was unique. He'd agree with that. His lack of skill or interest in the kitchen was no secret. He'd never tried to keep it one. But the tension Markus felt with his friends was a new discovery. Conrad's single status shouldn't take such a toll on his son. If only there was something he could do about finding his son just the right mother. The women he knew paraded through his mind. Kate Vander Will? Her son had fought with Markus. As step-brothers, their friendship might deteriorate. Carlin Reese? She couldn't bake either. Miss Harper? Too flirty. Miss Jones?

The thought of her pierced him. He'd made plain to his brother the fact that he wasn't courting her. Not even entertaining the idea. Just because she dominated his thoughts didn't mean he had any intention of wanting her for himself. Definitely not. She wouldn't want him anyway. As a young woman less than twenty years of age, the last thing she'd welcome is a life with an old man like him raising two children.

At home, Conrad lifted Markus onto the kitchen table and cleaned his knee.

"Is it still bleeding?" Markus tugged on his trousers for a better look.

"Not too bad. I'll put a bandage on it for now and take you to the doctor's this afternoon." Conrad finished cleaning and then applied a bandage. "Go change your clothes and wash your face. Aunt Hannah is keeping food warm for us."

Markus did as he was told. His mood improved with a fresh change of clothes, and he found other things to talk about as he walked with Conrad to Nick and Hannah's.

"Oh, Markus! Hello. I'll get out another plate. You may sit here." Hannah pointed to a chair on her way to the cupboard.

Conrad helped him scoot his chair to the table and then settled into another one. "Thanks for keeping lunch warm for me. I appreciate it."

She smiled and then gave Markus a wary glance. "Everything get worked out?"

"Markus has to stay home for a couple days. He started a fight on the playground."

Hannah gasped. "Oh, dear. If you're busy, Conrad, he can come here."

"Thanks for offering, but depending on the doctor's opinion of his knee, I might take Markus with me to work at the orchard."

His speech produced a look of awe on Markus's face. "Could I, Dad?"

"It'll be good for you to get out of town for a little while. But it doesn't mean there aren't consequences for fighting and getting suspended from school. If the doctor feels you can handle the work, you'll get to be the orchard's number one stall mucker for the next two days."

"Cleaning the barn? Aw, Dad." Markus whined.

"But you'll get to help me pick apples. Helen and I plan to

make more cider."

Markus shrugged and focused on eating. When they finished, Conrad took Markus in the wagon to the clinic. Matthew was there, so Conrad took a seat in the waiting room.

"Mishap at school today?" Dr. Matthew Kaldenberg asked when Markus's turn came.

"A fight." The boy shrugged.

"Hmm." Matthew helped Markus onto the examination table and looked him over. "Some scratches on the face and one arm." He dropped Markus's arm and reached for his bandaged leg. "I'll pull your trouser leg up for a look." Careful inching of the trouser over Markus's shin revealed the white bandage.

Matthew removed it. "Still bleeding somewhat. I'll give it a stitch or two to help it heal." He collected materials and utensils and set to work. "All done. Now stay out of trouble." He rested a friendly hand on the boy's back.

"Yes, sir." Markus said in a respectful tone.

Conrad paid Matthew and led his son onto the street. They walked home together under a blue sky. A light breeze blew golden and red leaves from the trees and made them dance along the way. Conrad inhaled the dry fall air. A beautiful time of year in a lovely place. He and his brothers Dan and Nick had wanted to find a place in America with clean air and open spaces. Oswell City fit him well. But the new life as an immigrant hadn't been without tragedy. The gravestone in the cemetery reminded him of what he'd lost.

But he had Markus and Betje. His brother, Hannah, and their family were here in town so that Nick could hold his job at the bank. Dan, his wife Rachel, and their family were on a nearby farm. Conrad could do his work outdoors instead of crammed in a factory in a stuffy city. Some of Nick's friends had stopped in Chicago, but Nick, Dan, and Conrad kept going west. They had friends out here on the Iowa prairie, too, and the choice to settle here had been a good one.

Markus and Betje, along with their cousins, would grow up in a small town among people who knew them, cared about them, and ... fought with them.

Conrad bit back a wry smile as he led Markus into the house. "Go to your room and put your foot up for a while. Your knee should rest."

Markus didn't argue. The boy was probably tired from his misfortunes. Conrad turned away and took inventory of the last batch of goods he'd bought from the bakery. *Dry stuff out of a box*. Markus's words. More true than Conrad wanted to admit. He couldn't bake and he didn't even want to learn. Should he feel guilty about that? His children deserved a parent who saw to their nutrition and, according to Markus, had the ability to host a party.

Conrad shrugged. They were getting by just fine. Betje would be home from school soon, and he would have a snack all fixed for her. Proof that he was adequate as the overseer of nutrition. He stepped over to the counter and spread slices of bread with butter and jam, both products of Helen's labors at the orchard.

The door opened just as he finished up, but the visitor wasn't his daughter arrived home from school. It was Walter Brinks from the hotel. He held a note in his hand.

"This message came over the telephone for ya a few minutes ago." He gave the note to Conrad and sprinted from the house.

Conrad unfolded it and read the message that had come from Mr. Blaine. He held his breath as the news sank in. Some of his merchandise had arrived in Des Moines damaged and unfit for sale. Could he call the office right away?

Conrad sprinted down the hall to Markus's room, told him to serve the bread and jam to his sister when she came home, and raced to the hotel.

15

Ethel Brinks pointed at the black receiver lying on a small table. Picking it up, Conrad faced the wooden box on the wall and drew in a deep breath.

"Conrad Van Drunen here. I understand you called," he blurted as he held the receiver to his ear. His heart raced.

"Yes, I did." Mr. Blaine's voice carried over the line. "Two of the tables you shipped to us arrived with damaged legs. It was most likely caused by jostling on the train."

"We had everything tied down securely. The crewmen helped me." His mind spun in its search for reasons why experts at shipping freight would put his furniture at risk.

"I'm sure they did everything possible, but I'm not blaming you, Mr. Van Drunen. Train travel is rough at best. The hours of rumbling over the tracks bumps items around. There is great potential for fragile pieces to get damaged."

"Was anything else broken?"

"No. Our quota is complete except for those two tables," Mr. Blaine said.

"That's good to hear. Would you like for me to replace those tables? I'd be happy to."

"If you could construct replacement legs, that would be sufficient."

"Yes, of course. I'll send them to you as soon as possible."

"That won't be necessary. I'd like to pick them up."

"Pick them up?"

"Yes. Mr. Gresham and I are planning to take our wives out to dinner at the hotel in Clear Brook and then to a theater production at the college afterward. While we are in the area, we'd like to come to Oswell City and have you give us a tour of your facilities. We are always interested in the locations and situations from which our products come. This information assists us in making sales. We'd like that advantage where your products are concerned."

Conrad stared at the wall as he listened. Mr. Blaine wanted a tour of his facilities. But Conrad had no facilities to speak of unless this sophisticated businessman counted a repurposed barn in his back yard as a high functioning operation.

His knees trembled. He had very little to show these men that gave him even the slightest chance of impressing them.

Mr. Blaine kept talking so Conrad tuned back in. "We'll be staying at the Clear Brook Hotel, arriving Friday afternoon. We'd like to have you join us for the evening. I know the owner of the hotel restaurant. He's a good friend of mine, and he sent me tickets that will get us in at a discount. It's the married couples discount that he runs on special occasions. You have a wife, don't you, Conrad?"

Conrad's jaw dropped. "Uh." The pain of saying *no* struck him as sharply as if Angelien had died yesterday.

A chair creaked in the background. Mr. Blaine must have shifted his position while holding the receiving to his ear. "It really is such a nice time whenever the restaurant arranges these special meals for couples. I'd hate for you to miss it. Plus, we'd make such a nice party with an even number of six. Would it work for you if we came for a tour on Saturday?"

"Uh, yes ... yes, it does." Conrad found his voice even though his brain had been working so hard to take in the stunning information coming from Mr. Blaine. He thought Conrad might be married with someone in his life he'd feel perfectly comfortable inviting to share this formal evening.

"Very good. We'll see you Friday. Meet us at the hotel at five o'clock. Thank you for making those replacement table legs. Good-bye."

"Good-bye." Conrad's voice shook. After holding the silent receiver in his hand for several moments, he remembered to hang it back in its place and turned away.

He sensed Ethel Brinks watching him exit the room. Her gaze stayed on him as he smiled a greeting and left the hotel. If she wondered if a crisis had arisen, he wouldn't know how to answer her. The news of damaged goods certainly caused a problem, but the invitation to the social engagement created a larger one. He must find someone to share the evening with him, not as a partner for the children's activities at a school event, but for something much more grown up and intimate. Just like ... well, like he really was married.

His stomach tightened as he followed the sidewalk. If Angelien were alive, he'd treat this evening out as a special time for them to enjoy some romance. Maybe he'd give her flowers. She'd wear a pretty dress. They'd leave the children in someone else's care, giving them the chance to be together without any demands or interruptions.

He chased away the daydream. Conrad had no one in his life to fill that sort of a place. Memories of the women he knew flowed through his mind again. None of them came close as an appropriate companion for the evening. He might as well tell his business partner to keep the tickets and use them on someone else. But then Conrad would lose this important opportunity to deepen his business relationship with these men. If he didn't go, he might jeopardize the connection he already had.

With those damaged table legs figuring into the situation, he had to go. He didn't have a choice. Somewhere, somehow, he would have to find a woman willing to fake a marriage for an evening.

At home, Conrad shoved his predicament from his mind and turned his attention to his children. Betje had arrived home from school and was sitting at the table eating her snack.

"How was your day, sweetheart?" He placed a kiss on the top of her head.

"Fine, Daddy. The big girls taught us little girls a new game at recess. We put flowers in our hair and hold hands as we skip in a circle singing a song. It's fun."

Conrad hid a smile as Betje took a big bite of her bread and jam. "I'm glad you liked it. Sounds like you have lots of friends."

She gave him a grin between bites.

Conrad left the room to check on Markus but found him sleeping, so he collected the torn trousers and took them to the kitchen. He'd wash and dry them so that they'd be ready for a trip to the dress shop for repairs.

THE NEXT DAY, Conrad put in his full hours of work and then headed for Eva's shop. He could probably ask Hannah to make the repair on Markus's trousers, but she had her own family to sew for. Conrad wanted to make sure he didn't wear out his welcome with his sister-in-law. There was no reason why he shouldn't pay a seamstress for her help.

He pushed the door open and entered the shop.

"Good afternoon, Conrad. I'll be with you in a moment." Eva smiled at him and turned back to the customer at the counter.

He milled around as he waited, scanned the dresses on the rack and watched the activity through the window. The most astounding idea assaulted him. Eva Synderhoff was a single woman. Maybe he should invite her to use the tickets to the dinner.

Common sense caught up with him. He could never convince her to act like his wife. Besides, Eva was much older than him. Her children were grown men whereas his were grade-schoolers. He and Eva wouldn't make a good match.

He'd also run the risk of people seeing them together and drawing the conclusion that they were a couple. But he'd just had his picture in the paper with Lacy Jones. He couldn't go out with Eva while also appearing to court Miss Jones. In the span of a single evening, he'd go from obscure father minding his own business raising his two children to a lady's man.

The thought choked him.

Eva approached him. "What can I help you with?"

He gulped and showed her Markus's britches. "The knee needs patched."

"Miss Jones can help you with that. It shouldn't take her very long. Would you like for me to explain this project to her?"

"No, I'll talk to her." He had first-hand information on the subject. No point in involving Eva if she wasn't the one doing the sewing.

Eva's brows rose and she gave him a knowing smile. "Of course you would like a reason to see her. It's nearly the end of the day. Take as much time as you wish."

There it was again, the idea that Conrad had a reason for making excuses to spend time in Miss Jones's company. Eva must have read the newspaper.

He ventured over to Miss Jones, showed her Markus's clothing, and gave the explanation in the most businesslike tone he possessed.

"I'll take care of it right now." She hopped up and pulled a piece of dark cloth from a pile. Then she sat at the table and cut out a square.

The silence grew between them. Conrad should fill it so he didn't stand around awkward and uncomfortable like he didn't know what to do with himself.

"Having a good day?" He asked as he watched her guide the scissors.

"Um-hmm. I'm going over to the De Witt's home for supper and to stay overnight. Sara is feeling better and only one of the twins got sick, but he is better now too. I should be safe from catching the flu." She talked as she worked, her eyes staying on the fabric before her.

"Sounds like fun."

"It will be." Miss Jones flashed a smile as she turned to the sewing machine.

In a matter of minutes, she had a patch sewn on the underside of the trouser knee, making the garment suitable for school wear.

He thanked her, paid Eva, and left the shop. Out on the street, the sign above the door to the *Oswell Journal* caught his attention. He crossed the street, went inside, and asked for Jake.

"Good afternoon, Conrad. Something I can help you with?" Jake emerged from a doorway and glanced at him.

"There is. I'd like to know how you decide which pictures to put in the newspaper."

"They must be of good quality and capture the spirit of the article I pair with them." Jake stroked his moustache.

"Oh." Conrad glanced down.

"Why? Would you like to put a picture in the paper?"

"No. I've come to talk about one that was already printed."

"Which one?"

"The photo on the front page of this week's paper."

Jake's brow furrowed as he reached for a stack of papers. He unfolded the one on top.

"This picture." Conrad stabbed the front page with his finger.

"This one of you and Miss Jones?" Jake sounded puzzled.

"That's the one."

"But it captures the theme of the story our reporter put in so beautifully. A couple who cares about kids operating a booth at the carnival."

"But that's the problem. We're not a couple."

"You aren't?" Jake looked confused.

"No."

"But don't you see the children at the table and the cupcakes arranged down the center? Miss Jones submitted a very nice picture. It accurately depicts the activity at your booth that night."

Conrad ventured a closer look at the photo. Jake was right. Children with cupcakes were visible in the bottom portion of the photo. Maybe he was just too sensitive on the subject. Even Jake thought he and Miss Jones were a couple. If only he could correct the assumption. But he was too late. The newspaper had solidified the theory that he was in a relationship with Miss Jones.

"I can't edit this edition of the newspaper since it has already been printed. I'm sorry, Conrad. If I would have known sooner, I would have been most willing to make changes."

"I understand. That picture was taken and submitted without my knowledge. I didn't know any of the photos Miss Jones had submitted from the school carnival included me. I was surprised when I saw the paper."

"My apologies. I hope it won't happen again." Jake folded up the paper and returned it to the stack.

Conrad nodded and offered Jake a wave as he left the office.

A man in a trap. That's who he was. His acquaintance with Miss Jones had gone too far for him to pull out. The newspaper had helped their relationship along until Conrad stood at a crossroads. He must either cut off all association with this young lady or live up to the perception the newspaper article had created.

As he prepared the evening meal and ate it with his family, Conrad held a private debate over the direction of his future.

"Markus, could you stay home for a few minutes by yourself?" Conrad asked after he'd put Betje in bed.

"Sure, Dad. Where are you going?" Markus glanced up from his homework.

"Just sit right here and keep doing what you're doing. I'll come back soon." Conrad rested his hand on Markus's head a moment before he stole quietly from the house.

His feet carried him down the street and decided to turn on Fifth Street. Cutting across the neighbors' lawns and pausing at the clothesline wouldn't do tonight. He was on a knock-at-the-front-door kind of mission.

Past the church his feet continued to walk. Up the sidewalk and halting on the front step they led him. Then his fist, in full conspiracy with his feet, rose for a firm knock on the door.

His friend opened it. The lamplight from the room beyond illuminated the foyer behind him, darkening his face in the sharp relief of a silhouette. But his friend wasn't the one he'd come to see.

"Hi, Logan. Could I speak with Miss Jones, please?" Conrad asked.

"Sure. Won't you come in?" Logan gestured toward the lamplight.

The inviting warmth of the house tempted him, but with a cloud of frost forming on his breath, he said, "No. I'd prefer to speak with her out here."

Without another word, Logan went to call Miss Jones. The suggestion he gave her to wear a coat floated to Conrad's ears.

She entered the lamplight. Her dark form filled the space as she grew closer. "Conrad? What is it? What are you doing here?" She stepped outside and faced him.

"I've come to ask, well ... to ask you for a favor." Conrad rubbed his hands together and licked his lips.

"A favor?" She pulled her coat tighter around her.

"Two business partners are bringing their wives to Clear Brook on Friday evening for a dinner at the hotel and then a show at the college theater. They gave me tickets, so I wanted to ask you to go with me."

"You're inviting me to dinner and a show?" Miss Jones' hand fluttered to her chest.

"Yeah. There's just one thing." He shoved his hands in his pockets and took a deep breath. "You and I, we'll have to pretend that we're married."

A look of sheer horror crossed Miss Jones's face. "Conrad Van Drunen, have you gone crazy? What on earth has gotten into you?"

"Just listen to me." He pulled his hand from his pocket and held it up. "Mr. Blaine has invited me and my, well ... my wife to a special dinner for couples. My attendance, I mean, our attendance," he pointed to her, "is important to my professional relationship with both of these men."

She crossed her arms. "I can't pretend something like this."

He took a step closer and placed his hands on her shoulders. "Just for a few hours."

"You confuse me." She glanced up at him. "First you tell me to deny that the picture in the paper means anything, and now you ask me to pose as your wife for an evening out."

The lamplight glowed on her hair turning the strands to gold. Even in the dusk of the evening he could see how beautiful she was. That photo told the truth about him. Maybe that was why he found it so infuriating.

"I'm sorry. But will you come?" His voice dropped low. "I'd like to take you out Friday night."

She rubbed her eyes. "I'm going to have to think about this."

"I understand. Take all the time you need." He backed away.

She looked up at him. "Good night, Conrad." Her eyes glistened in the lamplight glowing from the window.

When she went inside, he turned and walked away into the darkness. He, Conrad Van Drunen, had asked a young woman out on a date. This wasn't just any date. It was an evening with Lacy Jones, the one who helped him see past his hurt to the beauty in the world around him, and to the beauty in her.

If she agreed to go with him, then Friday night may prove to be the beginning of his heart's awakening. Miss Lacy Jones may very well possess the power to raise it from the dead.

16

"What did Conrad want?" Mr. De Witt sat with his wife on the sofa. Sara lay asleep in Mrs. De Witt's lap.

"He came to ask me to go to a dinner and a show in Clear Brook on Friday night." Lacy closed the door and studied the floor. Conrad had wanted more than she could explain. Her heart thumped as she wrestled with how much to say.

Mr. De Witt exchanged a look with his wife and then looked at Lacy. "How do you feel about that?"

She eased into a chair. "Surprised. Nervous. Afraid." A single chuckle escaped.

"I can understand why. But Conrad is a gentleman. He will do everything he can to make you comfortable and help you enjoy yourself." Mrs. De Witt spoke softly with occasional glances at Sara to make sure she stayed sleeping.

"I hope so. But he's nervous too." Lacy stood. "I'm going to bed." She went to the room at the end of the hall that she used whenever she stayed here.

Her heart still fluttered. Conrad Van Drunen had asked her to share Friday evening with him. Not just as a girl of his acquaintance, but as someone he wanted these important people to think he was married to. Her blood heated and her heart melted all at the same time. The nerve of him. Coming over here and presuming that she'd want to live a lie. Parading around as his wife of all things. What in the world was he thinking? Lacy crossed her arms and gritted her teeth.

But maybe he was caught in a situation he couldn't change. Had these businessmen forced this upon him? He might just be trying to make the best of a circumstance beyond his control. Should she go along with it, as a sort of support to help him out? She squeezed her eyes shut. What an impossible situation. How had she gotten so tangled up?

Standing at the window, she looked out into the darkness. Thoughts of the man who'd come to the door flooded her mind. Conrad had to be at least ten years older than her since he'd been married before. Did he have any children, or did he live alone? There were so many things she didn't know about him. But if he was a friend of Mr. De Witt, then he couldn't be so bad. He'd proven that he wasn't the villain she'd first thought him to be. Maybe she could trust him. If Mrs. De Witt thought so highly of him, then shouldn't Lacy?

If she decided to go, then Friday night would be her first experience going out with a man. In high school, she'd gone to dances and other social events with the boys in her class, but those boys had nothing in common with Conrad. He was grown up, drove a car, and held a job building furniture.

He'd likely given careful thought to his invitation. A man close to thirty didn't ask a girl like her, only a few months out of high school, to share this sort of engagement with him unless he was open to the possibility of a serious attachment developing.

Her heart fluttered again. What if that happened? Maybe Conrad would care for her, or maybe she would start to care for him. But he'd asked her to go out with him as though she were his wife. Did that mean he already cared? The thought terrified her. There was so much she wanted to know about the world, so much she had yet to learn about herself. A mature man like Conrad deserved a woman who knew who she was and where she was going.

The phone rang. Lacy heard Mr. De Witt's voice when he answered it. Then he laid the receiver down and came to her room.

"That phone call is for you."

Lacy gulped in some air. Who would be calling her at this time of night? Maybe Conrad had changed his mind, so he'd slipped over to the hotel to place a quick call. Or maybe Eva had something she wanted Lacy to know before going to work in the morning.

In the dining room, she picked up the receiver. "Hello? This is Lacy Jones."

"Hi, Lacy. This is your father." His deep voice carried over the line.

Her heart lurched. Her father! Not the voice she'd expected. "Hi, Dad. It's nice to hear from you. Has something happened? Why are you calling?"

He cleared his throat. "Your mother and I are disappointed in the treatment you gave your brother when he came to Oswell City to bring you home. We want you to know that it is time you ended your visit with your teacher and returned to us."

"Oh, Dad." Her knees shook. How could she ever make him understand? She took a deep breath and plunged in. "In my last letter to Mama, I told you that I've found a job here. I enjoy it. I like this town, and I don't want to leave."

His sigh carried over the telephone. "Lacy, that wasn't our agreement. Your mother and I allowed you to go with your friend only for a short visit to your teacher. You have to come home now. We never would have let you go if we'd known you'd change your mind about the length of your stay."

"I didn't expect to stay either. But I met people who are my friends now. Mrs. De Witt helped me find a job at the dress shop. I'm doing well here, never getting sick. I don't need Mama and Cal watching out for me anymore." The impatience grew in her voice to the same level as her father's.

"But you've been staying with the minister and his wife. You shouldn't take advantage of people's kindness any longer."

"Oh, but I'm not. I have my own apartment downtown. It is right next door to the dress shop."

"An apartment? You're living alone? This is worse than I thought."

"Dad, please. I like living there. Cal knows all about it. He even saw it. Didn't he say anything to you?"

"He just said you'd been stubborn and wouldn't cooperate."

His words sliced through Lacy. Why couldn't her family understand her need for independence? All her life, she'd been coddled and protected. As a young, sickly child, she'd depended on them to help her succeed. But not anymore. She could live her life on her own, and she wanted to prove it.

"I didn't mean to be uncooperative. The best I could, I let Cal know why I couldn't go home with him. Let Mama know that I'm perfectly healthy, and that I'm having a good time."

The other end was silent for a moment. Lacy imagined her father covering the receiver and consulting with Mama. The farm didn't have a phone, so they must be in the back hall of the Carter's general store and spending precious coins on this long-distance call.

"Lacy? Are you still there?"

"Yes, Dad."

"Your mother and I want to check your situation out for ourselves, but we can't afford to come right now. Plan on us making a visit as soon as we can pull together the funds for it."

"Maybe Cal will help you." Encouraging her parents to come for a visit might put their minds at ease about her. If they came to Oswell City, they could see for themselves what Lacy's life had become.

"I don't think so. He barely has enough to pay his tuition. We have to help him with his room and board. I'm not sure how we'll make this trip happen."

"Maybe Grandpa and Grandma will give you some extra funds."

"No. I'm not asking them for money. I'll figure it out on my own."

"I'll look forward to seeing you. But until then, please know that I'm doing fine. Mama has no reason to worry about me."

"Well, all right then. Glad I called. You take care of yourself, and we'll see you soon." The concession in Dad's voice nearly broke Lacy's heart. He'd called intending to march her right onto the train back to Silver Grove, but instead had given in to a trip in her direction.

"Good-night."

He echoed it and hung up.

Lacy stood still for a moment staring at the phone. Had she said the right thing? She hated to see her parents struggle with money. They never had enough. Would poverty keep Lacy and her family apart? Maybe they would always be separated in this way. They'd all been so close before Cal went away to school. Money, or the lack of it, shouldn't have the power to dictate her relationships.

It was a lesson she'd remember. She'd make sure to always have enough of it to go where she wanted and to be with whomever she wanted for as long as she wanted. Her chin lifted and she glanced away.

Mrs. De Witt and her husband stood in the room with her. "You handled that conversation very well. From what I heard on your end, you are a young lady of wisdom and strength. I'm proud of you."

Lacy nodded while tears stung her eyes. Mrs. De Witt's encouragement poked at places in Lacy's heart that had wanted to display those qualities. Not until she'd heard the words said did she know what her goal had been. She turned and walked to her room.

Standing in front of the mirror, Lacy took her hair down. Mr. De Witt's voice drifted through the open door. He probably thought she'd closed it as she usually did, but her thoughts distracted her, so she'd forgotten. She wouldn't have listened to the conversation coming from the parlor, but her name came up, pricking her curiosity.

His interest returned to the previous topic of the evening, the one in discussion before the phone call. "Conrad and Lacy. Who would've thought?"

"Logan, you saw that picture of them in the paper."

"I sure did. Conrad was so embarrassed and shocked when he saw it that I didn't dare say much."

"I hope you didn't tease him."

"I couldn't."

"From the look on his face in that picture, Conrad has had feelings for Lacy for a long time."

"I wonder if she feels the same."

"I don't know. Might be too early to tell. But they make a good match. I can see it working out. Lacy would be good for him."

"I agree."

The lamplight and the voices moved to the stairs. Lacy stood alone in her room in the dark. Neither Mr. or Mrs. De Witt had said anything to her about that picture in the newspaper, but they'd talked about it with each other, and Mr. De Witt had even talked about it to Conrad.

A queasy feeling swelled in her stomach from these conversations going on around her. Was everyone trying to plan her life for her? Maybe the De Witts would fall to the temptation to play matchmaker between herself and Conrad. She'd have to keep watch.

Mr. De Witt's remark came back to her. *I wonder if she feels the same.* Lacy changed her clothes and lay in bed with the question on her mind. How did she feel about Conrad? She was still grieving the loss of her gift, but maybe the time had come to see him for who he was, and not as the perpetrator of her misfortune. He was a man, and he was separate from her troubles. He might deserve a release from her incorrect perceptions.

"Hi, Joy. Here is a copy of the picture I took of you at the picnic," Lacy said when she entered the library.

Her new friend smiled. "Thanks, Lacy." She took the picture and looked at it. "I had fun that day, didn't you?"

"Yes. I'm glad Pastor Logan invited me."

"You don't have to wait for an invitation to future gatherings. Just come. We'll have a great time." Joy turned her attention to a woman with a stack of books, so Lacy moved away from Joy's desk and went to the section of the library with books about photography.

She didn't have much time to linger since she'd come to the library during her lunch break. The dress she'd dreamed of owning waited for her to claim it. Eva had paid her that week, so if Lacy cut her library visit short, she'd have enough minutes left over to make her purchase before returning to work.

A shiver ran over her. The beautiful dress would be perfect for the outing Conrad had asked her to share with him. His words from the brisk evening on the De Witts' front step whispered through her memory. *I'd like to take you out Friday night.*

But he wanted to pretend they were married. They'd have

to put on an act that they meant more to each other than they really did. Her blood heated. Frustrating man.

Lacy stifled a groan. The library staff wouldn't appreciate her noisy protest to Conrad's motives. Maybe she shouldn't buy that gown at all but show up in an old dress with patches sprinkled over the skirt. That would teach him to ask her to live a lie. But he said they'd go to both the theater and the restaurant. She'd never been to the theater. How fun it would be to watch the show, hear the music, and share in an evening with people of a higher social class than hers. And that dress. She'd really love to have a reason to wear such a lovely garment.

Lacy sighed as she walked the aisle studying the spines of books. A title on the third shelf caught her attention. She pulled it out and leafed through it. The pages were full of detailed descriptions about focus and lighting, along with helpful diagrams. Lacy tucked the book under her arm and headed back to the circulation desk.

A little girl sat in one of the overstuffed chairs in the library's lobby. She hadn't been there when Lacy arrived. Her head rested in her hands and her small body slumped. Sadness hung over her as though she struggled with a weighty problem.

Lacy's heart constricted as she looked at her. No one was around to help the little girl, so Lacy eased onto the footstool and patted her knee. "Hi there. Is something the matter?"

A tear trickled down the smooth cheek. "My brother's in trouble again at the school. Dad's there now talkin' to the principal. Aunt Hannah came to see me when I ate lunch. She brought me here so I could pick out a favorite story for when I get home from school later, but I don't feel much like readin'."

"What happened to your brother?" Lacy gazed into the troubled and watery blue eyes.

"He's been fightin' with his friends. We don't have a mother anymore. Only Dad. Markus doesn't like that. He wants Dad to do the things the other mothers do, but he can't." Another tear slid down her face.

Lacy stroked the girl's arm. The poor, motherless child. She looked in need of time on someone's lap crying and talking until her problems went away. At least she had Aunt Hannah. Hopefully the woman was kind.

"Can I help you pick out your story?" Lacy asked.

The little girl studied her for a moment before nodding her head. She slid off the chair and let Lacy hold her hand as they walked to the children's section.

"My name is Lacy. What's yours?"

"Betje."

"That's a pretty name." Lacy knelt in front of a child-sized shelf painted in bright blue. "Do you like any of these stories?"

Betje studied the row of books. After a moment of silence, she pointed. "That one."

Lacy pulled it from the shelf and handed it to Betje.

The little girl glanced up. "There's Aunt Hannah. I need to go now."

Lacy stood and watched the child meet up with her aunt. The woman smiled at Betje and walked with her to the circulation desk. Surely she'd see Betje's need for comfort and take the time out of her evening to help the girl enjoy her book.

After checking out her own selection, Lacy hastened onto the street. Meeting Betje had cut into the minutes ticking away from her lunch break. If she wanted to purchase her dress, she must hurry.

"Lacy!"

She turned in the direction of the call.

Luke Barnaveldt, the young man she'd met at the Labor Day picnic, waved at her.

"Hi, Luke. I've been to the library and saw Joy." He might be interested in that piece of news since he'd spent most of the tennis match with Joy. "I gave her a print of the picture I took of her."

"She'll like that." He fell in step with her as she walked along. "I'm glad I saw you. I was on my way to the dress shop to talk to you."

Her brow furrowed. "Do you need a shirt?"

He laughed. "No. I wanted to ask you if you might, well ... there's this show at the theater in Clear Brook on Friday night, and I wondered if you might go with me." They stopped walking and he turned to her.

Energy zinged through Lacy. Two invitations for Friday night. She sucked in some air and studied him. "But what about Joy? Aren't you taking her?"

Dark pink crept up his neck. "No. Joy and I are just friends. I hadn't even given it a thought. I'd rather ask you."

Lacy's eyes widened. She couldn't think why Luke wouldn't want to go with Joy. The young woman was pretty with her dark hair, and had nice manners too.

But if Lacy agreed to go with Luke, she'd have a companion close to her own age. He laughed and took life in a light-hearted way. She'd never seen Conrad laugh. He'd only ever cracked a smile, and even those were reluctant to come out. Did the man ever have any fun? Did he ever find a reason to enjoy himself? Maybe he didn't know how.

But if she went with Luke, she wouldn't have to pretend to be anyone's wife. She could just be Lacy, out with a friend and having a good time. Luke's invitation was tempting. But Conrad had asked first. Maybe his invitation was the one she should honor.

She weighed the matter for a moment. "Can I think about it?"

Luke shrugged. "Sure."

"This is my second invitation, and I'm not sure whose I should accept."

"Oh." Disappointment erased the cheer from his voice.

"You and I would have a good time together. But this other person already has a ticket reserved for me."

"I see." The light of courage dimmed from his gaze. "May I ask who this other person is?"

"Conrad Van Drunen." Lacy held her breath against the mix of emotions churning on her insides.

A smile tugged at the corner of Luke's mouth. "I should have known."

"What is that supposed to mean?" Lacy frowned.

"Haven't you read the newspaper?"

Her cheeks flamed. "Well, yes, but—"

He thumped her on the upper arm like one buddy greeting another. "Have fun, Lacy. I'll try to find someone to go with me. It won't be the same as having you, but maybe I'll see you there." He nodded to her and then turned and walked away.

Lacy stared after him while dizziness spun her head, and a knot tightened her stomach. First the De Witts and now Luke. Probably his family too. Had Rose and her aunt and uncle seen that photo in the paper? Had Eva? They couldn't have missed the front-page display, so yes, they probably had noticed it. The whole town had likely seen it. Oh, she shouldn't have ever brought her camera along to that carnival.

And what had he meant by telling her to have fun? She hadn't accepted Conrad's invitation. She could go to the theater with whomever she pleased, couldn't she? Groaning, Lacy trudged to the dress shop. Her lunch break was gone, so she'd have to wait until the end of the day to purchase her new gown.

Removing her hat and coat, she went to her workstation. After hanging them up, she sat and resumed sewing buttons on a shirt. Out of the corner of her eye, she watched customers enter the shop and browse the racks. Her dress had stayed safe from shoppers over the past days. If it continued to hang there for a few more hours, Lacy could claim it as hers.

A woman and her daughter moved closer to the garment. They held it out and talked with each other. Then the mother pulled it from the rack. Adding it to the other dresses draped over her arm, she followed her daughter to the fitting room.

Lacy fought the tears welling in her eyes. Surely they wouldn't purchase it. She'd come so close to owning it. In fact, if she hadn't had such a busy noon hour, the dress would be hers. She sent up a fervent prayer that the mother and daughter would choose a different one. Maybe praying about such things was foolish. Her face heated as she dabbed at her eyes with her handkerchief.

After several long moments, the pair emerged from the fitting room. The daughter carried a pink dress. Eva took the rest of the gowns from the mother. Was the cream one in the collection? Lacy had to find out. She left her chair and moved closer to where Eva worked hanging dresses on the rack.

Lacy released her breath as she watched the gown return to its place. It wouldn't get away from her again. The risk was too high. She went to the rack and removed it.

"Eva, I simply must try on this dress. Excuse me for a moment." Lacy left the bewildered lady staring after her as she went to the fitting room.

Lacy slipped out of her garment and put the other one on. The mirror revealed a nice fit. She checked the price tag. The dress was marked down from the original cost. Smiling into the mirror, Lacy turned around to see the gown from every angle. It was beautiful, and it made her look stylish and elegant.

The cream dress would be the first one she'd ever paid money for. Her other clothes were ones Mama had remade from dresses given to her by aunts and cousins. Lacy straightened as she admired her reflection. No more hand-me-downs. If she'd gone with Cal, that wardrobe would have been at the farm waiting for her. She was a working woman now, with her own salary. A new life and standard of living was gradually becoming hers.

She slipped the dress off, put her clothes back on, and went to the counter to give Eva an explanation, and to make her own very first purchase.

"MISS JONES." Conrad's voice came from behind as she walked down the street. Gentle pressure on her arm brought her to a stop.

She turned around.

"I don't mean to rush you, but the Blaines and the Greshams are coming on Friday. If you want to go with me, I need to know. If not, then just say so." Conrad released his hold on her arm.

Here it was, the question she must answer, but didn't know how. To go with him was deceitful. To not go with him excluded her from an evening learning about the theater in the company of upper-class people. Turning him down would also rob her of the chance to wear her new dress.

"I'd be willing to go with you, but do we have to pretend anything?" Lacy looked up at him.

A smile tugged at the corner of his mouth. "Not really. You and I don't have to say a word about our relationship. We can just go and have a good time."

"But what about the businessmen and their wives? They'd still believe something about us that isn't true."

"Let me take care of that. I never told Mr. Blaine I had a wife. He assumed it and then offered me tickets. If we don't bring it up, then I doubt if he will." Confidence strengthened Conrad's voice.

"I guess." Lacy held out her purchase. "I bought this new dress today. I'll wear it."

"You'll look nice in it. Friday evening will be fine. You'll see." He gave her hand a quick squeeze and then walked away.

He'd better be right. Lacy hadn't done anything deceitful in her whole life, and she wasn't going to start now.

17

Friday evening, Lacy made one more twirl before the mirror. This cream dress fit her perfectly. The silky fabric draped from her shoulders and fell over her hips in graceful lines. The hat she'd borrowed from Mrs. De Witt lay on her bed. Delicate little flowers along the brim were a perfect match in color to her dress. She settled it on her head and pinned it securely in place.

A knock came on the door.

Grabbing her heaviest shawl from the closet, she hastened to the front room. Her stomach fluttered. The guest must certainly be Conrad. Had she done the right thing in saying she'd go with him? Maybe she should cancel out and stay home. She rested her hand on her midsection for moment to steady her nerves and then opened the door.

Conrad stood there clean-shaven and dressed in a dark suit. "Good evening, Miss Jones. These are for you." He handed her a cluster of flowers.

"They're beautiful. Thank you." Lacy took them and placed them in a jar of water.

"Let me help you with that." Conrad grasped the shawl slipping from her arm and settled it on her shoulders. "Shall we go?"

She nodded and followed him to the street. "This is my first time riding in a car." The words slipped out before she could stop her thoughts from getting spoken. "Driving looks like fun. I wish I knew how to do it."

"There's really nothing to it. I'd be happy to teach you sometime." Conrad's relaxed response confirmed that driving was enjoyable.

As they left town, farmland ripe for harvest stretched away in all directions. Lacy ventured a glance at Conrad's face. He looked straight ahead at the road in front of him. Contentment lit his brown eyes and the corner of his mouth tilted upward as though he felt willing to smile. What would it take for a truly spontaneous, happy smile to burst onto his face?

"Tell me about your business partners." Maybe asking about this topic would do it.

"They are from Des Moines and operate one of the largest department stores in the country. Gresham, Blaine and Company. Perhaps you've heard of them." Conrad spoke in his usual solemn manner. Talking of his partners didn't bring a smile.

"Doesn't sound familiar. But then, I haven't had much of a chance to visit city stores." Lacy shrugged as a strong longing overcame her to go to one of those shops in the city. Not just to visit, but as a wealthy woman with a regular account who wore only the newest clothing of the latest styles.

She sighed. This dress from Eva's shop was a start, but not anywhere close to the garments rich women wore.

"Their wives are probably elegant, well-dressed ladies." She was starting to feel out of place already.

The corner of Conrad's mouth rose a little higher. "I suppose they are. I've never met them."

They drove for several moments in silence. When Conrad

came to a stop at an intersection, he cleared his throat and turned to her. "Miss Jones, about the whole marriage thing. You may want this just in case ... well ... just in case someone asks." He pulled a slim gold ring from his pocket and slipped it on her finger. "It belongs to my daughter, and I want you to have it tonight. I forgot to give it to you at your apartment when I gave you the flowers." He cleared his throat again, shifted the car into gear, and picked up speed.

Lacy's eyes grew round. Conrad had placed a ring on her hand as though she really belonged to him. Words of protest pressed against her throat. She could feel the ring on her finger, but she shouldn't encourage this ruse. Maybe she could slip the ring off sometime when he wasn't looking.

Even if the ring meant something, she wasn't ready for a man of thirty to start paying serious attention to her. She still had to make more money so she could buy the wardrobe she'd always wanted. Maybe do a little traveling. Write for the newspaper.

This last thought reminded her of the notepad and pencil in her handbag. She'd slipped her camera in for a photo of the hotel and the theater. If she could snap some shots of these buildings, she'd submit them to the paper along with an article about the play and the food she ate for dinner.

"Here we are." Conrad pulled the car into the hotel's parking lot and came to a stop. After shutting off the engine, he turned to her. "Ready?"

No, she wasn't ready at all. She couldn't imagine what the evening had in store. Lacy opened the door and got out.

Conrad offered her his arm. "Oh, and if they ask about my children, their names are Markus and Betje." He lowered his voice. "Markus is nine and Betje is seven."

The little girl Lacy met at the library had the name Betje. Was Conrad her father?

They walked to the grand entrance together and then

Conrad led her into the elegant lobby where a cluster of stylish people stood surrounded by brocade furniture beneath a chandelier.

"Good evening, Conrad." One of the men shook hands.

"Mr. Blaine." Conrad nodded.

"Ah, and this must be Mrs. Van Drunen." Mr. Gresham smiled at Lacy. "So nice to meet you."

"Please, just call me Lacy." She flashed a smile back at Mr. Gresham but scowled at Conrad.

He shook his head ever so slightly and then shifted his attention back to Mr. Blaine. "These women must be your wives."

Mr. Blaine extended his hand to the woman at his side. "This is my wife, Gretta, and Gresham's wife, Penelope." He gestured to the woman next to Mrs. Blaine.

Perfect hair and immaculate dress met Lacy's eyes. Her face heated. To think she dared to show up to this outing in a simple little dress off the rack of Eva's shop. These women were much more suited to the company of someone like Margaret Kaldenberg, not her.

"We'll make a lovely party this evening." Mr. Gresham smiled with contentment. "I believe the chef has steak and baked chicken on the menu tonight."

"Shall we?" Mr. Blaine motioned down the hall.

Lacy followed along at Conrad's side until they arrived at the restaurant. A high, domed ceiling arched overhead. Palms filled the corners. Soft light shone from the lamps on the tables.

A man in a dark suit and bowtie met them at the entrance. He showed them to a corner table perfectly arranged for a party of six.

Conrad pulled a chair out for Lacy and helped her to the table when she sat down. Then he settled in the chair on her left. Her hand under the table, she felt for the ring on her finger and slipped it off. Everyone would be so busy eating that they wouldn't have time to look for a wedding band.

The waiter brought menus, so Lacy picked one up and studied it. The prices listed next to the entrees made her heart stop. So expensive! If she were out with her father, he'd leave and take her to a more economical establishment.

"Ah, Conrad! It's so nice to finally get to meet your wife," Mr. Blaine said in a breezy, lighthearted manner.

Lacy grimaced. "I'm not—"

"Uh." Conrad interrupted her. "We are, I mean, she is quite happy to be here with us, aren't you?" He glanced at her with a look in his eyes that said he depended on her.

Gritting her teeth, Lacy shifted her attention back to the over-priced entrees listed in the menu.

"Tell us a little about yourself, my dear. Help us get more acquainted." Penelope Gresham looked down her nose at Lacy.

Already she knew she didn't like this woman. Her tone held condescension and the length her gaze had to travel down that long nose warned Lacy that Mrs. Gresham considered herself above the rest of the world.

"I work as a seamstress in the Oswell City dress shop. I came to town ..." her words faded away when Conrad's warm hand reached into her lap to hold hers.

"With a friend." Conrad finished the sentence for her. "That's how we met, isn't it? You came to town with a friend, and that's when we got to know each other."

"He nearly ran over me first. You could say I was in his way." Lacy raised a brow as she glanced at Conrad. If he wasn't worried about telling the truth tonight, then she'd make up for his failings.

Mrs. Blaine joined the others in laughter. "This sounds like an entertaining story. Tell us more."

The ring slipped onto her finger. Somehow, Conrad had found it in the folds of her skirt and put it back in place. Lacy sucked in a ragged breath and turned to him. His eyes glowed as he nodded at her in a manner that said he'd sure appreciate it if she'd leave the gold band alone. She let go of his hand and twisted the ring around her finger. Maybe she'd just keep her hand under the table.

"You work in a shop in town?" Mrs. Gresham's condescending voice demanded attention.

"I do. I enjoy sewing, and I've helped the owner out by doing the more tedious jobs so that she can manage the cash register and take orders when people come in." Lacy sat up straighter. She had purpose and skill, and Mrs. Gresham couldn't look down on that.

"My goodness. A married woman holding a job in a store." Mrs. Gresham rested her hand on her bodice. "I've never been a strong believer in women holding jobs. The idea. They are much better off at home managing the servants and planning menus."

Her husband chuckled good-naturedly. "Not everyone is as fortunate as you, darling."

She sent him a glare then turned her attention back on Lacy. "But what does your husband think? I can't imagine that he'd approve of you being gone from home so much."

"I don't have a—" Lacy's word got lost in Conrad's.

He cut in and spoke at the same time as her. "I love that—"

They both stopped talking and looked at each other.

Conrad cleared his throat. "She's talented and efficient. Eva Synderhof is very fortunate to have her in the shop. I love the fact that she can hold a job." He picked up her hand, the one with the ring on it, and kissed her fingers. "I'm proud of you, Lacy, my love."

"We're still waiting to hear more about how the two of you met." Mrs. Blaine gave her hands a light clap as though she were having fun.

Lacy heard the request, and she knew the woman deserved

the truth, but she couldn't find her voice. Conrad's words echoed in her mind, and his kiss burned on her hand. She'd received both on this evening of falsehood, but each action carried its own whisper of truth. Conrad had revealed his heart to her in that moment of cover-up.

The waiter came to take their orders. His question of what she wished to have snapped her back to the group. When he left, Conrad relaxed. The menus out of the way, he draped his arm along the back of her chair. Then he launched into a retelling of that summer day when he saw her in the street. He left out the part that it had happened just a few weeks ago. The way he told the story left the listener believing it was way in the past, and that she and Conrad had known each other, had shared a life together, for a long time.

The group laughed at the appropriate places and sympathized when Conrad described the damage done to her frame. The memory came back, but the feelings of dislike were gone.

Their food arrived just in time. Conrad would never know how close she came to pushing away from the table and stomping out of the hotel.

She'd only taken a few bites of the delectable roasted chicken when Mr. Gresham asked a question.

"Do you have children?"

Lacy coughed. The businessman probably expected her, as the assumed mother, to answer. But she wasn't the mother, and she couldn't mislead him in thinking so.

Conrad put down his fork. "Yes. Markus and Betje."

Glances roved between Conrad and Lacy. Finally, Mrs. Gresham spoke. "But you are awfully young, my dear, to mother children. How old—"

Conrad cleared his throat. "My son is nine, and my daughter is seven."

Mrs. Blaine exchanged a disbelieving glance with Mrs. Gresham. "They must be from a different mother."

Lacy choked down her food. Conrad shouldn't have ever tried to pull off this ruse. He was bound to get found out, and then his relationship with these businessmen would be damaged. She looked at him as an ache grew in the back of her throat. She didn't want to help him lie, but neither did she want to help him get found out.

"They are." Conrad leaned back in his chair. "Markus and Betje are from my first marriage."

Lacy's eyes misted over. The tenderness in his voice could make anyone believe he told the truth.

He reached over once more and clasped her hand. "Lacy is my ... is my second ..." His voice trailed away as he reached for his napkin and wiped it across his mouth.

The ache in her throat strengthened. Conrad's conscience must be starting to bother him for the way he stumbled over his words.

"Tell us about you, Mrs. Blaine. Do you have children?" Conrad recovered nicely and shifted the conversation away from him.

Lacy drew in a deep breath as Mrs. Blaine took full advantage of the moment. She talked all about her children and of her grandchildren. The conversation stayed on the topic of the Blaines' and the Greshams' grandchildren, allowing Lacy to enjoy her dinner in peace.

When she'd finished. she slipped her notepad from her handbag and took a few notes. Readers in Oswell City might be interested in her thoughts on the meal and the surroundings.

"What are you writing?" Mrs. Blaine asked.

"I'm making notes for an article I hope to write for the *Oswell City Journal*." Lacy finished the sentence she'd written and laid her pencil down.

"Writing for the newspaper?" Mrs. Gresham asked with condescension.

"Maybe for the gossip column." Mrs. Blaine sounded

excited about the possibility.

"But that means she'd say something about us. It had better be flattering." Mrs. Gresham's voice rose as though the idea scared her.

Lacy shook her head. "I'm writing an article to go along with the pictures I'll take of the hotel and the theater."

"Pictures?" Mrs. Gresham said as she turned to her friend.

"See. Right here, with the camera I brought." Lacy slipped the camera from her bag and held it up.

"Lacy takes sensational photos for our local paper." Conrad glanced at her as an invitation to share a private joke.

She rolled her eyes in teasing.

A single chuckle came from him. Not a smile, but at least it was an attempt to laugh. She'd take it.

"A camera? How interesting." Mr. Gresham reached over and picked it up. Then he turned it to study it from every angle.

"I've thought about getting one of those," Mr. Blaine said.

"You should. I've gotten so much enjoyment from taking pictures of scenery and wildlife." Lacy accepted the camera when he handed it back to her.

The waiter came and took everyone's payment in the form of the tickets for their discounted, married couples' meal.

Lacy held her breath as Conrad handed over his tickets, one for him and one for her. After this one last act of deception, the lie could end. She and Conrad weren't married. Now that they were headed to the theater, she could move past the discomfort of pretending to be something she wasn't.

"Shall we?" Conrad offered her his arm.

She accepted and walked out of the hotel restaurant with a new sense of liberation settling over her.

Outdoors, Lacy turned and raised her camera. "Hold on just a minute, Conrad. I want to take a picture." She snapped a few shots and then placed her hand back in the crook of his arm.

He led her to the car and opened the door to get in. She

followed and watched as he started the car. She should say something about their fake marriage, but what? She'd done her best to tell the truth, but did Conrad know that? Maybe she should point it out to him.

He spoke first. "That didn't go too bad." He turned to glance at her. "Did you have a nice time?"

How should she answer that? Lacy stiffened. "The food was good, but really, Conrad, should we have pretended to be married? You almost got found out when those women started asking about your children. What if Mr. Gresham and Mr. Blaine learn the truth? You could lose your business with them."

A smile tugged at the corner of his mouth. "It went better than I expected. Neither one of us said anything about being married, not really. And wasn't I entirely honest about my children?" His brow rose as he turned to look at her.

"Yes, you were, and I tried to be as well. But what about the appearance? You know we gave the impression of something false."

By this time, they'd reached the theater. Conrad parked his car, turned off the engine, and reached for her hand. Holding it to his lips he said in a quiet voice, "I did not."

Her eyes grew round as he gazed into them for a long moment. What was he saying? Did he want to be married to her? Maybe his pretending had turned into something real. Her heart skipped a few beats.

They entered the theater and found their seats next to the other couples. Conrad held her hand for a long while. His endearment, *Lacy my love*, pounded through her mind. He'd encouraged her to have a good time. His special attention to her were becoming a vital part of that good time. Were she and Conrad learning to care for one another? What if the lie Conrad had asked her to live tonight actually turned out to be the truth?

18

Conrad settled into a theater seat at Lacy's side. The lights dimmed until the hall went completely dark. Music played as the first cluster of actors came onto the stage. He sucked in a deep breath and allowed himself to relax. He hadn't enjoyed an evening this much in a long time.

A light touch came to his chest in the exact area of his suit-coat's pocket. He glanced down to see Lacy's slim fingers slip into it and back out again. That pocket was empty, or had been. He patted it and felt a circular object resting under the layers of fabric. Betje's ring. A grin stretched his mouth. The ring he fought to keep on Lacy's finger had come off and landed in his coat pocket. Well, he'd let her win. She'd been a good sport through the whole evening, and now that they were sitting in the dark theater, no one would be able to see that her ring had mysteriously disappeared.

Neither was anyone likely to care. Maybe he'd tried too hard to impress the men he did business with. The gain he'd secured in going out to dinner and a show with them this evening might get lost if they were ever to reproach him.

He wasn't opposed to telling the truth. It was an easy

truth to tell. A few hours in Lacy's company had altered his world. The idea of sharing his life with another woman frightened him less than it had before he'd taken the risk to ask her out. Settling back in his chair, he pushed these thoughts from his mind and watched the scenes getting acted out on stage.

At intermission, Conrad stood. "Enjoying the play?" he asked Lacy as he stretched.

"Oh, yes!" Her eyes glittered. "I'd read Shakespeare in my high school English class, but I've never seen it acted out."

"This is my first time seeing it too."

Lacy turned eyes full of disbelief on him.

"Don't look so shocked." He smiled. "You have to remember that I've only lived around here for a few years and didn't know any English before I came. There are many things I'm still learning."

A smile flashed across her face, but then disappeared when understanding of his move to a new country dawned.

"Hi, Lacy. I'd hoped I'd bump into you at some point tonight." Luke Barnaveldt stood in the aisle.

Lacy turned around and gave him a bright smile.

Conrad no longer thought of her as a formal and distant "Miss Jones." Ever since that little term of endearment had slipped from his mouth at dinner, she'd been Lacy to him. He couldn't take the endearment back. *Lacy my love* had been manufactured in his heart to fit the occasion and had been said for all to hear. He hadn't prepared for the term to stick in his mind as the permanent way he viewed her. But there it was—Lacy my love. He'd do his best to keep the love part inside and only let the Lacy part sneak out.

"Luke! Where are you sitting? Did you bring anyone with you?" Lacy gave her full attention to the young man.

"I asked Joy to come like you said I should. She knows we're only here as friends, but we're enjoying the show."

"It's good, isn't it? Conrad and I are enjoying it too." She gestured to him as she spoke.

"We're sitting up there, four rows behind you." Luke pointed to the place where Joy Haverkamp sat.

She waved at them, and Lacy waved back. The lights flickered so Luke left. When Lacy sat down, Conrad leaned over and whispered, "How did you know Luke was coming to the play?"

"He asked me to come with him, but I told him you'd asked me first." Lacy turned her attention to the orchestra as they started to play.

Conrad tried to do the same, but Lacy's words ricocheted around on his insides. She'd had another invitation to tonight's theater production. The thought had never occurred to him that other young men might have interest in her. He'd thought of her as connected to him somehow since he'd come to her rescue more than once. She'd become someone he had special rights to, like her time and attention was at his disposal.

Conrad scowled as he watched the actors parade onto the stage for the next act. What a selfish and conceited heel he was. Maybe Lacy should have gone with Luke instead of him, if that was what she really wanted.

But the idea of missing out on this evening with her brought a pain to his midsection. He was enjoying himself. Lacy made him feel at ease and comfortable. She was gracious and kind, even when he mortified her with his attempts to help others see what he saw in her.

He made his best effort to follow the story getting acted out in front of him, but Lacy stayed on his mind.

The show went on for another hour. When it ended, Conrad thanked his colleagues and gave them directions to his house for their meeting in the morning. Then he drove Lacy back to Oswell City. The hour was late, so the trip was quiet, broken only by occasional comments about the play.

On Main Street, Conrad parked his car and walked Lacy to the door. "Thanks for coming with me."

"I had a good time."

"I'm glad you decided to come with me instead of with Luke."

"You asked first, and I wanted to keep my word to you." The light of a harvest moon glistened in her eyes.

She shivered, so Conrad grasped a corner of her shawl and drew it more tightly around her.

"Luke probably wouldn't have asked you to pretend you were married to him."

She smiled. "No, probably not."

They stared at each other for a solemn moment.

"I enjoy spending time with you, and well, I'd like to ask if you would consider allowing me to court you, Lacy ... my love." Those words popped out. Conrad could kick himself. His heart raced and dizziness set in. This might be harder than he first thought.

"Courting?" Lacy's eyes grew round and then she lowered her gaze. "I'm honored. Can I think about it?"

"Of course. I don't need an answer right away." He picked up her hand and kissed the back of it. "Good-night."

THE NEXT MORNING, Conrad fed Markus and Betje breakfast and then took them to Nick and Hannah's. Mr. Gresham and Mr. Blaine arrived soon after Conrad returned home. He welcomed them and took them to the back yard.

"This is my workshop." Conrad unlatched the door and led the men inside. "You can see that I have furniture in all stages of completion in here."

The two men walked around analyzing everything. Mr.

Gresham pointed to the saws and the lathes on the wall. "Your tools?"

"Yes, they are. I brought them with me from Holland. I built furniture there too." Conrad moved to the middle of the shop so that he was available to answer more questions.

"You do all of your work in here?" Mr. Blaine asked as he paced, kicking up sawdust.

"Yes, sir, I do. I keep a few completed items in storage at the orchard, along with my supply of building materials, but the majority of the construction happens here."

"The orchard?" Mr. Blaine looked away from a table top he checked for smoothness.

"It's a farm a mile out of town to the south. Owned by the church. I'm the handyman there. If you're ready, I'll drive you out."

Mr. Blaine nodded and moved toward the door. Mr. Gresham followed him into the yard while Conrad secured the lock. They got in the car and made the trip out of town to the orchard.

Conrad parked and led the way to the barn. He pushed the heavy door to the side and went in. "Woodworking supplies and lumber are over here." He led the way to a walled area under the haymow. Stacks of wood, a bin of nails, and two completed tables filled the space.

"This is all so interesting. Your workshop in town is quite small. Have you ever thought of expanding and maybe hiring people to help you? I didn't expect to find out that you do all of the work yourself." Mr. Blaine said as he dusted straw from his coat.

"I haven't been able to afford hiring anyone. And my children are school age. I need somewhere close to my house where I can work. That barn in my backyard works perfectly." Conrad led the men outdoors and shoved the barn door closed.

"We admire your ingenuity and resourcefulness, but let me

tell you that the day is coming when you will have too many orders to fill on your own," Mr. Blaine said.

"For sure. You are at a point in your career when expansion is a very good idea." Mr. Gresham leaned against the car as he talked.

"Show us the shipping location and then we must be off." Mr. Blaine opened a car door and got in.

"You have a fine young wife, Conrad." Mr. Gresham talked as he watched the scenery speed by.

Conrad's stomach clenched as Lacy's rebukes came back to him. "I'm afraid I owe both of you an apology. You see, Lacy and I aren't really, well ..." He gulped. Would telling the truth only cause misunderstanding? He'd led these men to believe that he was married to Lacy. If he were to try to correct that, would he give the impression that he was living in an inappropriate relationship with her?

He puffed out a breath. This situation could get complicated in a hurry. "What I mean to say is, Lacy is very special to me. We aren't married yet, but I hope that we will be very soon." His pulse throbbed. Was that the truth? By attempting to give these men an accurate description of his standing with Lacy, had he told another falsehood?

"Well, when you do finally tie the knot, be sure and let us know. We'd like to come to Clear Brook more often. Gretta really enjoyed your company last night. I can see us taking in social events as a group quite frequently, wouldn't you say?" Mr. Blaine turned to his colleague.

"Definitely. Penelope felt the same way." Mr. Gresham smiled. "We could cut some excellent business deals over dinner at that fine hotel. You know we don't have many people like you in this area that we do business with, Conrad. Our partnership could open up a whole new avenue of sales in this part of the country."

The words from these men were more than he could have

expected. Apparently, they were impressed last night, not just with Conrad's willingness to go to dinner with them, but with the location in general, including the hotel and the quality of the show they'd watched in Clear Brook. A vision of his future formed in his mind. He could see himself and Lacy as a couple sharing social engagements with these men and their wives. They could be a great help to each other as his business and their influence expanded.

On Monday afternoon, golden fields beckoned. The outcome of his tour with his business partners on Saturday had swirled in his mind over the weekend. Bits of conversation repeated in his thoughts stirring up questions. Conrad needed a chance to think. Leaving his afternoon duties, he walked through the orchard to the open field on the other side. A long strip of grass ran parallel to the fence. He walked and walked, allowing his mind to process.

Gresham and Blaine had both agreed that he must expand. But how? Where? The only time he had available to build furniture was in the evenings. Would he have to quit his handyman job to keep up with demand? His children needed him at home in the evenings. He couldn't move his workshop because then he'd be gone during the hours Markus and Betje were home from school. He'd never see them.

The dilemma chased around and around in his head unbroken by a solution. He couldn't think what he should do. The situation had no answer. A car rumbled up the road behind, but Conrad kept walking. The driver was probably one of the neighbors, and would speed by at any moment. But the automobile stopped. Conrad turned to look.

Logan rolled down the window. "Hey, Conrad."

He waved.

"You all right? Did a cow get out?"

"No, I'm not chasing any cows."

"What happened?" Logan's brow furrowed.

"Out taking a walk. That's all." Conrad broke off a dry cane from a weed and whacked the grass with it.

"Oh, I see. You've got girl troubles," Logan teased.

Conrad's cheeks heated. Not if Lacy agreed to a courtship. No trouble with his girl. "No, that's not it either."

"You're looking pretty down. Something is wrong." Logan got out of his car and strode over.

He was a good friend. Conrad could trust him with his problem. Logan might even have some answers.

Conrad shrugged. "My business partners from Des Moines visited on Saturday. They took a tour of my workshop, and now they think I should expand. Get more workspace. Hire some people. But I don't know. Where would I go?"

"You already store some things in the barn. Use it for production." Logan pointed in the general direction of the barn partially hidden behind the apple trees.

"Yeah, I could I guess. But the barn belongs to the orchard. I don't want to clutter it up with all my stuff."

"You have a job here and access to the barn for your work with the orchard. I don't see why you can't make room in it for your business."

"I don't know." Conrad took a whack at more weeds. "It seems like taking advantage of my situation."

"Have you heard that construction on the new highway is wrapping up?" Logan asked.

"Jake ran an article about it in the paper."

"The company wants to get finished before snow comes. They'll be moving out of the house which means it will stand empty for the first time since we started this ministry to immigrant families."

"What will Helen do?"

"Her brother-in-law might give her a job at the hotel."

"Oh. That probably means you won't need me around to keep doing the maintenance and the chores."

"The church board is in a discussion about the next step we should take. Immigration from European countries has slowed because of the war. We don't know if it will resume again when the war is over or if this is a new trend. But one thing we do know is that we can't neglect the house and the other buildings on the farm. They still require upkeep, so we were planning to keep you on at the orchard, at least until we know which direction to go in finding a new use for it."

Conrad nodded as he listened. Change might be coming, so he must prepare to make adjustments. "I'm glad you told me. If my use of the orchard's barn helps you keep the orchard running, then I'll use it."

"I think it would. Doing your wood working in the barn gives you a reason to spend time at the orchard, and that would help us because there would be someone around to keep an eye on the place. You might find that you have extra hours available during the day to work on your projects. We might have to adjust your pay a bit, but maybe the sales you are getting from your furniture will make up for the loss."

"Yes, it would. I recently received a generous payment from Gresham and Blaine. From the things they said on Saturday, they expect my income to keep increasing."

Logan smiled. "Sound like we have an arrangement that helps everyone."

"Sure does. Thanks for helping me find a solution."

"You're welcome." Logan looked at the horizon where the sun hung low. "I'd better be on my way. Fred Ackerman is recovering from surgery, so I'm headed over to pay him a visit."

"I should go too. Markus and Betje are out of school by now and I must pick them up from Nick and Hannah's." Conrad waved to Logan as he returned to his car.

When his friend left, Conrad followed his trail back to the barn, got in his own car, and drove back to town.

At Hannah's house, Betje burst into the kitchen with a book in her hands. "Look Daddy. Aunt Hannah helped me finish this book. It's such a good story. A new friend I made at the library helped me pick it out." She thrust the book into his hands.

Conrad glanced at the cover. "Good for you, Betje. Do you need to take the book back to the library?"

"Aunt Hannah said she would help me do it," Betje said with a glance at her aunt.

Conrad nodded and turned to his son. "How about you, young man? Did you stay out of trouble today?"

Markus shrugged.

"Since I didn't get a call from the principal, I will take that as a yes," Conrad said sternly. "Come, let's go home."

He thanked Hannah and led his children out the door. After driving them home, he went to the kitchen to begin the usual marathon of placing a meal before his family.

Betje changed out of her school dress and Markus started on homework while Conrad worked in the kitchen. He reviewed the events of the weekend and his talk with Logan. A possible courtship with Lacy, an expansion of his business, and a decrease in his work at the orchard. What was the Lord saying to him through these changes? Would his choices work for everyone's best interest? His children and his business partners depended on him.

19

"Someone is here to see you." Eva leaned over and whispered in Lacy's ear.

Lacy lifted her eyes from the buttonholes she worked on and glanced at the shop's entrance.

Jake Harmsen from the newspaper stood there with his hat in his hands. He nodded at Lacy and offered her a smile.

Her stomach fluttered. Was he here to talk to her about the article she'd submitted to the paper? Maybe he'd come to say he didn't want to use it.

Lacy rose to her feet and crossed the room on shaky legs. "Mr. Harmsen, good afternoon." She kept the tremble from her voice as she shook his hand.

"Good afternoon, Miss Jones. I've come to talk with you about the photos and the article you submitted about your evening in Clear Brook. There are a few changes I would like for you to make, and then I'd like to publish it in the paper." He held a collection of typed pages out to her.

She took them. "Why, yes of course. I'll do whatever you want."

"Good." He smiled. "You have talent for journalism, and

with a little guidance, your writing will make a fine contribution to the newspaper."

"Thank you." Lacy glanced at him as a joyful ripple of laughter slipped from her mouth.

"Bring those revised copies to the office by tomorrow morning. I want to include your article in this week's paper." He put his hat on his head and left the shop.

Lacy returned to work in a daze. Mr. Harmsen liked her work, and he wanted a final draft by tomorrow. Pastor Logan had allowed her the use of his typewriter to create her first draft. Maybe he would let her use it again to complete this assignment. She focused as much as she possibly could on the shirt she'd left undone, and then rushed to the church when Eva closed the shop.

Pastor Logan met her in the hall. "Hi, Lacy. Something wrong?"

"No, not at all," She heaved breathlessly. "Could I use the typewriter? Mr. Harmsen has asked for revisions, and I must get them finished by tomorrow morning."

"Go right ahead." Pastor Logan led the way to his study. "I have to go out on a call for a while, so I won't need to use my desk or the typewriter." He took blank pages from a drawer and stacked them on the desk.

"Thank you." Lacy sat in his large, cushioned chair and rolled a page into the typewriter.

She set to work tapping the keys and placing words on the paper until she had the revisions done. Then she put the extra paper away and left the church.

"Lacy!" Mrs. De Witt waved from her front step where she swept.

Lacy returned the wave.

"It's getting late. Have you eaten yet?" Mrs. De Witt asked.

"No." A smile tugged at one corner of her mouth. Maybe she'd receive an invitation.

"Then come join us. We have some special visitors tonight."

Lacy adjusted her direction toward the parsonage instead of downtown to her apartment. The delight of sharing a meal with the De Witts and the mystery of her guests were too much to refuse.

"Come right inside." Mrs. De Witt held the door open so Lacy could enter.

She stepped into a house enlivened with children's voices and graced with the presence of Conrad Van Drunen.

He gave her a warm smile. "What a pleasant surprise. I didn't know you'd be joining us."

She laughed. "Neither did I."

"We'll eat as soon as Logan gets back in town." Mrs. De Witt put her broom away and stirred a pot in the kitchen. A lovely aroma of simmering meat and gravy filled the air.

"Come." Conrad grasped her hand and led her through a boisterous game Mrs. De Witt's twins played with two other children.

Lacy recognized the little girl as Betje from the library.

"Lacy!" Betje gave her an energetic hug in the moment before she sat with Conrad on the sofa.

"You two know each other?" Conrad asked.

"This is Lacy, my friend from the library I told you about." Betje beamed as she made the introduction.

"She's your daughter?" Lacy asked in an incredulous voice. This man kept throwing surprises her way.

"She is." Conrad smoothed Betje's hair.

"Lacy helped me pick out the book Aunt Hannah read to me." Betje's eyes shone as she talked to her father.

"You have a very sweet daughter." Lacy smiled at the little girl.

Conrad didn't reply as she expected him to. She glanced at him and discovered his attention on her. The same light glowed in his eyes as she'd seen for the first time on the night they spent together in Clear Brook. She looked away when Pastor Logan entered the house.

Mrs. De Witt called everyone to the table for the meal. Sharing it with the two families was the most fun Lacy had enjoyed in a long time. The children jabbered with simple little stories while the adults teased and laughed. Lacy found herself caught up in a warm circle of love and acceptance. When Mrs. De Witt served the dessert, she was truly sorry to see the meal end.

But Lacy must be at work in the morning. Reluctantly, she pushed away from the table. "I should go. Thanks so much for inviting me. I had a wonderful time."

Conrad also left the table. "Markus, Betje, could you please stay and play with John and Simon? I want to walk Lacy home."

He went to get her coat and helped her put it on. Out in the darkness, Conrad held her hand as they walked down Main Street. Lacy didn't pull away. She liked the safe feeling of having him close.

At her door, Conrad drew a package out of the bag he carried. "I'd hoped to bring this past your apartment tonight." He gave the package to her.

Lacy opened it. "An Angel Frame!" Pleasure and confusion warred on her insides. "You got me an Angel Frame?"

Conrad shrugged. "It's my gift to you to say thanks for going with me to Clear Brook and for putting up with my clumsy attempts to show you what you mean to me."

A tingling sensation broke out all over her as she looked into his eyes. She mattered to him. In this moment, nothing else was more important.

He grasped her upper arms and pulled her to him. The words, *Lacy my love*, whispered from his lips as they found hers. Conrad's mouth pressed hers for a brief, sweet moment. Then he pulled away.

A carload of raucous young people drove by. The windows

were rolled down and faces hung out of the car leering and gawking.

The obnoxious disruption failed to spoil the moment. Conrad looked deeply into her eyes for a moment before he whispered, "Good night." Then he brushed his thumb over her cheek.

Lacy watched him turn away and walk down the street. Conrad had kissed her right there in the street. Darkness had already fallen, but they'd managed to attract the attention of those people driving by. She covered her mouth as if to protect Conrad's kiss from the rowdy bunch and rushed inside.

She must find a picture to display in her new frame, and then put it in a special place. The photo in her broken frame would work perfectly, but somehow it didn't belong in the gift Conrad had given her. She went to her kitchen drawer for her scissors and cut out of the newspaper the photo of her and Conrad at the school carnival.

A few words from the story showed around the edges since the image wasn't quite the same size as the frame, but it looked nice enough to deserve a place of prominence. Lacy set the picture in its frame on the small table near her rocking chair. She took a step back to assess her work. Were they courting now?

Conrad still waited for her answer, but the delay hadn't stopped him from pursuing her. Maybe she should say yes to a formal courtship. But then an engagement and a marriage would surely follow. Lacy had only just begun to live independently. Must she give that all up now that she'd found it? What about her desire to travel and to buy her own pretty clothes?

She must work and save toward those goals. Courtship didn't fit very well into the ambitions of an independent young lady. Conrad would just have to be content with things the way they were. A walk home after an occasional night out, gifts, and polite kisses.

Lacy covered her mouth again. She could get used to the idea of receiving Conrad's kisses for the rest of her life. He was a gentleman and he regarded her with a tender respect. She turned away from the photo and its frame. The complex feelings it churned to the surface were too much to deal with at this time of night.

~

JAKE HARMSEN LEANED against the counter as he read over Lacy's revisions. "This is really good." He shifted his attention to her. "I've been thinking of making an offer to you, but I wanted to see how this article turned out first."

Lacy's chest tightened. "What sort of an offer?"

He smiled. "How would you like to work freelance for the *Oswell Journal*? I'll give you assigned topics to report on. You can take the photos and write the articles to go with them. How does that sound?"

Like a dream come true, that's how his offer sounded. Her eyes widened. "I'd love to do that. Yes, I'm willing to write freelance articles for you, Mr. Harmsen."

"Good." He moved to his desk. "I'll put your article about Clear Brook in the paper this week. I'd like to give you the topic of writing about the harvest going on in our area. Take some pictures and talk to a few farmers. Can you handle that?"

She nodded. "Yes."

"You've got some time to get it completed. Bring it in by the third week of November. It will be a nice article to run for the Thanksgiving holiday." Jake handed her a sheet of paper with suggested ideas for the article.

"That sounds fine. I'll get it turned in with plenty of time." She said good-bye to him and left the office.

As she headed to work at Eva's shop, Lacy couldn't contain the squeal of excitement pressing on her throat. She had a job writing for the newspaper! It had come about so easily. Years and years of higher education hadn't been necessary. She'd only had to take the risk to show the editor her photography. There were things she could do in this town. Lots of things. Between her job at Eva's shop, her friendship with the De Witt family, and her opportunity with the newspaper, she'd found her place. It was a good place, comfortable and satisfying.

"I saw you with him." A familiar voice from behind slashed through Lacy's thoughts.

She turned to find Rose scowling at her. She paused. "Good morning, Rose. Where did you come from?"

"I'm helping Aunt Helen at the hotel today." A hint of defiance edged Rose's voice.

"Shouldn't you be in school?" Lacy asked.

Rose shrugged. "I only have two classes today, and they aren't until this afternoon."

Lacy nodded as she studied her friend. Rose looked tired and very pale. "Are you feeling all right? You don't look well."

"A bit of a headache, but I'll get over it." Rose blinked as if the ache in her head interfered with her ability to focus.

"Rose?" Lacy reached a hand to her.

"I'm fine. In a few hours I'll be back to normal." Rose pressed her hand to her stomach.

That pale face had been among others hanging out the car window that passed her and Conrad the night before. Lacy gasped. "Were you with those people who drove through town late last night?"

Rose's scowl deepened. "How dare he kiss you."

The evasion of her question confirmed Lacy's suspicions, but the fact that Rose knew about the kiss was all the proof Lacy needed. The only way Rose would have known was to witness it. "You were with that group. And you were drinking, weren't you?"

"I said I'm fine." Rose blinked in an attempt to focus.

"Rose, how could you?" Lacy failed to keep her hurt and disappointment from surfacing. "You said you wouldn't drink. What changed?" Rose kept blinking, so Lacy steered her to one of the benches along the street. "Sit down. You need to rest."

"Why did he do it?" Rose asked as she followed Lacy's direction. "Why would he kiss you like that?"

Lacy sat next to her friend. "Conrad and I care about each other, and he wanted to say thanks for my willingness to help him out."

"But he's supposed to like me." Rose jabbed her chest with her index finger. "I'm the one he drove home our first night in town. I'm the one he invited to the farm to make cider." Rose's scowl transformed into sorrow and her eyes shimmered with tears. "I thought ... well, Conrad is one of the nicest men I've ever met. I like him a lot. I thought he liked me too. But he's chosen you instead." Rose's scowl transformed into sorrow. Her eyes shimmered with tears.

"Oh, Rose." Lacy clasped her shoulder. "I'm sure he never meant to confuse you. He probably saw you in much the same way as he saw me, as a girl new to town that he wanted to help get settled and make a few friends. I'm sorry your relationship with him hasn't turned out the way you wanted."

"It isn't fair." Rose's cheeks flushed as she crossed her arms over her chest. Then she stood and glared at Lacy for a moment before walking away.

Lacy's stomach tightened as she watched her friend stomp down the sidewalk. Conrad's interest in her may have just cost her the friendship she shared with Rose. What if Rose stayed mad and her envy of Lacy ruined their relationship? It had been Rose's idea for Lacy to come along to Oswell City. Now Rose's feelings were hurt. Did she regret inviting Lacy to come with her? Rose may have met Conrad without any interference and been the girl he wished to court.

But Conrad had given Rose a ride because of Lacy's fall in

the street. Rose wouldn't have lost her ticket if she'd been alone, which meant she wouldn't have crossed paths with Conrad. Even if she would have met Conrad after arriving in town, Rose probably wouldn't have attracted his interest. He was a father of two children, whereas Rose liked to go out with her college friends.

Lacy got to know him because she'd stayed with Mrs. De Witt. Rose had a place to stay with her aunt. The chances were slim that Rose would have gotten to know Conrad without her connection to Lacy. She may have seen him at church or at the orchard if she ever went there with her aunt Helen, but he may not have paid any attention to her without Lacy around.

Heaving a deep breath to clear her conscience, Lacy stood. She'd done nothing to compete with Rose for Conrad's attention. If her friendship with Rose suffered, it wouldn't be because of anything Lacy had done. This was just the way things had happened. Rose must accept it and move on.

But Lacy's heart hurt at the thought of a change in her friendship with Rose. Had she lost her best friend? A loud clang from the church's bell rang out, then a second one followed it. Six more would follow alerting everyone in town that eight o'clock had arrived. Lacy hastened to the dress shop. Maybe she could get inside and seated at the sewing machine before the last chime.

20

"My mother is coming to town." Lacy sat across from Conrad at a table in the corner of the church's fellowship hall.

Luke Barnaveldt and Joy Haverkamp led a group of young people in a game. Others clustered at the snacks. A few couples were sprinkled around the room at tables. Energy and lively conversation filled the wide hall, but in this corner, a quiet peace settled.

"You don't sound happy about it." Conrad reached for one of Lacy's hands and held it.

"I'm not sure how I should feel." Lacy traced the floral pattern in the tablecloth. "Dad and Mama don't approve of my choice to stay in Oswell City. Mama is probably going to try to make me go home with her. But I don't want to. Oswell City has become my home. The De Witts are here. So is Eva and my job at the dress shop. I have friends here, and I have you." Lacy sat up straight and met Conrad's gaze.

His eyes filled with gentle kindness. "I'd hate to see you go. Don't let your mother or anyone else steal you away."

"I'm not going anywhere."

A spontaneous smile stretched Conrad's lips. That long-awaited shift in his demeanor brought a glow to Lacy's insides. Maybe her determination to stay in this town provided the key that was starting to unlock Conrad's happiness.

"I'm surprised to see you here tonight," she said in a quiet voice.

"Logan made me do it." Conrad shrugged. "Markus and Betje are at a sleepover with their cousins, which left me with a free evening. Logan found out somehow and twisted my arm to get me to come, so here I am." He smiled a little wider. "When Karen told me you were coming, that helped me make up my mind."

Lacy's internal glow radiated stronger. "I'm glad you took the risk."

Conrad glanced at the activity around them. "It isn't so bad. I've had a good time." He looked at her again. "How did you find out your mother is coming? Do you know this for sure?"

"Oh, yes. She's coming with Rose's parents. Rose told me. She found out from her aunt Helen who found out from Ethel Brinks when Rose's mother called the hotel. She just told me yesterday. They are arriving tomorrow."

"Tomorrow?" Conrad's brows shot to his hairline. "You didn't get much notice."

"None." Lacy's jaw grew tight. "And now my mother will be in town for two days, and I don't know how to make her understand I belong here, not on the farm in Silver Grove." Lacy lowered her gaze and her brow creased with a frown.

"Would it help, I mean, would you like for me to come with you to meet the train? Rose will have her aunt and uncle with her, and if I came, then you wouldn't be alone." Conrad spoke so softly that his words were drowned out by a cheer from the group playing games.

"If you have time, I would appreciate that very much." Lacy's grasp on his hand tightened.

"I have time. When does the train arrive?"

"Four o'clock."

"I'll drive to your apartment and pick you up."

"Thank you." Lacy released her hold on Conrad's hand when Pastor Logan came to their table.

He held a stack of cups. "Hot cider fresh from the orchard's press. Would you like some?"

"Please." Conrad accepted a cup. "Did you know that Lacy and her friend Rose will have guests in town over the weekend?"

"I didn't. Who are they?" Pastor Logan asked as he poured cider into their cups.

"Rose's parents and my mother," Lacy said.

"Invite them to the parsonage for supper tomorrow night. Karen would love to see them again, and so would I."

"Thanks. Are you sure Mrs. De Witt won't mind?"

"I'll tell her about it, but I know my wife well enough to confidently say that any guests from Silver Grove are welcome in our house at a moment's notice." Pastor Logan flashed a grin and moved to another table with his stack of cups.

Conrad stayed by her side the rest of the evening, and again the next afternoon when he took her in his car to the train station. For as much as Lacy loved her mother, the dread of this visit from her loomed large and powerful. She didn't know what she would have done without Conrad's calming presence.

"Mama." Lacy welcomed her mother with a hug in spite of the tension pulling at her insides.

"You look well, but a little tired." Mama stepped back to examine Lacy. "And I do believe you're thinner. Hmm. We'll have to do something about that." She frowned at Lacy for a moment as though seeing her as a problem to solve.

"I'm fine, Mama, and I'm getting along quite well. You'll see." The smile Lacy conjured up didn't wipe Mama's frown away.

"Who are you, young man?" she peered at Conrad.

"This is Conrad Van Drunen, Mama. He's a friend of Mr. and Mrs. De Witt, and he is a friend of Rose and me as well." Lacy gestured to Conrad as Rose brought her parents closer.

"Hi, Conrad," Rose sidled up to him. "I'm so glad you came to the station today. Let me introduce you to my parents too."

"Jack and Amelia Harper, this is Conrad. He is the carpenter at the orchard where Aunt Helen works. He can do anything." Rose sent Conrad a look full of admiration.

He responded only with a pink flush to his cheek.

"Nice to meet you." Rose's mother smiled at him and turned to Rose. "Could you show us to the hotel?"

Lacy, Conrad, and Mama followed. As they walked, Lacy stole glances at Rose. Her friend seemed much more alert than she had on that morning they met on the street. Maybe Rose's improved condition was due to the time of day, and she was naturally in better shape by the afternoon. Had Rose been drinking with her friends last night? Lacy couldn't say. Disagreements had grown the distance between them. The change in their friendship brought a sharp prick to Lacy's heart. Would their parents notice? Would Rose be able to hide her drinking habits while her mother and father were in town?

"Do you have room for me to stay with you? Jack and Amelia reserved a hotel room, but I don't have the money to stay there. That's why your father didn't come. We could only spare the funds for one train ticket." Mama's words cut into Lacy's thoughts.

Her apartment was small, but she could try and find room for a guest. "You may have my bed and I'll sleep in the main living room area." Probably scrunched up on the loveseat is where she'd end up.

Mama responded with a smile. It brought a new thought to Lacy's mind. Mama's request to stay with her might be her way of keeping tabs on Lacy so that she could coerce her into a new plan, like Cal had tried to do.

Well, it wouldn't work. Lacy stretched to her full height and held her chin high as she walked with the group to the hotel. "We will meet you at the De Witts. I want to help Mama get settled while you are at the hotel," Lacy said to Rose.

She nodded and gave Conrad one more admiring glance.

Lacy, Mama, and Conrad covered the length of one more block until arriving at Lacy's apartment.

"I must go home. Markus and Betje will be out of school by now," Conrad said. "See you tomorrow?"

Lacy nodded. "Sure. I work in the morning, but maybe we can get together for the evening meal."

"I'd like that." Conrad gave her a brief smile, lifted his hat to Mama, and walked away.

Lacy opened the door, led Mama up the stairs, and opened a second door to her apartment. "Here it is."

Mama entered and looked around.

"The bedroom is right through here." Lacy led her across the living area.

Mama followed with an air of disapproval about her. "Where will you sleep?" She asked as they worked together opening Mama's luggage.

"Out there on the loveseat." Lacy pointed through the doorway.

Mama straightened and sighed. "Lacy, this place is awfully small. Are you sure this is the best way for you to live?"

The question brought a sharp pain to Lacy's middle. "But it's mine, and I can afford it. Mrs. De Witt and her mother helped me find the furniture. The grocery store is just down the street. I can handle it."

Mama jutted her chin. "I don't know. You'd be better off living at home with us. What if something happened to you when you're up here all alone? How would you get help?"

Lacy bit back the impatient words that wanted to fly from her mouth. "Nothing is going to happen to me. Plus, I have friends here who care."

Mama's gaze slid over every inch of Lacy's abode. "Your father is right. You need to come home."

Lacy's veins heated. She refused to leave everything she'd worked for and the friendships she cherished. She drew in a long, deep breath. "It's time to have supper with the De Witts. They would like to see you again and invited us over tonight. Let's go." Lacy replaced her hat and walked in silence with Mama down the street.

The Harpers were already there. Much laughter and chatter filled the house as everyone became reacquainted with Mrs. De Witt and her husband. The mothers enjoyed meeting the children and watched as they showed off their newest toys. Sara giggled and allowed these strangers to hold her.

Happy conversation and good cheer filled every minute of the evening. Sad to leave, Lacy gave Mrs. De Witt one more hug and promised to come spend the night again as soon as she could.

The group left and split off at the jewelry store. The Harpers moved on to the hotel, and Lacy and Mama went upstairs to the apartment.

"They're nice people. I enjoyed seeing your schoolteacher again. Such adorable children! Her husband was a good preacher. I miss him in Silver Grove. It'll be nice to hear him again Sunday morning." Mama removed her hat and set it on the table. "I could do with a little snack before I go to bed." She opened the door of Lacy's ice box.

"See my new frame, Mama? Conrad replaced it for me." Lacy held up the cherished frame.

"Very nice. He seems like a proper young man." Mama glanced at Lacy and then turned her attention back to the ice box. "You hardly have anything to eat in here." Mama shut the door and straightened. "Don't you make enough money to buy food? You shouldn't work for such a pittance. Your father and I could take much better care of you on the farm."

"Mama." Lacy clenched her fists at her sides. "Of course I make enough money to buy food. I just don't keep much around because it spoils. One person like me doesn't eat meat and cheese fast enough to use it up before it gets bad. I buy small portions so that I won't waste anything."

"Hmm." Mama studied Lacy as though searching for signs of starvation.

"Let me fix you a sandwich. It will take no time at all." Lacy moved to the cupboard and cut slices from the loaf of bread she'd baked two nights before.

"Tell me about Conrad." Mama settled in a chair.

"He's a friend of the De Witts."

"Did I hear him say he has two children?"

"That's right." Lacy took some leftover roast beef and the crock of butter from the ice box.

"A widower?"

"Yes. He lost his wife a few years ago."

"He likes you."

Lacy shrugged. "I like him."

"No, I mean he *likes* you. I saw the look in his eyes. He thinks you're special. But be careful, Lacy. Does he know about your delicate health? He might not be so interested in you if he knew how easy it is for you to get sick." Mama crossed her arms and raised her brow.

"But, Mama, I haven't been sick since February. That was several months ago. I've felt perfectly fine all summer." Lacy placed the sandwich on a plate and brought it to Mama.

"You get started coughing and can't quit. Ever since you had whooping cough as a child, your congestion hangs on. If Conrad is serious about courting you, then he should know how sickly you are." Mama took a bite of her sandwich.

"I'm not sickly. Not anymore. Everyone gets sick in the winter from time to time. Just because I fought bronchitis in February doesn't mean I'm in worse health than anyone else." Lacy's voice rose as she fought her impatience.

"The life you're trying to lead here will only make it worse. You'll wear yourself out and get run down. Then you'll get sick and can't work." Mama's gaze bore into Lacy. "You'll have to leave when I leave on Sunday. This whole business of holding a job and living on your own won't last. You'll have to go back home."

Lacy held her breath against the heated words that wanted to pour out. Mama couldn't see Lacy's accomplishments or her success at achieving independence. The woman sitting across the table from her would never understand. Lacy had no way of making her change. The only thing she could do now was to follow Conrad's suggestion to not let Mama or anyone else steal what was hers.

She stood. "I'm not going back to Silver Grove."

Mama gave her a sharp look. "Oh, yes you are."

Lacy's vision blurred with hot tears. She stomped into the bedroom to change into a nightgown. When she returned to the main room, Mama stood at the sink washing her plate.

"I'm working at the dress shop in the morning. Please entertain yourself however you like. I'm going to sleep now. Good night." Lacy turned away and lay down. The sounds of Mama working in the kitchen drifted to Lacy's ears and kept her from sleep. Mama finished in the kitchen and went to the bedroom. The apartment fell quiet. Even then, Lacy lay awake.

~

THE STIFF SILENCE between Lacy and her mother continued into Sunday morning. They prepared for church, made the walk to the building, and sat through the service without saying a word to each other. Pastor Logan preached a beautiful message and then shook their hands at the back of the church after the service.

Lacy talked with Joy and Luke while Mrs. De Witt led Mama over to Eva Synderhoff so that she could introduce them to each other. Mama and Eva visited for a few moments. Then a sorrowful expression claimed Eva's features. What had Mama said to Eva?

"Look at this." A child tugged on Lacy's dress.

Lacy glanced down to find Betje Van Drunen holding up a book.

"Aunt Hannah took me to the library again. She helped me pick it out. Do you like to read? Maybe we can read it together."

Conrad arrived and gave a light chuckle. "Lacy may not have time to read you a book."

Betje turned to him with a pout.

"Of course, I would. I'd love to read you a story sometime." Lacy smiled at the girl.

"Do you and your mother have lunch plans?" Conrad asked.

"I'm afraid not. Mama and the Harpers must catch the early afternoon train. We won't have time to eat very much."

"I hope they have a safe trip home." He gave her a quick nod and then led Betje away.

Mama hastened to Lacy's side. Breaking the silent treatment they'd given one another, Mama blurted out her first words to Lacy, "We must go. There isn't much time to pack."

Lacy frowned. "But most of your clothes are already folded in your suitcase. You did that before we left for church."

"There's still much to be done. Come on." Mama grasped Lacy's arm and tugged her along.

At the apartment, Mama flew into action. She pulled the satchel and suitcase from the closet and began filling them with garments from the dresser.

"Mama, what are you doing?" Lacy gasped in horror at the scene unfolding before her.

"I'm getting you packed to return to Silver Grove. That's what I'm doing." Mama stuffed a petticoat into the suitcase.

Lacy sprang forward and grasped Mama's wrist. "Stop. I need to wear those clothes to work."

"Oh no, you won't." Mama opened a new drawer and pulled out a blouse.

"What do you mean?" Lacy's grip on Mama's arm loosened.

Mama looked Lacy in the eye. "You won't be wearing these clothes to work because you don't have a job anymore. I told Eva you were leaving town with me today."

Lacy's heart stopped. "You what?"

Mama pointed to a pair of stockings draped over the back of a chair. "Get those things picked up and in your satchel. Time is running out."

"You had no right to speak to my employer. This town is my home, and I'm staying." Lacy went to the kitchen for her shawl and flung it over her shoulders.

"Where do you think you're going?" Frustration edged Mama's voice.

"To Eva's. She needs to know that I'm keeping my job and that I'm coming to work in the morning." Lacy yanked the door open and slammed it shut behind her.

How dare Mama do this to her? Her family had no right to order her around. She'd show them. She could live on her own, hold a job, and stay healthy.

Lacy stomped down the street and around the corner to Eva's house. After Lacy explained the situation, Eva assured her that she still had a job. Relieved, Lacy returned to her apartment. Mama was still working on Lacy's clothes.

She cleared her throat. "It's time to meet the Harpers at the station, Mama."

"But you have to come. I told your father I'd bring you home." Mama looked up from the overflowing suitcase.

"I'm sorry to disappoint him." Lacy's heart throbbed. She hated to upset her parents. Why did they have to make this so difficult?

A knock came at the door, so Lacy went to answer it.

Conrad stood at the top of the stairs. "I thought I'd come by and offer to drive your mother to the station."

"That's very kind of you." She lowered her voice. "I could use your help. Mama refuses to leave without me." Lacy held her breath. The idea of leaving so abruptly made her dizzy.

Conrad's gaze softened. He bent and placed a kiss on Lacy's cheek. Then he entered the room and picked up a suitcase. "Mrs. Jones, I've come to give you a ride to the station. What other bags do you have?"

"These two, plus that suitcase and satchel for Lacy." She pointed to the mess she'd made on the bed.

"We'll worry about those another time." Keeping a gentle pressure on Mama's back, Conrad guided her away from Lacy's dresser and into the kitchen.

Lacy picked up the satchel. "Come on, Mama. Time to go."

"But wait! What about Lacy's things?" Mama's eyes grew round, and she resisted Conrad's assistance.

"Lacy can look after those. My car is waiting." Conrad gestured at the street beyond the window.

"Lacy." Mama grumbled at her. "You have to come."

"Yes, Mama." Lacy held the door open.

Together, she and Conrad got Mama down the stairs to the car. At the station, they met up with Rose's parents just as the train pulled in.

Lacy gave Mama a hug. "I'm glad you came. It was good to see you."

"Your father will be upset. Expect a telephone call from him." Mama gave Lacy another sharp look.

Conrad wrapped his arm around Lacy's waist. "Lacy's in a good place, Mrs. Jones. You and your husband don't need to worry about her. She has friends here."

Mama said nothing as she followed the Harpers to the coach car, but Lacy could see the hurt in her eyes. How she hated parting with Mama in this way. Why couldn't they have reached a resolution? What would it take for her brother and her parents to accept the choices she made for herself?

The whistle blew and the train inched forward. After one last wave, Lacy laid her head on Conrad's shoulder. "Thank you. You came just in time. She was determined to take me along. She even had my suitcase packed."

A chuckled rumbled in Conrad's chest. "I'm keeping you right here with me."

Lacy closed her eyes and savored his words. She'd found her home, and no one could drag her away from it.

21

Conrad took a break from work for a late lunch so that he had time to deposit his paycheck from the orchard. He parked along the curb and entered the bank. After completing his business with the teller at the window, he turned away.

"Hey, Conrad!" His brother Nick leaned over his desk and waved.

Conrad changed direction and went to Nick's office. Nick worked in investments and estate planning at the Oswell City State Bank. "What is it?" he asked as he leaned on the doorjamb.

"Do you have time to meet for a few minutes? There's something I want to ask you."

"Sure." Conrad sat in one of the chairs that faced Nick's desk.

"I saw the amount of that check from Gresham and Blaine in a report that came through. You must have deposited it last week." Nick leaned back in his leather chair.

"I brought it in as soon as it came in the mail."

Nick pointed his pen at Conrad. "You're a wealthy man."

"I know." The weight of responsibility hung on him.

"You won't need that handyman job at the orchard anymore. In fact, you could buy the orchard."

"From what Logan has told me, the church might be looking for a business deal. The construction crew left this morning. Helen plans to start working at the hotel which means that the house will sit empty. It requires too much upkeep to have no one living in it for very long."

"Keep it in mind. You could definitely afford a larger home than the one you have now."

Conrad shrugged. "I hadn't really thought about moving."

"There are other matters you'll want to consider too. You should invest some of your money. You should also set up a savings account to fund an education for Markus and Betje."

"I hadn't thought about that either. They're both pretty young."

"It's never too early to start. Can you come over tomorrow night? We'll have supper and talk about this beforehand."

"I guess. What about Markus and Betje? Should I bring them too?"

"Probably, but let me talk it over with Hannah. I'll get back to you."

Conrad nodded and stood up. "See you later."

After a quick stop at home to eat a sandwich, he returned to work for the rest of the afternoon. Later that evening, Nick and Hannah's son Earl came to the door.

Conrad let him in.

"Mama sent me over with this note for you." He handed a folded slip of paper to Conrad.

"What's it say, Dad? Do we get to sleep over at Aunt Hannah's again?" Betje bounced on her feet and glanced at him with hope in her eyes.

He sat down to read. "Your aunt says she is going to hire Joy Haverkamp to babysit for you tomorrow night so that we adults can have a nice meal together."

Betje cheered. "I'll get to play with my cousins! Joy is nice. I like her."

Conrad's brow furrowed as he read. "Your aunt Hannah tells me to make sure and dress up. That's interesting. Wonder why she's being so formal just so Nick and I can talk about finances." He folded the note and turned to Earl. "Thanks for bringing this over."

The boy waved on his way out the door. "See you tomorrow!"

~

THE FOLLOWING EVENING, Conrad left work exactly on time and went home. His two children met him in the kitchen pent up with excitement.

"How soon until we leave, Dad?" Markus asked.

"Less than an hour. Give me some time to change." Conrad took the stairs to his room for a bath and a careful shave. Attired in his best suit, he returned to the kitchen.

Betje giggled. "You look nice, Daddy, just like you do when you go somewhere with Lacy."

Her observation shot a dart through him. He'd gladly spend his evening with her. "No, sweetheart. Daddy and Nick will spend the night talking about money."

"Oh, that sounds boring." Betje wrinkled her nose.

Conrad couldn't agree more. If only he could conjure up a reason to share a nice meal at the hotel dining room with Lacy. He'd rest his arm on the back of her chair again and savor every chance he got to gaze into her clear blue eyes.

"Time to go. Get your coats." He patted the shoulders of both children.

The walk to his brother's house was a short one. Hannah welcomed them in, and then Joy whisked Markus and Betje off with their cousins to her house across the street.

Hannah led Conrad to the dining room where the table was set for four. He frowned. Had she invited more people than just him for supper? Maybe one of Nick's colleagues from the bank would be participating in their conversation. If that was the case, then it was a good thing he'd worn his nicest suit.

Nick entered and led Conrad to the comfortable chairs near the fireplace. He settled in with a notebook and started to ask questions.

Conrad's answers fueled their discussion of investment possibilities and interest rates on savings accounts. Nick helped him put together a plan. As Conrad studied the column of numbers Nick had made, his confidence rose. If these figures affected his life in the way Nick expected, Conrad's whole existence was about to change. He'd be able to afford a standard of living he hadn't even known was possible in those days prior to his emigration.

He and his brothers had come to America for new opportunities. All three of them had discovered these opportunities and now lived comfortable, successful lives. But Conrad was about to venture higher in the realm of financial security. His early years in his native country had provided him with no point of reference for this new affluence. Thank goodness he had his brother's wisdom and foresight by which to navigate this new life.

The front door opened. Hannah's voice and that of another woman carried into the dining room. Conrad recognized that voice. Surely, she hadn't come for supper.

But she did. Hannah brought her to the dining room.

"I'll serve the food now. You may all take a seat at the table." Hannah flashed a smile to her guest and left the room.

Nick stood so Conrad did too. His knees shook a little, but they still managed to hold his weight.

"Conrad, you probably know Hannah's good friend, Kate Vander Will." Nick gestured to the woman in the room.

He nodded. "Yes. Her son Burt is in the same class with Markus."

"Oh, yes. They are both a year behind Earl," Nick said.

"That's right." Kate smiled. Her eyes lit with interest as she looked at Conrad.

Heat crept into his face. As the pieces of this puzzle came together, Conrad suspected his brother and sister-in-law had set him up. The request to dress up, the babysitter for the children, and the use of the dining room with a table set for four confirmed that the two of them had plotted to get him and Kate together tonight. Conrad stifled a groan as he followed his brother to the table.

"Your children must be at Joy's." Nick pulled a chair out for Kate.

Conrad bit his lip. According to Hannah's plan for him, he probably should have been the one to do that.

"Yes. I took them there on my way." Kate reached for her napkin and put it on her lap.

"Conrad and I were just discussing finances," Nick said as he settled into his chair. "My big brother is doing quite well for himself as a furniture builder. He'll soon be the most eligible bachelor in town if he isn't already."

Kate's eyes held admiration added to the already present interest he'd read there earlier.

"Come on, Nick." Conrad tried his best not to squirm under Kate's gaze. If Nick's assessment became the accepted opinion of him, more women than just Kate would get interested in him.

Hannah came to the table which gave Kate someone else to look at. He sucked in a breath of fresh air while Nick prayed to begin the meal. Eating didn't go so bad. The food on his plate gave him something to do. The women carried most of the conversation, so all that was required of him was the use of his silverware, sips from his glass, and the occasional reply whenever a question came his direction.

He enjoyed smooth sailing until the dessert was gone and Hannah refilled everyone's coffee cups.

"Nick promised to help me in the kitchen, so why don't the two of you take your coffee to the parlor? We will join you as soon as we can." Hannah picked up a stack of plates and disappeared into the kitchen.

Nick did the same.

Conrad's chest tightened. After his success at surviving the meal, he'd been abandoned. The people he'd thought were his allies had actually implemented another strategy to get him alone with Kate. His financial talk with Nick appeared to have come to an end. Conrad wanted nothing more than to flee the house and shed his stiff suitcoat.

Kate bounced up and came to him. "What a lovely idea! I'd been hoping we'd have time to ourselves tonight."

Conrad dragged himself out of his chair and offered Kate his arm. As much he wanted to, he couldn't forsake his inbred awareness of how a gentleman should act.

"How has the school year been going for your family?" He asked as he escorted her to the parlor.

"Quite well. Burt struggles a bit with math, but he's receiving help. How about your children?"

"Betje is an outgoing little girl with lots of friends, but Markus has been getting in fights. Perhaps you've heard about them."

Kate laughed. "The boys have had some scuffles." She turned serious and glanced at him. "Burt told me the reason for Markus's fighting. Do you know what it is?"

"The poor boy doesn't have a mother to cook for his friends when they come for slumber parties." Conrad answered in a low voice as his gaze locked with Kate's. He gulped in some air and took a seat.

Conrad chose the location at the end of the loveseat. A nice little table sat between it and a wingback chair. Conrad envisioned Kate choosing the chair. Then they could maintain a bit of distance while still enjoying a leisurely conversation.

But Kate didn't follow that plan at all. She set her coffee down on the table and then joined Conrad on the loveseat. She pressed so close to his side that enough space remained on her other side for another person.

If he had any room at all he would have scooted far away from her. But he was cornered. He sucked in a breath and made sure his hands stayed folded in his own lap.

Kate wasn't so scrupulous. She settled one of her hands on his lapel. "Conrad, you could solve Markus's problem by giving him a new mother."

"I could." His cheeks flamed.

"Don't you ever think of getting married again?" Her breath whispered around his chin.

"I do."

"What's holding you back?" She gazed up at him.

"It's a big decision."

"True, but when you've met the right one, marriage isn't so scary." Her lips were mere inches from his. How easy it would be for him to turn and meet them with his own.

But he didn't dare move. Kate would interpret the slightest shift in his stiff posture as consent to her influence.

"Take us, for example. I'm a widow with young children, and I'm in need of a man who could help me raise them. You're a widower with children who need a mother. You and I are the same age, Conrad. We could blend our families and start a new life together." Kate slid her hand over his shoulder and down his arm.

"That would make sense, wouldn't it?" He stared straight ahead. "But do you love me?"

Kate gasped as though his question caught her off guard.

"Well, I'm sure our affection for one another would grow over time. I admire you very much. Yes, I guess you could say I love you."

He turned to her with an apology in the sober lines of his face. "But I don't love you. I'm sorry. My first wife and I had a special relationship. We were deeply in love. I won't marry again unless I can find that with someone."

Kate's eyes widened. "What do you mean?"

Conrad looked at her while his energy drained away, leaving him with a heavy feeling. "There is no future for us."

Kate's lids slid painfully over her eyes. She leaned and planted a kiss on his cheek. "I wish I could have that special kind of love with you."

"I know. I'm sorry."

"Is there someone else?" she glanced up at him.

Yes, there was. Lacy Jones filled his heart. He'd found in her what he'd lost from Angelien's death. She wasn't a widow with children who needed a father. Rather, Lacy was artistic and sensitive. She understood his need to create and could share in it with him. But Kate could not. From what Conrad could see, she didn't have even one creative bone in her body.

Kate knew how to work hard, and she had to in order to care for four children alone. Conrad commended her for that. But life was more than just the work of completing pragmatic tasks, routine jobs that would need done again the next day and the days following. His life included an appreciation of the beauty around him. He wanted to share in it with someone who loved it as much as he did.

For Conrad, creating art happened by forming the natural substance of wood into quality furniture. For Lacy, art was capturing a scene of nature in a photo. She understood him and had in common with him this desire to create.

He freed himself from Kate's suffocating touch and moved to the chair. He should have done that a long time ago so that he was distanced from her much earlier in the conversation. But he hadn't expected her to claim him so fully. Before he'd caught on, he'd been trapped.

Conrad cleared his throat. "There is someone else. Miss Lacy Jones and I have been spending time together. I've asked to court her and I'm waiting on her answer."

"Oh." Kate sounded offended. She fingered the lace on her dress's neckline. "I wish I could change your mind. Maybe you'd court me instead."

The heaviness spread to his arms and legs. "That won't work out between us. I'm sorry."

Pounding came on the front door. Footsteps hastened from the kitchen, thumping on the hall's wood floor. The door swished open. Loud voices and crying erupted.

"I'm so sorry to come back early, Mrs. Van Drunen, but I had to bring Burt and Markus. They've been fighting." Joy Haverkamp's anxious voice filled the parlor.

Conrad shot to his feet and abandoned Kate. He rushed into the hallway. "Markus, is this true?"

"Yes." Markus crossed his arms as defiant tears slid down his cheeks.

Kate rushed to Conrad's side. Markus glared at her.

"Why were you fighting?" Conrad shot Markus a stern look.

"Burt said you came here tonight so you and his mama could talk about getting married. Earl said so, too, but it's not true." Markus glowered at Conrad.

"Sure it is, you dummy. Just look at them." Burt shoved Markus.

"Markus is gettin' a new mama." Earl snickered and gave Markus a shove of his own.

"Now, boys." Hannah intervened and pulled them apart.

"Say it isn't true, Dad. I don't want Burt's mama for a mother. That means Burt and his sisters would come live with us. We'd fight all the time. Please say you won't do it."

Markus looked up through watery eyes as he pleaded with Conrad.

Joy glanced about with a guilty air as though she'd heard something she shouldn't have. Hannah pulled her children indoors and away from the chilly night air.

Conrad scanned the group to make sure he had their attention. Nick appeared from the kitchen, so Conrad included him. "Mrs. Vander Will and I are not getting married. We talked it over and I think she understands why it won't work."

Markus flung his arms around Conrad's waist while Betje and her girl cousins looked at him in pity.

Conrad patted his back. "It's time to go home. Thank Miss Haverkamp for taking care of you." He leaned over and stage whispered in Markus's ear. "And no more fights." When he began walking, Markus released his hold and turned to thank Joy.

Burt and his sisters gathered around Kate as Hannah herded her children to the kitchen along with their father.

Conrad's eyes met Kate's. "Good night." He spoke in a way that put a finality on the evening's events. They wouldn't be courting, and their families wouldn't be blending.

She glanced back at him with a hint of resentment in her eyes.

"Thank you for the meal and for the helpful financial advice." Conrad said to Nick and Hannah as he walked through the kitchen to the back door. It was the entrance he always used on visits to their house, and it felt like the most appropriate exit to use for his discreet escape from the evening's mess.

"This didn't go at all like I intended. I didn't mean for you and Kate or your children to have an argument." Hannah crossed her arms.

"I hope we've all learned that I don't need any help finding a mother for my children." Conrad cast a solemn glance at

Hannah and swung Betje into his arms. "Come on, Markus." He guided his son out the door.

Conrad imagined Hannah returning to the parlor and talking the evening over with her friend. He'd probably receive a harsh evaluation for messing up their plans. But he could live with that. He'd rather endure one evening of misunderstanding than fill the rest of his life with regret. Reaching for Markus's hand, he led his children home.

22

"Hi, Lacy." Conrad caught up to her on the sidewalk after the Sunday morning service.

"You look tired." She matched his pace as he fell in step with her.

"Nick and I helped our brother Dan harvest his corn crop yesterday. I admit I was rather slow getting started this morning."

"Did you get finished?"

"No. I'll take some time to go back out there this week. What about you? Do you have a busy week ahead?" Conrad asked.

"Yes. Eva continues to get more and more business in her shop, so I know there will be plenty of orders for me to fill. I also want to get started on an assignment Jake gave me for the newspaper. It involves interviewing area farmers about the progress of their harvest."

"Do you have a ride?" Conrad waved at a couple across the street.

Lacy shrugged. "I plan to walk."

"But you'll have to go several miles by the time you returned home. Let me take you in my car."

She glanced at him. "You don't have to do that. When would you have time? You said you'd be helping your brother this week, plus you've got your job at the orchard."

"Let's go today."

"But what about your children? And don't you want to rest from the work you did yesterday?"

"Driving isn't hard. It's rather relaxing. And Markus and Betje are going to the orchard this afternoon with their Sunday School class. Logan is hosting a hayride for them. I have the day to myself, and I'd like to spend it with you."

The look in Conrad's eyes tugged at her. Over the weekend, the weather had been perfect with blue skies, warm temperatures, and lovely fall colors on the trees that beckoned her to find any excuse to spend time outside. A drive in Conrad's car would save her mountains of time and would keep her from exhausting herself on long treks down country roads.

She stopped walking and returned the warmth present in his gaze. "You probably need lunch just like I do."

He nodded. "You read my mind."

"How about I pack some food and we enjoy a picnic somewhere along the way?"

"I know just the place." He raised a brow. "See you in an hour?"

"I'll be ready."

They parted at the corner. Conrad turned to go to his house while Lacy continued down Main Street to her apartment. Inside, she made sandwiches, filled a jug with water, and collected food from her icebox. Their picnic would include the remaining cookies from a batch she'd baked on Friday, apples Pastor Logan had brought from the orchard, and the leftovers of a potato salad Mrs. De Witt had sent home with her from the meal she'd shared with their family the night before.

A car puttered to the curb and shut off. Lacy glanced out the window to see Conrad emerge from the passenger's side of a Model T Ford. After tossing a blanket over her arm, she lifted her basket of food from the counter and hastened out to meet him.

"Put those in here." Conrad situated her basket and blanket on the seat. Then he shut the door and faced her. "On my way over, I realized this would be a perfect day for you to learn how to drive. Would you like to give it a try?"

Lacy's heart pounded. Sit in the seat behind the steering wheel and maneuver the levers and pedals to control the automobile? She might have landed a job freelance writing for the newspaper, but she couldn't possibly be intelligent enough to drive a car.

"You said you wanted to learn." He held his hands out, palms up.

Lacy gulped. "Well, yes, but I didn't think, I mean, I didn't expect to ever have the chance."

"It's not hard. I'll teach you." Conrad opened the door and patted the seat as an indicator that she should get in. "Come on."

Lacy willed her feet to respond. They did with slow, heavy steps while her mouth went dry.

Conrad smiled at her. "I'll help you. It will be fine."

She slid over to the driver's side and studied the variety of levers and pedals while Conrad slid in next to her.

"This is the throttle that gives the engine fuel. On the other side is the spark." He pointed at levers extending from both sides of the steering wheel. Then he pointed at the pedals on the floor. "These are your clutch, reverse, and the brake. Over there is the parking brake. Use it to help control the clutch."

Dizziness settled over her. "I don't know about this, Conrad. So many pedals and everything. What if I use the wrong one?"

He squeezed her upper arm. "You'll do fine. We'll be driving on flat land, so once we get the car in motion, the only thing you'll have to worry about is stopping."

"Stopping?" Her pulse throbbed in her temples. "What if I can't get the car stopped in time? I'll crash!"

"No, you won't. I was nervous the first time, too, but you will get the feel for it. I promise." He cleared his throat. "Now, about the clutch. All the way in is low gear to slow down. All the way out is high gear to go fast. I don't use that very much unless I'm out in the country on straight roads."

Lacy's stomach churned. Even if Conrad found the straightest, flattest road for her to drive on, low gear still sounded like a very good idea.

He leaned over and reached in front of her. "The spark should be all the way up. Give it a little throttle. There we go." After Conrad maneuvered the levers on the steering wheel, he straightened and looked at her. "Turn the key."

She sucked in a breath, and with shaking fingers, reached for the gold key near her knee. Turning it made the car buzz.

Conrad smiled. "Good job. I'm going to go out and give the car a crank. I'll be right back." He left her side and bent in front of the car. On the third crank, the engine began to putter. Conrad came around to her side, reached in the open window, and fiddled with the levers on the wheel. "That sounds good. I'll get in and then we'll take off." He walked around the front of the car, slid onto the seat, and pointed at her feet.

"What should I do?" Her voice wavered.

"Relax, Lacy, my love. This will be fun." A grin split his face. For the first time since she'd met him, the man actually grinned. She'd store it away as a special memory, that is if she could get her heart to stop pounding and her stomach to stop rolling.

"I trust you, Conrad," she whispered. And she did. As soon as the words were out of her mouth, her stomach stopped complaining.

He rested his hand on her shoulder. "Keep your foot on the clutch and let out the parking brake."

"All right." Lacy moved her left foot and reached for the lever at her side.

"Push the brake forward. That's right." Conrad watched her every move. "Put your foot all the way down and give it some fuel right here." He tapped the steering wheel near the throttle.

"Like this?" Lacy gave the throttle a gentle nudge which made the engine run at a higher pitch. The car crept forward. "Oh! We're moving!"

Conrad laughed. "Of course we are." He settled one of his hands on hers. "This is how you steer." The steering wheel turned under her grasp as Conrad guided the car into the street. "Lift your foot off the clutch."

The car sped up, taking her pulse along with it.

"You're driving!" Conrad removed his hand from the wheel and leaned against the seat.

"Where do you want to go?" A little less shaky, her voice carried over the noise of the motor.

"Head out of town a little way. I want you to get a good feel for the spark and the throttle before trying anything harder. The road to Clear Brook is nice and straight. Let's keep going that way."

Lacy gripped the wheel with everything she had. She'd been on this road twice, once with Rose and her friends, and once with Conrad. How different this trip was from either of those. She was the one behind the wheel this time. In charge. Never in her life had she ever been put in control of anything. Her parents made decisions for her. Cal ran interference for her. Fragile health and restrictive poverty had set the rest of the boundaries in her life.

But today she broke free. She had a job that supplied her with plenty of her own money. Her health was the best it had ever been. Friends surrounded her, and Conrad had given this entire day to her. Lacy had taken control of her own life and her efforts had reaped satisfying benefits.

"Stop up here at this intersection and turn right. I'll show you how." Conrad reached over and bumped the throttle lever until the car puttered at a lower pitch. "Put on your brake. Push down on the clutch."

Lacy did as he instructed and brought the car to a graceful stop.

"Nicely done. Now press the clutch in while I accelerate." Conrad tapped the throttle again while Lacy turned the wheel.

They drove on for a while along a route through golden corn fields in all stages of harvest. Trees on distant hills radiated rich hues of rust, plum, orange, and yellow. Puffy white clouds sailed overhead, and the sun shone warm and cheery. It was the kind of fall day Lacy wished she could save for a dreary day in February. Then she'd open her supply and release the autumn loveliness to color her world, covering the dark and the cold.

"Turn in here." Conrad pointed to the left and then reached over to adjust the spark and the throttle. "Use your clutch and your brake again like you did at the intersection."

Lacy followed directions as she drove the car over the uneven grasses of a pasture.

"This is some of Dan's land, and he doesn't mind if we are here. Go down to the pond by those trees."

Lacy bounced the car down an incline until reaching the edge of a meadow. She'd heard of Model T Fords being built sturdy enough to get driven anywhere, on roads or off. This trip through the pasture proved the theory as true.

"Park here." Conrad adjusted the throttle again as Lacy brought the car to a stop. "Nice driving. You're a natural."

"Thanks." Lacy loosened her grip on the steering wheel and flexed her fingers. They were stiff from the tight hold she'd kept since leaving town.

Conrad got out and retrieved the items from the back. Lacy followed him to a partially shaded spot on the pond bank. She helped him spread out the blanket and opened the basket.

"You catch on quick. You'll be driving all by yourself in no time." Conrad lounged on his side and stretched his legs out.

"I don't have a car. The only way I could drive again is to use yours." She took the food from the basket and set it out.

"My car is available to you anytime." Conrad picked up a sandwich.

"That's very generous of you, but I couldn't."

"Why not?" he asked around a bite of food.

She glanced at him. "Aren't you afraid I'd crash it or damage it in any way?"

He maintained a serious expression. "That's not as important to me as making sure you know I'm here for you, and I enjoy being with you."

No one had ever said anything like that to her before. Not even Rose. Yes, they were best friends, or had been until Conrad came on the scene, but it made little difference. Rose cared about her as much as an eighteen-year-old girlfriend could. But Conrad's maturity, his additional years of life experience, and the mark a deep grief had left on him gave him a clearer insight into who she was. She couldn't decide if she liked that or not.

She risked shifting her attention off her lunch and onto his face. But she shouldn't have done that. The tender warmth in his eyes radiated all through her and brought tears to her eyes.

Blinking, she pushed some potato salad around on her plate with a fork.

"Lacy?" Conrad's low voice rasped with sensitivity, bringing on more tears.

"It's nothing." She wiped one eye. A sense of great blessings beyond what she deserved swept over her. The gorgeous fall day, the town she loved and called home, and this man who called her "Lacy, my love," all blended together in a beautiful picture of the vast mercy God poured over her.

Conrad reached to hold her hand. "It's something. What is it?"

Her throat swelled and threatened to cut off her speech, but she must try. "This. You. Here." A sweeping gesture in every direction her affections lay did the work of filling in the meaning that her tongue could not.

Conrad gave her an empathetic smile. "I know just how you feel." With his thumb, he stroked the back of her hand. "My offer of a courtship still stands."

"I know." Through a misty blur, she watched his thumb trail over her fingers. "But you wouldn't want me after you got to know me." The truth cleared her clogged throat and helped her speak easier.

"What's that supposed to mean?" Conrad gave a gentle chuckle like she was a child trying to convince a parent of a tall tale.

"I'm not who you think I am." Lacy pulled her hand away and reached for her camera. "I'm not so hungry after all. I think I'll go get some photos of those yellow leaves against the blue sky." She pointed to a tree by the wood fence separating the pasture from a harvested field.

Wandering away through the grass, she left Conrad on the blanket munching sandwiches. She felt his gaze on her but there was nowhere to go and hide. He watched her as she turned and crossed the pond bank to the other side where the tree she wished to photograph grew straight and tall in the afternoon sun.

Lifting her camera, she aimed for just the right picture.

"Hold that pose." A distinctively male voice floated to her ears. She turned to find Conrad in his Sunday trousers, tie, and white shirt, swishing through the grass.

She cocked her head to discern his meaning.

He came to her and caught a strand of her hair wavering in the breeze. Slipping it behind her ear, he looked deeply into her eyes. "Don't ever change, Lacy, my love. You are perfect just the way you are."

She dropped her attention to the grass as her cheeks flushed. "No, Conrad. I'm not perfect. If you only knew."

"Knew what?"

Working up her courage, she looked him in the eye. "I'm a stupid, sickly child from a poor family. I only came to Oswell City in the first place because Rose coerced me into it. I never would have had the money or the confidence to travel on my own if I hadn't been with her. Beautiful things like the clothes I help Eva sew and the Angel Frame you ran over will never be mine. I only had that frame because my parents scraped together every last penny to buy a gift for a milestone birthday. I'm not who you think I am. A man like you shouldn't want to court a girl like me."

"Lacy." He grasped her upper arms and drew her closer to him. "That isn't what I see."

"It isn't?" Did she dare to believe him?

His eyes softened as they looked into her. "You're an artist, Lacy. A true creator. You understand how to look for the beauty in everything. You've helped me find it too. We share the delight in making something meaningful out of nothing." He caught that same strand of hair again, after the wind teased it loose. "Plus, you've got this gorgeous hair. Every time I see you, I want to pull the pins out and let it fall over your shoulders." His gaze traveled over the twists of hair pinned securely to her head as if he might try now to make that wish come true.

Her eyes widened at his openness. Was he serious? No one had ever said anything like that to her either.

"You're so beautiful, Lacy." He gathered her into his arms. "Say yes, you'll let me court you." He kissed her nose.

Safety and confidence, that's what she found here in

Conrad's embrace. She didn't want to lose those feelings, so she rested her hands on his shoulders allowing his kisses to travel over her cheek, to her mouth, and down her neck.

"Say yes, Lacy, my love," Conrad whispered.

How could she refuse a man with so much practice at making a woman feel cherished?

But her independence. Her wish to travel. Would courting Conrad tie her to a new set of limitations? It might. He had a job and a family. But he also had a car, and he'd let her drive it. Maybe she could use it to travel. And oh, could he kiss. Her knees were turning to jelly with every touch of his lips on her skin.

"You make it hard for a woman to resist you," she said in the moment before Conrad covered her mouth with his own.

"Don't try." He spoke with his lips on hers.

Several moments passed before she had enough breath to reply. "I like having my job. It provides me with a salary. I've never had any money of my own before I came to Oswell City and started working for Eva. It's made all the difference. If I save long enough, I'll be able to travel. I might even be able to afford beautiful gowns, like the kind that the doctor's wife wears."

"Is that all that's holding you back?" He gazed at her with amusement playing about his lips.

She nodded. "Yes, I suppose it is."

"Come on. I want to show you something." His embrace loosened as he settled his hands on her waist. After planting a kiss on her forehead, he clasped her hand and led her to the car.

23

"Where are you taking me?" Lacy asked as she occupied the passenger seat of Conrad's Model T.

"Back to town." He tapped the spark and then the throttle.

"But I still have to interview farmers. That's why we drove out here." Lacy turned for a glance out the back window.

"I know, but this is more important. You'll have time to interview people later. Just take my car. You know how to drive it." Conrad worked the levers and the pedals to slow the car down for a stop at the intersection.

Driving looked easy when Conrad sat behind the wheel. For Lacy, the new skill required much concentration and effort. He might regret offering his car to her when the day actually came for her to take it out for the first time.

Conrad turned the corner and puttered the rest of the distance into town. On Main Street, he drove right by the jewelry store without stopping. If he wasn't taking her home, then where was he headed?

At the law office, Conrad turned onto Sixth Street. Another block and he slowed down before guiding the car into a narrow driveway.

He brought the car to a stop and turned to her. "Come with me. This is my home." He reached across her to open the door. When she got out, he followed. Then he led her across the lawn. But they didn't go inside the house. Instead, he brought her to the back yard, the place where he found her lying in the grass on the night of her adventurous ride with Rose's friends.

Conrad went to a small barn near the street and paused to hold Lacy's hand. "Welcome to my workshop."

Why would Conrad change their afternoon plans to drive her to his house and show her his workshop? She entered behind him and waited while he lit the lamps.

Their glow joined the sunlight from the small windows in revealing walls hung with tools and gadgets. On the floor solid pieces of furniture stood in rows—tables, bedsteads, bookcases, desks, and chairs. Everything appeared excellently built and of the best quality.

"Come up here." Conrad took a lamp and climbed a ladder on the wall at the other end to an area above that looked similar to the haymow in her father's barn.

But hay didn't fill this haymow. Conrad helped her up the last rungs until she settled on a clean, swept, wooden floor. The light from the lamp in his hand gleamed on the faces of clocks and the glass of picture frames. All sizes were on display from the smallest to fit a nightstand to the largest for covering a wall.

In the corners of each frame, a tiny piece of metal caught the light. She stepped closer to inspect. Angels. Just like the one on the frame Dad and Mama had given her for her birthday, and like the one Conrad had given her to replace it.

The pieces fell into place. She turned to look at him. "You make these?"

"I do." He took a smaller one off the wall. "When my wife died, I needed a project to keep my mind and my hands busy. I also wanted to keep her alive in some way, so I started making frames. One for our wedding picture. More for our children's baby pictures. A larger one for our family picture. I sold a few to help generate profit for the orchard. The business grew until now I sell them in Gresham and Blaine's department stores along with the furniture I make."

"Mama and Dad bought my frame at the general store in Silver Grove." Lacy caressed the wood on the frame in Conrad's hands.

"Yes, I believe they are sold all across the country. Gresham and Blaine supply small town stores in addition to their larger city department stores."

Lacy heard what Conrad wasn't directly telling her. He had a good business going selling his frames and his furniture in the city and in small towns alike. His name and his craft were likely well-known.

"See this?" He pointed to the metal angel in the corner. "These frames are named Angel Frames after my wife Angelien. The angel makes me think of her, as if she's still here with me and our children. Manufacturing these Angel Frames helped me get through some pretty dark days. But it's better now. You've helped me." He hung the frame back up and turned to her. "Come with me to the house."

He picked up the lamp to light their descent to the ground level. After extinguishing the lamps, he took her across the lawn.

She entered a neat, well-kept but austere kitchen, followed Conrad through a simple parlor, and joined him behind the desk in an office down a hallway. Windows filled one wall with a view of the street that ran in front of the house. The other walls were lined with shelves holding ships. Many were in bottles. Others were displayed on their own with no glass confinement of their masts and sails.

"This is my hobby. It also pulled me out of a dark, dark, hole in those days when Markus and Betje were very small. Model ship building taught me to see furniture construction as a craft, an expression of art in which even the smallest details contribute to the authenticity and distinction of my work." He picked up a bottle containing a ship and turned it around.

"The *Valkenburg*. A Dutch battleship built in 1725. I worked on this ship during a time when Betje might have been lost to me. She'd fallen and hit her head, but Dr. Kaldenberg brought her back to good health."

Lacy drew in a breath. Precious Betje had been in an accident? She didn't know what she would have done if she'd been Conrad watching his little girl suffer.

He put the bottle with the *Valkenburg* back on the shelf. "But those days are past. Sometimes I miss them, and sometimes I'm glad they're gone. Do you ever feel that way?"

Lacy admitted to herself that she did. Her entire grade school and high school career affected her that way. The struggles with her health and with learning she didn't miss, but the friendships she did. Why did life have to be such a complex mix of the good and bad, the easy and the hard, the pain and the joy?

Conrad took a ledger book from a drawer. Black and sleek with gold lettering, it looked official and important. "This is my account book for the business I do with Gresham and Blaine. I won't burden you with the numbers, but I will tell you that I've become a wealthy man. My brother and I met this past week to talk about investing and savings accounts. These are issues I've never had a reason to think about until now. Markus and Betje will be living a privileged lifestyle, very different from the one their mother and I envisioned for them." He put the book away and reached for her hand. "Come. I have one more thing to show you."

Lacy walked with him out to the car and rode in silence as Conrad drove north of town. She knew where he was going. Somehow, she felt it in her bones. It was fitting for an introduction to the famous Angel Frames to precede a visit to the grave of the Angel herself.

Conrad parked beneath a tree and slid out of the passenger side after her. Soberly, purposefully, he led her to stand before a gravestone bearing the name of Angelien Van Drunen. In the corner, a silhouette of an angel had been engraved into the stone, just like it was a frame surrounding a special memory.

"Angelien's grave." Conrad's voice rasped.

All day he'd been reaching to hold her hand, but now she reached to hold his.

His jaw worked for a moment before he spoke. "She was a good wife. We had a special love. But I've found with you what I'd lost with her." Conrad stopped talking to the gravestone and looked at Lacy. "Hold the pose. I don't mean the posture you had beneath the tree during our picnic. I'm talking instead about who you are. Your beautiful, artistic, gentle self. You've helped me find my laugh and given me the courage to dare to love again."

"Look over here." He pointed to a tiny stone near Angelien's. There was no name on it, only the date December 25, 1912. "That's our baby, the one we lost. The one ... the one who took Angelien's life." His voice cracked.

"Your wife died in childbirth?" Lacy asked.

He gave a somber nod.

"Oh, Conrad, I'm so sorry. I didn't know." She laid a hand on his chest.

"Not many people do. Or if they did, they've forgotten. My brothers know. Eva, the De Witts, and the doctor know. They were all there the night it happened. I've never said anything to Markus and Betje. Don't know how. They've never heard of ... of the sister who died with their mother." Conrad made a quick swipe of his hand over one eye.

Lacy stood in silence as she listened. There was nothing she could do. The pain Conrad still felt over his family getting ripped apart lay very heavy on her heart and threatened to crush it. Her head lowered to his shoulder and large tears rolled down her face.

Conrad shifted so that he could gather her into his arms. They stood there for a long time weeping silently, grieving together.

"Thank you," he whispered and then kissed the top of her head.

"Are you ready to go?" She glanced up at him.

"I think so. Now you know the truth about me. My secrets, my sadness, and my struggles. Maybe I'm the one who should be saying to you that a girl like you shouldn't court a man like me." Conrad caught her hand and walked at her side to the car.

"I'm beginning to understand." Lacy stared straight ahead while Conrad drove to his house. "I want to travel. I want a lifestyle in which I could afford nice dresses. My desire for independence is really my wish to live free from the burden of poverty. If I shared my life with you, then you could give me all of that. It's what you've been trying to tell me and show me, isn't it?" She turned to look at him.

He shifted his focus away from the view out the windshield to look at her long enough to give her a solemn nod.

His silent answer sent tingles to the tips of her toes and the ends of her hair. If she gave him permission to court her, would he later want to marry her? Could she bring herself to do it? What would her life be like as the wife of a rich man like Conrad? He was wealthy not only in his finances, but in his relationships and in his faith. She had every confidence that the things she was striving for would find satisfaction in a life shared with him.

They returned to his house at the same time his sister-in-law Hannah arrived. She walked with her children plus Markus and Betje. They ran to Conrad when they saw him.

"Hey, there," he said as he knelt to return their hugs. "Did you have a good time?"

"The best." Betje's eyes shone. "Pastor Logan took us on a ride, and then Mrs. De Witt helped us sing songs. We made little dolls from corn husks and had a picnic. It was so fun!" Betje spun around as she said the last sentence.

Conrad's gaze met Lacy's at the word *picnic*. The memory of his kisses flooded her mind. From the look in his eyes, she guessed he was thinking about them too.

"How about you, Markus? Did you have fun?" Conrad tousled his son's hair.

"Yeah. Earl and I stayed together. We sat in the back of the hayrack." Markus smirked at his cousin Earl as though he was remembering his own share of mischief.

"I see. You better not have been causing trouble. I'll ask Pastor Logan about you." Conrad spoke in a stern voice.

"Aw, don't worry about it. We were fine, weren't we, Earl?" Markus swaggered over to his cousin.

"Thanks for bringing them home." Conrad waved to Hannah as he guided the children to the house.

She waved back and took her children down the street in the direction of their house.

"Can Lacy stay for supper?" Betje asked as she skipped along at Conrad's side.

"I was planning on it." He leaned over and whispered in her ear. "Will you, Lacy, my love?"

The intimate whisper sent shivers through her. "I'd love to."

Conrad's grin returned. In the house, he went to the stove to check the flame. "Markus, please go to the cellar for more wood."

"Sure, Dad." The boy went down the stairs while Conrad hastened around the kitchen setting out bowls and dry ingredients.

"Come read a story with me." Betje tugged on Lacy's hand.

The girl's father looked as though he could use a hand in the kitchen, but she'd told Betje long ago that she'd read to her sometime. The chance may not come again for a long while. Lacy had better stand behind her promise. Conrad had likely prepared many meals over the years. He could handle this one too.

Lacy smiled at Betje. "Lead the way."

The little girl scampered into the parlor and picked a book from the library up from a table. "This one."

Lacy took the book and sat down on the sofa. Betje climbed into Lacy's lap and leaned on her just like they'd sat this way often.

Opening the book, Lacy found the first page of the story and began to read. Three pages later, Betje stirred in her arms.

"Are you going to marry my daddy?" The little girl peered up at her.

"What?" Lacy's eyes widened, and her breath caught in her throat.

"He likes you. He dresses up to go places with you. Last week, he went to Uncle Nick and Aunt Hannah's to eat with Burt's mama, but he doesn't like her. I can tell. And besides, Burt and Markus fight. They wouldn't make very good brothers, would they?"

"No." Lacy glanced over Betje's head to find Conrad standing in the doorway. How much of Betje's thoughts had he overheard? She gave him a secret smile.

"Who would you want your daddy to marry?" Lacy asked.

"You." The little girl poked a playful finger at Lacy's chest and giggled. "He's happy when he's with you."

Conrad's brows shot to his hairline while Lacy bit her lip against a laugh.

"I'm happy when I'm with him too." She smiled at him.

"And I'm happy when I'm with you." Betje pointed at Lacy again.

"I'm glad, because I like being with you. How about we read some more?" She turned a page in the book to find her place.

"All right." Betje settled down and listened to Lacy's voice.

She glanced up to discover that Conrad had disappeared. Clinking utensils in pans told Lacy where he'd gone. By the time she'd covered the next page and turned to a new one, smoke rolled through the doorway from the kitchen.

24

"I have to get up," Lacy said to Betje.

The little girl tumbled onto the sofa.

Lacy hastened to the kitchen and found the smoke streaming from the cracks around the oven door. Grabbing a hot pad, she knelt down and opened the door. Heat rushed out along with more black billows. Coughing, Lacy reached for the square pan in the oven and carried it to the door. The thing continued to smolder even after she dumped it in the grass.

What had Conrad put in that pan? She wrinkled her nose as the smoke streamed into the air. Waving it away from her face, Lacy returned to the kitchen.

"What's going on?" Markus stood in the doorway. "Where's Dad?"

"Right here." Conrad emerged from the cellar with two jars in his hand. "I went down there for some vegetables Hannah gave us. What happened?" He looked around at the hazy kitchen.

"A pan in the oven burned so I took it outside. Markus, could you open a window in the parlor?" Coughing, Lacy moved to the kitchen window while she gave directions.

He nodded and left the room.

"That was our cornbread." Conrad slumped and went to the door to look at the smoking pan.

"We can make more. What else is on your menu?" In the absence of an apron, Lacy tied a tea towel around her waist.

"Now, Lacy, you don't have to cook. I wanted to prepare something special for you. Go finish your story with Betje." Conrad came over and tried to take the towel.

Lacy turned away. "I want to help. I know how to cook. It'll be easy for me to whip up a meal. What else are you fixing?"

"Beans and potatoes from Hannah. Pork chops and the cornbread." Waving smoke away from his face, Conrad went to the icebox. "Here's the pork chops."

"Put them in the skillet. I'll take care of the cornbread." She opened the door to the firebox. "For one thing, you have your oven way too hot." Lacy adjusted a lever on the pipe, poked at the burning wood, and then mixed up the cornbread.

Conrad put the meat on the stove and then went to open the jars. They soon settled into a rhythm. Conrad set the table and washed up some dishes while Lacy supervised the stove.

"You can call in Markus and Betje," Lacy said to Conrad after one last peek in the oven.

Conrad smiled and then left the room. Soon the whole family appeared.

Markus scooted up to the table and licked his lips. "This looks really good. A full meal, and with cornbread."

"It's a special treat I'd hoped to bake properly for once, but Lacy is the one who made it turn out right." Conrad set the pan from the oven on the table.

"Let's eat." Markus grabbed his fork.

"Wait until after I pray." Conrad laid the fork down. He prayed and then the meal started.

"Can you make pie too?" Markus peered up at Lacy.

"Yes," she answered as she spooned beans onto her plate.

"Pancakes?"

"Yes."

"Doughnuts?"

"My favorite. They're easy."

"What about cake and cookies?"

"I know how to make those too."

"Markus, that's enough." Conrad scowled at him.

"Wow. Just like Chris's mama. She knows how to make all of those." Markus stuffed a bite of food in his mouth.

"Markus." Impatience edged Conrad's voice.

His father's displeasure rolled right off Markus. He kept up a steady pace shoveling food into his mouth.

Conrad cleared his throat. "Never mind him," he said with a brief glance at Lacy.

She shrugged, but the tension between father and son was unmistakable. Maybe conversations about baked goods led to arguments between the two of them.

The meal continued until the food was gone. Conrad read a passage of Scripture and then dismissed the children. He hung around bringing dirty dishes to Lacy at the wash basin. Then he pulled out a towel and dried the clean dishes.

"I'm afraid I've let Markus down with my lack of baking skills," Conrad said as he placed a plate on a growing stack. "That's why he quizzed you."

His meaning got lost on her. She shook her head to tell him of her confusion.

"You've impressed my children. They are as eager to have a mother as I am to give them one." He laid the towel down and leaned against the counter. "They see you as someone they'd like as their mother."

"And what about you? Do you want me to be their mother?" Lacy kept her hands busy in the dish water as she talked.

"My heart decided for me a long time ago." Conrad didn't resume the dish drying but stayed in place at the wash basin.

"The choice is up to you. You're young, Lacy, hardly ten years older than Markus. Can you see yourself tied down to a widower and his two children? Is that what you want for your life?"

Lacy paused. The pots and pans along with a mess of silverware waited for their turn in the dishwater, but Conrad's answers deserved the truth from her.

She dried her hands. "I've been on a search for freedom from poverty and the chance to make my own decisions. But the people in my life are becoming just as important to me. Eva, Mrs. De Witt and her husband, and you. I hope that I have something to give back."

"You do. You are giving in so many ways." He tucked the strand of hair he'd been enamored with all day behind her ear.

"How?" She'd been so busy trying out her experiment of independent living that she couldn't think of any ways that she gave to the people she cared about.

"With your photography and writing for the newspaper. Your dependability at Eva's shop. The kind of friend you are for Rose. The feelings you have for me." Conrad laid his hand on his chest over his heart.

Heat crept into her face. "They're growing."

He gave her a tender smile. "You know how I feel about you, but ultimately, the choice is yours. Just know that should we decide to marry someday, I'll buy you the most stylish, elegant wardrobe anyone has ever seen. We'll take trips all over the place to see my furniture on sale in fancy department stores. We'll raise Markus and Betje, and maybe have more children of our own."

This was a topic that hadn't entered her thoughts. Marriage meant children. She knew that, but she was still grappling with the courtship question. The image of his first wife's gravestone also stayed on her mind. Maybe she shouldn't take the same risks that Angelien had.

"I ... I need time. More time." Her voice shook.

He straightened away from the sink. "Sure. All right. The last thing I want to do is pressure you."

She reached for a pan and resumed washing the dishes. Conrad wiped them dry in silence. The tension hung in the room like a heavy curtain. She didn't want this beautiful day to end this way. What had started out as a pragmatic trip to gather information for a newspaper article turned into a romantic, revealing adventure. Conrad's secrets had come out. They included his exquisite ability to kiss, his creation of Angel frames, and his lost newborn.

The truth screamed at her. Conrad was a man of integrity, of endurance and of wealth. She'd never find anyone better. But his good qualities didn't change her weaknesses.

She finished with the pans and sank the silverware into the water. He'd called her an artist, a creator of meaning and beauty. Is that really what she'd done for him in the short time they'd known each other? Is that really who she was? Maybe she shouldn't believe him. He might have said those things to flatter her. But Conrad didn't act that way. He said things only if he meant them. Lacy's childhood and teen years played through her mind. Had anyone ever called her an artist? No one that she could recall, not even Grandma Jones, who of all of Lacy's relatives, was the most outgoing and encouraging. Nothing in her experience aligned with Conrad's words.

Except one episode hazy in her memory. Mrs. De Witt had admired a painting Lacy made in art class long ago. Her teacher's compliment had stayed with her, prompting her to purchase her used camera from a traveling salesman. Besides Conrad, Mrs. De Witt was the only other one who saw these gifts in her.

"Finished." Lacy laid the last of the silverware in the sink and removed her towel apron.

Conrad dried them and then shuffled around as if

dreaming up excuses for Lacy to stay. But darkness was approaching. The fall twilight wouldn't last long.

"I've had a fun time today. Thanks for teaching me how to drive. I hope I wasn't too terrible at it."

Conrad chuckled. "You're a natural. I had fun too. We didn't get around to interviewing anyone, but borrow my car sometime. It's usually available in the evenings. I'll show you how to use the headlights."

Headlights. Another thing to worry about. The pedals and the levers kept her plenty occupied. She'd stick to driving in the daylight if she could help it.

"I'll remember that. Thanks." She moved around him to the door.

"Have a good week," he called after her.

"You too," she said back.

In the driveway, she took the picnic basket and blanket from the backseat of Conrad's car. Then she started her walk home. A block later, she met a couple in the growing darkness.

The man called out to her. "Good evening, Lacy." The voice belonged to Pastor Logan.

"Hello."

"I hope you don't have far to go," Mrs. De Witt said.

"I'm on my way back to my apartment."

"Good." Mrs. De Witt smiled.

"I've come from the Van Drunens'. Markus and Betje had a good time at the orchard today."

Pastor Logan laughed. "Our annual hayride is fun for the children, but we adults enjoy it too."

Lacy bid them good night and continued on her way. As she drew closer to home, her steps slowed, and her heart grew heavy. Something about that meeting with Mrs. De Witt and Pastor Logan made her sad. Was it something they said? Lacy analyzed the meeting as she climbed the stairs. What had happened to steal her joy?

She moved about the kitchen area emptying the basket and putting things away. Her eyes caught a glimpse of the shiny angel on the corner of the frame on the table. It was the frame which held the photo of her and Conrad at the carnival.

Alone. The word drifted through her mind. That's what bothered her about the meeting with the De Witts. They weren't alone. They were together. A couple. If she chose her independence over Conrad, she'd be alone. Sure, she might take some unforgettable trips, and she might buy a few articles of stylish clothing in her lifetime, but what would it matter if she lived her life alone?

Her parents had each other. Cal and Rose both had friends in college. The De Witts had each other plus their young family. But Lacy was, well, just Lacy. Didn't she want that? Conrad had asked her that question about helping him raise his children. But they'd do it together.

Lacy didn't want to be alone. She wanted a family, a husband, a life she shared with him. Conrad sat in his house this very minute as a man who'd offered her everything from safe embraces to the use of his car. She must do something about this if she didn't want to watch this journey she was on lead her to a future of isolation.

Throwing a shawl around her shoulders, she hastened back out into the night. Down Main Street, then a turn onto Sixth Street and walking two blocks brought her to Conrad's door.

She knocked.

He answered. His tie was gone. The buttons of his shirt were undone at the neck and his sleeves were rolled up. Obviously, he wasn't expecting to entertain any more visitors today.

But this was important. She sucked in a deep breath. "Yes."

He raised a brow. "Yes what?"

"Court me, Conrad."

A smile broke through. "You mean it?"

"Yes."

He came outside and wrapped his arms around her waist. “Flowers, kisses, and more driving lessons. They’re all yours, Lacy, my love.”

How she loved the sound of his nickname for her. Made up in a moment of falsehood, it told her tonight of yet another truth about Conrad.

He loved her.

And she was pretty sure she loved him back.

25

"I brought your mail for you." Hannah entered the house and set a stack of envelopes on the table.

"Thanks." Conrad leaned against the stove with arms crossed. His scowl remained in place as he watched Hannah's movements.

"What's wrong. More trouble?" She asked.

Conrad cocked his head in Markus's direction.

Her gaze followed.

Markus sat in a chair pouting. His hair was messed up and his shirt sleeve was ripped. Dust on his cheeks turned to dirty streams from the tears in his eyes.

"What happened?" She whispered.

Conrad sighed and rolled his eyes. "Something about me refusing to marry Burt's mother. I didn't get the whole story, but I caught enough to know that Markus's friends have stopped inviting him over."

"It isn't fair!" Markus burst out.

"Conrad." Hannah's impatient voice implored him to fix the situation.

He turned his hands palms up. "What do you want me to do about it?"

Hannah's mouth flattened into a thin line. "Nick and I gave you every opportunity to improve your situation."

"Improve?" His brows shot up.

"Yes, but you walked out of our house leaving Kate feeling like she'd made a fool of herself."

"She did." The scowl returned along with the memory of Kate's encouragements.

Hannah's bottom lip trembled. "Kate is a lovely woman and a wonderful friend. She'd make a good mother for Markus and Betje."

Markus shot out of his chair and ran from the room. A door slammed in another part of the house.

If only Conrad could do the same. How he'd love to bolt from this conversation, the entire situation, and slam the door on the quest of finding his children a mother. But his life remained incomplete. The longing for a true companion, a special love, gnawed at him. But it laid beneath the surface in hidden and quiet places his sister-in-law and her friend couldn't see. Bringing it to the light cheapened it somehow, like the exposure would mock him or cheat him of something precious.

He exhaled in a long, tired sigh. "You're right, but I don't have feelings for Kate."

"You haven't tried."

Conrad shrugged. "I don't have to. I just know." Now would be a good time to tell her about Lacy, but Hannah would only compare her to Kate, finding ways to prove that Kate shone as the best choice.

Hannah sighed too. "You can't stay single forever. Your children are growing up too fast."

"Let me worry about that." Conrad opened the door as a hint that they'd spent too much time on the subject.

Hannah slipped past him and followed the sidewalk to her house. He hadn't heard the end of this. His brother and sister-in-law weren't ones to give up on a cause for which they held strong feelings. Conrad, his money, and his single status had become their mission. They wouldn't abandon it until they felt satisfied with the outcome. He couldn't decide if he should feel gratitude for his family sharing the same town with him seeing his every movement, or if he should resent this battle growing between them.

He flipped through the envelopes. Bills. But the envelope on the bottom displayed a return address of Gresham and Blaine, Des Moines. Conrad ripped it open. The document inside unfolded to reveal the terms of a new contract. He held his breath and his eyes widened. The typed words requested twice as many items delivered monthly for the upcoming year than what he'd done during the current year. The contract was effective starting January one.

January!

That gave him barely two months to prepare. He'd have to expand and hire help just like the two men had suggested during their visit. Conrad scanned the words again. He'd never be ready. Where would he find the extra workers? How could he spend any more time building furniture?

Conrad sank into a chair. This was a disaster. To leave the contract unsigned sent the message that he wasn't interested in the relationship he'd built with the businessmen. But to sign it plunged Conrad in over his head.

"Dad?" A whine came down the hall.

Markus. Conrad had forgotten about him. "I'll be right there." He folded up the contract and stuffed it in the torn envelope.

"You're not going to make Burt's mama mine, too, are you?" Markus looked up at him through wet eyes. Fear hung on his face.

Conrad settled next to him on the bed. "No, I'm not. I made that clear to Aunt Hannah. She didn't like it, but I won't change my mind." Conrad settled a hand on his son's.

"Good." Markus stared at the quilt on his bed. "Burt started the fight today. He got everyone on his side and then made fun of me." Tears trickled over his cheeks.

A conniver and a traitor, Burt sounded like a boy who could use a father. As much as Conrad wanted to teach the young man a lesson, he wouldn't be the one to assume the role. Kate would have to find someone else to train her son.

"It sounds to me like we need to change our approach." Conrad rested his arm on the pillow and patted Markus's shoulder.

The boy looked at him with questions in his eyes.

"I'm going to ask Lacy if she will help us host a sleepover for your friends." The idea hadn't occurred to him until this moment. But Markus needed a way to save some face with his buddies. If getting Lacy to come over for an evening would solve the problem, then he'd give it a try.

"Really? You'd do that?" Markus shifted on the bed as enthusiasm tinted his voice.

Conrad nodded.

Markus turned somber. "But do I have to invite Burt? We'd have more fun without him here."

"Maybe you can ask him to come over in the morning, after you and the rest of your friends have had a chance to play."

"I guess." Markus still wasn't entirely sold on spending any time with Burt at all.

"You can't leave him out completely, or you'd be doing to him what he's done to you," Conrad said in a quiet voice.

"Having lots of friends is really hard." Markus grunted.

Conrad chuckled. "I suppose it is. What's most important is to keep the ones you have."

Markus studied Conrad's face for a moment before a smile

broke out. "Yeah. I'll be able to keep my friends if Lacy helps out, won't I?"

Conrad patted his back and nodded. If Markus continued to welcome Lacy into his family, and if she could provide the piece of their home that Conrad and his son were sorely missing, then he'd know beyond a doubt that asking Lacy to court him was one of the smartest things he'd ever done.

"Take a look at this." Conrad handed the contract over to Nick. Here he sat again, in his brother's bank office asking for advice. His questions strengthened Nick and Hannah's interest in his life, but he needed them. Nick had proven himself a successful banker, and Hannah cared about Markus and Betje as if they were her own. Conrad figured he could put up with their attempts at improving his life, as Hannah called it, for the sake of soliciting Nick's wisdom on financial matters.

Nick flipped a page as he read. "Impressive." He looked at Conrad. "If you could pull this off, we'd recalculate the figures I'd suggest you reserve for investing."

"That's the problem. I don't know how to meet the demand." Conrad gestured at the document in Nick's hand.

"Logan is letting you use the barn at the orchard."

Conrad nodded. "I still won't keep up."

"You'll have to hire someone." Nick handed the contract back to Conrad.

"Who?"

"Put a notice in the paper. See who answers."

"I'll consider it, but I'd rather have a referral or work with someone I already know."

"Check around with the businesses or with people at church. They might give you some names." Nick made notes on a piece of paper.

Conrad stood. "Your ideas give me a good start." He left the bank and went to the newspaper office.

The responses he received weren't too promising. One applicant didn't have enough experience with woodworking. Another one smelled too strongly like a tavern, and two more had other jobs that demanded a large amount of their time.

Conrad repressed his disappointment as he and his children went to Nick's house for Earl's birthday party.

"How is the employee search going?" Nick asked as they sat around the dining room table eating cake.

"Slow." Conrad told them of the applicants he'd met.

"I saw your ad in the paper." Conrad's other brother, Dan, sat with his wife on the other side of the table. "What sorts of jobs would your assistant do?"

"The sanding, finishing, and the assembly take the most time. I would design the furniture and cut the pieces, but if I had someone to do the other tasks, I could work much faster."

Dan pointed to his wife. "Ruth and I have been talking about me finding projects to do this winter after the crops are harvested. I could be your assistant until spring, sort of as temporary help, and then go back to farming in time for the planting season."

Conrad's brows rose. "That should be enough to get me started and to give me time to find the right person permanently."

"I'll handle your finances. We can make it a family business. Maybe it's time for your furniture sales to have an official name," Nick suggested.

"Van Drunen Brothers Furniture Company." Conrad glanced at the others to gauge their approval.

"I like it." Dan smiled. "Maybe I'll come back and help you out again next winter."

"Let's meet in my office tomorrow and talk through the plan," Nick said.

Conrad nodded as pleasure welled up in him. With Dan as his assistant, Conrad could work with someone he knew and trusted. Like they'd done with the move to America, he and his brothers would help each other make this new and unknown venture a success.

THE NEXT MORNING, Conrad visited the lumber store to put in an order for wood. He needed a supply to fill the requests for furniture until the end of the year, and also to get started on a surplus for the next one. Then he went to the bank for his meeting with Nick and Dan.

Plans were made, documents signed, and the contract mailed. Dan came to the orchard the following week, along with the fresh shipment of lumber. The two of them dove in measuring, sawing, and sanding. The work went much faster, and soon the barn was stuffed with furniture in various stages of completion. Dan and Conrad worked together over the course of the next two weeks to get ahead of the demand.

Finished items were moved into the house. Helen had long ago accepted a position at the hotel. Conrad did maintenance on the house to keep it in good condition, but with no one living there, the jobs were few and the ones he had to do were simple. More time was gradually becoming available to him for the furniture business.

He'd take it. Even with two of them at work, Conrad feared they wouldn't have enough items ready for sale by January one. The house filled so full of tables, chairs, and dressers that it began to resemble a furniture store. Conrad and Dan searched for another warehouse and chose to clean out a smaller barn that had been used to shelter horses.

Before long, they filled it too. Conrad made his November shipment of furniture which freed up some space and also rewarded him with a handsome payment. After the shipment had been sent, Conrad and Dan settled into a nice pattern. Conrad arrived at the orchard at his usual time, milked the cow, took care of any maintenance or repairs on the house and barns, and then worked with Dan building furniture until late afternoon.

Then he went home, fixed a meal for his children, oversaw their homework, and spent a couple hours on smaller projects like shelves and picture frames in his backyard workshop.

His business began to revolve around the barn at the orchard where production happened. He couldn't imagine what he would have done without Logan's offer to use the space for his own work. It was a good arrangement, giving Conrad a place to work and continuing to give the orchard a purpose.

He hadn't heard any more about the prospect of the church changing ownership of the property. Conrad worked on, taking care of the house and barns while nurturing the hope that his activity here would provide a sufficient reason for the church to keep the orchard.

But one blustery November day Logan drove out in his car and came to the barn. He held a bill of sale in his hand. Conrad paused in his work at the saw and his chest tightened. His setup here had been too good to be true. This visit from Logan and the paper in his hand indicated change. Big, lasting change.

Conrad licked dry lips and forced a greeting. "Hi, Logan. Is there something I can help you with?"

"No. Actually, I was hoping to help you." Logan held up the bill of sale. "I've been posting these around town, and I wanted to bring one out to show you so that you knew. The church board has decided to put the orchard up for sale. The auction is next week, and I think you should bid on it."

26

Conrad's breath came in short gasps. The property he used for his furniture business was getting sold. He could lose it. But then Logan had said Conrad should bid on it. That meant he could keep it as his own. But he'd have to move out of his house in town if he made such a large purchase. What would his children say? What would Nick say? What about Lacy?

These thoughts crashing through his head made him feel as if he might pass out.

"Whoa, steady there, Conrad. You look like you could fall down." Logan reached his hand out to him. "Come, sit over here." Logan led him to a chair waiting for a final coat of stain.

Dan emerged from the back of the barn where he'd been working on the assembly of a chest of drawers. "What's all this?"

Logan showed him the poster and repeated his suggestion of Conrad's bid.

"I need to talk with Nick first. It's a big decision. How do you know no one else is interested in the property?" Conrad turned to Logan.

"I can't say that for sure. The sale might generate a lot of interest. But you've worked here for several years, and now that you have your furniture business set up in the barn, you have a strong chance at buying it."

"I don't know. This is a prime property after the church fixed it up, and it's only a mile from town. Someone is sure to want it." Conrad made a fist with one hand and held it to his mouth.

"Bidding on it is still worth a try. I have to get back to town, so I'll see you later." Logan waved and returned to his car.

Conrad looked up at Dan. "What do you think I should do?"

"Like Pastor Logan said, you might as well try. Talk to Nick. He'll help you." Dan returned to work leaving Conrad to mull the new information over in his mind.

He tried to go back to work as well, but he was too distracted. An hour later he gave up and called out to Dan. "I'm going to talk to Nick. You may quit early if you want."

Conrad took off his apron, tossed it in a corner, and headed for town. At the bank, he went to Nick's office and dropped into a chair.

"What happened?" Nick asked.

"Logan informed me today that the orchard is for sale and that he thinks I should bid on it at the auction next week."

"One of my colleagues was helping the mayor and the lawyer get the arrangements finalized. I've told you that you could afford to quit being the handyman and buy both the land and the buildings. It's quite possible."

"Do you really think I have a chance?" Conrad peered at him.

"Oh, yes. You have a connection to it, and you have the bank account to drive the price as high as you want." Nick grinned.

"But I'd have to move." Not only would he have to leave his house in town, but he'd have to face the upstairs room where

Angelien and their baby died. He'd gone in that room in the past to paint or make repairs. But a short stay as part of his job was much different from living in the house with the eternal reminder hovering above him at the top of the stairs.

What if Markus or Betje claimed it as their room? Would he have to go in there to tuck them in every night knowing, remembering the sorrow? Or what if he married again and his new wife wanted to use that same room? He shuddered. He couldn't do that, nor could he allow it. Lacy knew, and she understood. If she was that new wife, maybe she would let him choose the room they shared.

"Conrad?" Nick looked at him with concern in his eyes.

He shook his head to clear it. "Sorry. I was ... uh ..."

"Thinking of Angelien?" Nick asked in a soft voice.

"Yeah."

"Would living there again be too hard?"

Conrad considered the question for a moment. "It depends on who I live there with."

"Kate?"

Conrad wrinkled his nose as he rubbed his hand over his shirt.

"Do you have someone else in mind?" Nick's brows rose.

"Lacy Jones." Conrad gulped in some air. "She's agreed to let me court her."

Nick frowned. "You mean the young lady from that article in the newspaper?"

"That's the one."

"But you told me you weren't courting her." Nick leaned forward.

"Things change." Conrad sent his brother a solemn glance.

Nick gave him an amused look and then shuffled around in his desk until retrieving a pen and some notepaper. He began to write. "Here's the amount of money I would suggest as a down payment." He turned the paper around to show Conrad and then wrote on it again. "This is the amount that would be a fair price to pay as the total cost for the land and the buildings." He showed the new numbers to Conrad. "Think about it. Talk it over with people you trust. You've got time to decide."

Conrad nodded and went home. He arrived as Markus and Betje were returning from school. They talked about their studies and the happenings of the day.

"When are we going to have our sleepover?" Markus asked around a slice of apple Conrad had cut for him.

"I'll ask Lacy today. There are some things I need to talk to her about when she comes to help us with your slumber party," Conrad said.

"Will you get dressed up again?" Betje asked.

He hadn't thought of that. It sounded like a good idea, but he didn't have time to change. "No, I don't think so. I'm just going to stop in and catch her at the dress shop before she goes home."

"What do you need to talk to her about?" Betje's face wore a worried look. "Is it us?"

"No, it isn't you." Conrad tweaked her nose. "I have a big decision to make, and I want her to help me with it."

"What is it, Dad?" Markus propped his elbows on the table.

"Pastor Logan told me today of some property for sale. He thinks I should buy it. If I did, we would have to move to that big house at the orchard where I work." Conrad watched his children for their responses.

"Would we still go to school?" Betje asked.

"Yes. That wouldn't change." Conrad cut another apple into slices.

"Could I still play with Earl?" Markus sounded worried.

"Of course, you could. We might not see your cousins as often as we do now, but that doesn't mean you couldn't still play with them." He laid the knife down.

"I'd miss our treehouse." Markus frowned.

"I'd miss my room." Betje looked at her brother as if she sympathized with him.

Conrad agreed with them. There were things about the house he'd miss, too, like the nearness of the neighbors, and his office. If he bought the house in the orchard, he'd have to convert one of the parlors into an office.

"Markus, can I put you in charge while I run to the dress shop?" Conrad looked at his son.

"Sure, Dad." He nodded.

"Betje, go ahead and change out of your dress, and then choose a book to read. I'll be home again soon." He turned to the little girl.

She scooted off her chair and went to the parlor while Conrad cleared the table. Then he followed the sidewalk to the dress shop.

Lacy glanced at him from her place at the sewing machine. "Hi, Conrad. Let me finish this row of gathers and then I'll be done for the day."

He waited through the steady whirr of the sewing machine and Lacy putting her supplies away. "I'd like to invite you over to my house." He held her coat as she slipped her arms into it.

"What's the occasion?" She settled her hat on her head.

"Markus is having a sleepover with his friends, and I was hoping you'd rescue me." He cracked a smile.

"Sounds like fun. What do you need me to help with?" Lacy put on her gloves.

"Cooking the evening meal. Would you be willing to do that?" He raised a brow.

"What would Markus like?" Lacy gave him a thoughtful look.

"Is roast beef sandwiches and potato salad too much to ask?" He sucked in a breath.

Lacy chuckled. "Not at all. Those are easy."

"Friday night?" He held the door for her and followed her into the street.

"Fine." Her cheeks glowed pink in the cold.

"Markus might ask for pancakes. Be prepared." A smile tugged at the corner of his mouth.

"I'll make them Friday night and leave them for you to heat up Saturday morning. Surely you can handle that."

"On the stove top? I'll try."

Lacy laughed as they parted ways.

FRIDAY NIGHT, the house swarmed with the activity and noise of school-aged boys. Betje had gone to Hannah's to play with her girl cousins, leaving Conrad and Lacy alone in the kitchen after the supper dishes had been washed and put away.

They sat at the table sipping apple cider when Conrad reached for Lacy's hand. "Tell me what I should do."

"About what?"

"The orchard is for sale. Logan thinks I should try to buy it. Do you think I should?"

"How do Markus and Betje feel about it?"

"A move to the country would be a change. They were concerned about their cousins, the school, and the treehouse." Conrad twisted his mug in his hands.

"I can understand that. Do you think they would be willing to move?" Lacy lifted her mug to her lips.

"Probably. They'd just need time to get used to the idea."

"What about you?"

Conrad huffed out some air. "The move makes sense, I guess. But I wouldn't want to rattle around in a big house like that by myself. Plus, the neighbors are farther away than they are in town. I could get used to it, though. I might even like it after some time has passed."

"A house of that style and size fits a man like you with your income. I can see that home being made into a lovely place, like a mansion." Lacy's eyes glowed.

Lacy should be the one who got to do the job of decorating that large, beautiful house. With her childhood of poverty, she'd probably never had the chance to enjoy new furniture, rich carpets, and stylish drapes. If only she was ready to accept a proposal of marriage. She'd only recently given her consent to a courtship. He mustn't rush things.

She was still the one he wanted there with him. Whenever he envisioned himself and his children living in the grand home, Lacy was in the picture sharing their life and making his home complete.

"Then perhaps I ought to buy it. My brother Nick thinks like you. He feels that I should be a little more ... what should I say ... comfortable with my wealth." He took a sip of cider.

"He's right." Lacy shrugged. "Go to the sale and just see what happens."

"Would you come with me?"

"If you like." She nodded.

THE DAY OF THE SALE, Conrad led Lacy into the crowded parlor of the house at the orchard. Farmers, businessmen from town, and strangers Conrad didn't recognize hung on every syllable the auctioneer said. Hands raised. The price went higher. Conrad waved his number in the air in steady competition with the other bidders. A few of them dropped out but the auctioneer kept going.

He pointed to a couple in the corner, then to Conrad. He nodded and the price climbed. Then the auctioneer pointed to others that had kept up with the bidding and the price went up even more.

Keeping in mind the dollar figures Nick had given him, Conrad waved his number with each price change. But this sale was rapidly driving the cost beyond what he and Nick had discussed. What if he spent more than Nick thought was wise?

But what if someone else got the property instead of him? Could he live with that? He'd have to retreat to town and find another location for his business. But he knew the orchard better than anyone.

He had memories here. It was the first place he'd held a job after his arrival in America. A stranger to this land and not yet knowing the language, he'd been offered the chance to put down roots, settle in, and make a better future for himself. He'd lived here with Angelien. He'd worked with her here and he lost her here. In a way, this house and Conrad belonged to each other. He may have difficult days ahead when the room upstairs reminded him of his grief, but the pain of severing all ties would be much worse.

People were dropping out of the bidding as the auctioneer pointed to him again. He raised his hand. The auctioneer nodded and pointed to the couple in the corner. They raised their number. The bidding returned to Conrad. It was down to the two of them. The price was high, but so were the stakes. His future depended on yet another raise of his hand.

The auctioneer pointed to the couple. They looked at each other, and the man shook his head. One more time, the auctioneer pointed to Conrad. He nodded. The crowd cheered.

"Sold!" The auctioneer's voice boomed out. "To Conrad Van Drunen. Go to the kitchen and talk to James Koelman about the details."

People clapped and then milled around visiting with others and searching for the exit.

"Congratulations." Logan found him in the crowd and slapped him on the back.

"I hope Nick doesn't complain too loudly about the amount of money I spent."

Logan chuckled. "A worthy investment. He should be proud of you for staying in until the very end."

A smile stretched Conrad's mouth. This affirmation from his friend went a long way in building both his confidence and his excitement. Conrad inched through the crowd to the table where James sat. The lawyer handed Conrad a pen and showed him the lines on several different documents where he should sign his name. He was a man of means with a sizeable house and property in his possession.

27

Lacy raised her hand to knock on Conrad's door. Shuffling steps and energetic voices reached her ears as someone in the family responded to her request for entrance on this Saturday morning.

A moment later, Betje answered the door. "Lacy!"

"Hi, Betje. I brought something for you."

"Really? What is it?"

Lacy went inside and pulled a book from her bag. "I checked it out from the library last night."

With shining eyes, Betje took the book and turned it over, studying the cover.

"I remembered that you are reading that series, so I got you the next one." Lacy pointed to it.

Betje looked up at Lacy. "I'll read it right away, maybe even today."

"Hi, Lacy." Markus sauntered into the room.

"Good morning. Is your father here?"

"In his office." Markus pointed down the hall.

Lacy followed his direction and found Conrad seated at his desk. "Would it be all right with you if I asked Markus and

Betje to come with me into the country today? I need to finish my assignment interviewing farmers for the article I'm writing for the paper, and I thought it would be fun to take them along." Jake wanted to run this article in the Thanksgiving week edition of the *Oswell Journal*, so today was her last Saturday available to finish the project.

Conrad shrugged. "I don't see why not. They'd probably like that. I'll ask them." He called the children in and explained Lacy's plans.

"Yeah. That sounds like fun!" Markus yelled and punched the air.

Betje offered a wide smile. "Let's take our lunch for a little picnic."

"It might be too chilly for that, but we might find somewhere to eat indoors." Lacy chuckled at the small girl's enthusiasm.

"How will you travel?" Conrad asked.

"I thought I'd ask Pastor Logan for his horse and buggy if he isn't using it."

"Take my car. You know how to drive it," Conrad offered.

"Oh, but ... I've only driven with your help, and never when I'm alone." Lacy's eyes grew wide, and her hand fluttered to her chest.

"You'll do fine. It has plenty of fuel. Markus knows a little bit about the car. He can help you." Conrad stood and approached her.

"Let's take the car!" Markus, along with his sister, had arrived to hear Conrad's suggestion.

"Oh!" Lacy's chest tightened. "What if I can't get stopped, or I don't get the throttle right? I don't know, Conrad. This seems risky."

"But you know how to do those things. Today will give you a chance to practice. The roads are straight without too many hills. You'll remember how to drive. I have every confidence in you." Conrad smiled at her.

Lacy took a deep breath. "I'll go to the nearest farm first, and if that trip doesn't go well, I'll bring the car back and ask Pastor Logan for his buggy."

"That's fair," Conrad said and turned to Betje. "Get Markus to help you pack a lunch."

The little girl had been watching the adults with fear in her eyes as if she was worried about how the discussion would turn out. But with this instruction from her father, joy broke out on her face, and she turned to race down the hall with an excited "Yay!"

Lacy shifted her attention to Conrad. He gazed at her with pride and affection glowing in his eyes. "You'll get along fine," he said in a low voice before planting a kiss on her forehead. Taking her hand, he led her to the kitchen where excited children slapped bread and meat together in thick, sloppy sandwiches.

Lacy wrapped up the sandwiches and placed them in the basket Conrad held open. Apples, a block of cheese, and a container of water finished their meal. Conrad took the basket to the car, backed it onto the street, and helped the children settle in the back seat.

"Have fun!" He waved and shut the door.

Lacy sat behind the wheel of the idling automobile. What should she do first? In a moment of panic, she stared at the many levers and pedals.

Conrad was crazy. She'd never remember how to drive his car. In that moment, the afternoon of their picnic in the country flashed into her mind. "Hold the pose," Conrad had said. He hadn't been talking only of how she looked standing under the brilliant yellow tree. He'd meant her character, who she was, and the talents she had.

Holding the pose meant freedom. Isn't that what she'd

stayed in Oswell City to find? She'd met a man who helped her to that goal. He trusted her, cheered her on, and offered her his car to drive.

Freedom couldn't take on a freer expression than that.

Lacy gripped the steering wheel. She'd possess that freedom and she would live in it. This was her life, and today she was on her own assignment writing her own article for the newspaper. Freedom was hers, as much as she wanted of it as she could ever want.

But in order to complete her assignment, she must get this car moving. Her gaze traveled over the levers on the steering column to the parking brake and then to the floor. She remembered now. She must do something with those floor pedals.

In slow motion, she eased her foot onto the clutch. Nothing happened. What else had Conrad told her to do? The parking brake? That made sense since brakes kept vehicles from moving. She pushed on the parking brake. Still nothing happened. What must she do now? Maybe the throttle would work. She tapped it.

The car crept forward.

"Oh!" All of her air left her lungs. She quick grabbed hold of the steering wheel and turned the car into the street. After tapping the throttle a little more, she puttered to the intersection.

Recalling the lessons Conrad had given her, she maneuvered the car through town. Pedestrians crossed in front of her. Other cars pulled in and out of parking spaces along the downtown square. Buggies got in front of her slowing her down. But Conrad was a good teacher. He'd given her the tools to help her in every situation. Clear of the main street congestion, she drove the car onto an open country road.

Her first stop was coming up at the Dan Van Drunen farm. This trip acted as her test. If she had confidence in her driving by the time this interview was complete, she'd continue on with

Conrad's car. But if fear set in, she'd take it back to him and find another way to travel to the farms.

Hold the pose rumbled through her mind again. Driving Conrad's car on her own was one of the ways in which she held the pose of freedom, of choosing for herself, and of standing in her own successes, experiments, and failures.

At the Van Drunen farm, she parked the car and shut off the engine. Markus and Betje bounded from the back seat to play with a puppy in the yard. Ruth met her at the door and took her to the barn to find Dan.

Lacy asked him questions about the harvest, the number of acres he planted to certain crops, and about the yield. After collecting her information, she thanked him for the interview and left the barn.

He followed her into the yard. "I see that you're driving Conrad's car."

"He taught me to drive." Lacy waved to Markus and Betje.

"How about if I start it for you?"

"Thank you." Lacy slid over to the driver's side and turned the key. She hadn't thought of how to start the car every time she visited a farm. Would she have to depend on help with cranking from every person she interviewed?

Markus and Betje ran to the car and got in. The puppy jumped and yelped as though it wanted to come along.

"No, Toby. You stay here. This is your house. We'll come another day." Betje shook her finger at the dog through the open window.

The car puttered. Dan straightened and saluted. "She's running," he called out.

Lacy used the clutch and the throttle as Conrad had shown her and drove to the road. A decision faced her. Should she turn left and take the car back to Conrad, or should she turn right and venture on to another farm?

The trip to Dan's farm had gone smoothly. Except for

paying attention to the activity downtown, Lacy had faced few challenges. Maybe that meant she really could drive. In addition to her skills of sewing and writing for the paper, did she dare add driving to the list of her accomplishments?

The Haverkamp farm lay two miles farther down the road. If she completed that visit, she'd be half done with her assignment. The road to the Haverkamps was straight with only one curve around a small pond. This next leg of her journey shouldn't be too difficult. She'd just have to concentrate.

Lacy increased the throttle and turned the car to the right. "One more stop, and then we'll have lunch," she said to her passengers.

The comment interrupted the conversation Betje carried with her brother about Toby, Uncle Dan's dog.

Down the road, around the curve, following a horse pulling a wagon, and then the turn onto the Haverkamp's driveway, Lacy drove with increasing confidence. Controlling a car was becoming easier, even fun, as long as she didn't meet another car or a speeding truck that clouded her in dust.

Both of the Haverkamp brothers, Dirk and Joost, were in the field when Lacy arrived. Their harvest wasn't finished, so Lacy crossed the cornfield and waited for them at the end of a row.

"May I ask you a few questions? I'm Lacy Jones, and I'm writing an article for the newspaper." She pulled out her pen and notebook.

"I can only spare a few minutes." Dirk leaped off the wagon while his brother guided the horse to turn around. At a slow pace, he made his way down the row of corn, pulling off the ears and tossing them into the wagon.

Lacy asked Dirk the same questions she'd asked Dan but received different answers. She thanked him for taking time for her, gathered Markus and Betje, and returned to the car.

The motor was shut off, so it had to be cranked. But the

men were in the field and no one else was around. What could she do? Was she strong enough to turn the crank?

"Um ..." Lacy scanned the farmyard in search of someone to help, but no one appeared. "Markus, come here." She beckoned to him. "Turn the key in the ignition. Do you know how to do that?"

He nodded and went to do as she asked.

Lacy grasped the crank and tugged on it, but it moved only a small distance. She straightened and huffed. Starting a car was hard work. Wiping her hands on her skirt, she took a breath and tried again. The stubborn crank refused to cooperate. She looked around. The time had come to find someone stronger than herself. But her only choices were out in the field.

"Come, children. We're going to have our lunch." Maybe by the time they'd finished eating, the men would return to this side of the field and be willing to help her out.

"Yay, lunch!" Betje and Markus scrambled into the backseat and opened the basket. They pulled food out and unwrapped it with great eagerness.

Lacy had her sandwich half-eaten when the horse and wagon emerged from the corn rows and turned toward them. "They're coming this way. Markus, go ask if one of them could please help us start the car." Lacy tapped his shoulder.

Carrying his sandwich, Markus slid from the backseat and approached the heaping full wagon. One of the men stopped to talk to him while the other one drove the wagon to the corn crib.

Dirk crossed the yard with Markus and came to Lacy. "You need your car started?"

"Yes, please."

He nodded and went to the front of the car as Lacy turned the key. He bent and cranked until the engine came alive. After waving at her he went to join his brother.

"Go ahead and keep eating while I drive." Lacy finished her sandwich and then put the car in motion.

She might not possess the strength to start the car, but she had the skill to drive it. Two more farmers were on her list of interviews. If she remembered to ask for help during her visit, she should have no problems driving. Lacy guided the car onto the road, down a small hill and over a bridge to Fred Akerman's farm. So far, this was the trickiest part of her journey. Lacy maneuvered the levers in preparation for crossing the bridge, and then increased her speed to climb the hill on the other side.

Breathing in a sigh of relief, she turned the car into Fred's driveway. He was also in the field, so Lacy and the children walked out to him. He agreed to answer her questions and to help her with the motor crank.

"I'll look forward to seeing your article in the paper." He smiled as she put the car in gear.

The last farm on her list was Tim Van Kley. He lived on the other side of town, so Lacy drove down Main Street and followed the road to the north past the mayor's house. When she turned the last corner, chaos met her eyes. Cows ran as a black mass in her direction, bellowing and bawling as they came.

Lacy screamed and her mind went blank. Conrad hadn't tutored her for a stampede. Weakness claimed her arms and legs. She turned the wheel. The car swerved sharply to the side, but it didn't do what she expected it to. Instead of using all four of its wheels to carry her and the children along the shoulder of the road, it tumbled into the ditch. Lacy rolled around and around, struck her head, and melted into an ocean of blackness.

28

Conrad unloaded the stack of boxes he'd brought with him to his new house. The absence of his children on this Saturday afternoon gave him free time to get started on the mammoth task of hauling his entire life out to the orchard.

Furniture, clothing, pots and pans, and everything else that comprised a home would have to get transported over the coming days. Nick had offered to help him with the sale of the house in town, so Conrad had a little time to make the move, but not much. Whomever bought his house would want to settle in before the weather turned to winter. Conrad felt the same way. He wanted to get his family moved before the snow fell, if possible, and before the holidays arrived. If he could have Markus and Betje used to a new place in time to enjoy Christmas, the transition would go much easier for him.

The last time he'd spent Christmas Day in this house was the night Angelien died. The reality of moving here at this time of year brought with it the burden of facing his past. He'd loved and he'd lost. Could he pick up and move on in the same place with his children and maybe even a new wife? He'd give it his best effort, but only time would tell.

He opened a box of ledgers and other supplies he'd brought from town and took the first steps into converting a downstairs room into his office.

Pounding came on the front door. "Conrad! Hey, Conrad. Are you here?"

The shouting jerked him to attention. He raced from the room and tripped on the hall rug.

"Conrad!" The shouting continued.

"I'm coming!" He shouted as he got back on his feet. They grew heavy, carrying him in slow motion. He couldn't make them move fast enough.

The pounding on the door stopped, but the throbbing in Conrad's head had just begun. He fumbled with the doorknob. It slipped through his fingers and wouldn't turn. "What is it?"

"Lacy Jones had an accident!" The visitor yelled.

Conrad managed to turn the knob and then he yanked the door open.

Tim Van Kley stared him in the face.

"What?" Had he heard correctly? Lacy in an accident? Surely one of them had this wrong.

"You're a tough guy to track down. I went to your house in town first, but when I didn't find you there, I went to your brother's and then the Pastor's to see if anyone knew where you were. Logan said you might be here working." Tim ran his hand through his hair. "I towed your car out of the ditch. It's in pretty bad shape. You might want to come get it and look it over. Not sure you can drive it."

His car? Had Lacy been in an accident with it? A tremor shook his knees.

"Lacy and your kids are at my house. The doctor is there too. I fetched him on my way to find you." Tim shifted his weight from one foot to the other.

His kids? Did Tim mean that they'd been hurt in the accident? If the car was so damaged he couldn't drive it, then how serious was their condition?

"What ... how bad ..." The shock stole his breath and his speech.

"Not sure. I think I heard the doctor say one of them had a broken arm, but I don't know."

Broken bones? What if the injuries were worse and the doctor was just now discovering the extent of them?

"And Lacy ... what about ... how much..." The tremble in his lip made speaking nearly impossible. But he had to know.

Tim dipped his head as a somber expression crossed his face. "I pulled her from the car unconscious."

Conrad's eyes widened and his heart pounded. "Does that mean ..."

"She was breathing when I left the house." Tim's voice wavered.

An ache grew in Conrad's throat. If Lacy ... but he couldn't think of it. He covered his face with his hands.

"Come with me and see for yourself." Tim's voice had fallen from the high-pitched yell to a whisper.

Conrad nodded, closed the door behind him, and followed Tim to his wagon.

As they traveled, Conrad's thoughts shifted away from the wagon he'd left half-filled with items for his move and the unfinished rearranging of the parlor-turned-office. His mind raced ahead to the scene unfolding on Tim's farm. He pictured his children lying in borrowed beds suffering in pain. The word *unconscious* beat a steady rhythm through his mind and in his heart. Lacy was injured. How badly? Where on her head had she received a blow? How had it happened? So many questions for which he had no answers. Tim drove too slowly. Conrad had to get there now.

"This is the spot where the accident happened. You can see

the tire marks going off the road right here." Tim pointed to the tracks that veered through the shoulder.

"Stop a second, Tim. I see something in the grass." Conrad held up his hand as a signal to the driver.

Tim heeded and brought his team to a stop. On the opposite bank, a sheet of paper fluttered. He snatched it up and glanced at it. Notes about Dan's harvest covered the page in Lacy's neat handwriting. This must be one of the pages to the article she was writing for the newspaper.

He looked around. Were any more pieces of paper caught in the grass? One waved at him from the fence row. Another had gotten snagged in a bush. Conrad collected them and returned to the wagon.

"Ready to keep going?" Tim asked.

Conrad nodded. The best he could, he smoothed the wrinkles and the punctures from the papers. They shone bright and white like and affirmation that the people he cared about were resting comfortably and safely. But he wouldn't be at ease until he knew if this was really the truth.

Tim turned into his driveway. Along the side sat a twisted, dented Ford car.

"There's your car." Tim pointed at the wreck.

Conrad didn't recognize it. The car he drove was shiny and sleek. This car appeared damaged beyond repair.

Before Tim parked his wagon, Conrad climbed over the wheel and leaped to the ground. He took off for the house on a run.

Tim's wife Rebecca met him at the door.

"Follow me." She led him through the kitchen and up the stairs to the first bedroom.

Betje lay on the bed.

Conrad's heart lurched at the sight of her. A bandage covered one cheek and wrapped over her chin.

"Daddy," Betje said in a weak voice.

Conrad went down on his knees next to her. "Sweetheart, are you all right? What happened?"

"Doctor Matt says I have cuts on my face. He gave me some stitches. Lacy drove your car off the road, Daddy. We rolled around and around. It was kind of fun, but scary. Especially when Lacy lay limp and sleeping in the grass. I couldn't help her. Neither could Markus. His arm hurt him a lot. Lots of cows were going by and then one of those loud tractors. The man driving turned around and helped us come here." Betje yawned while Conrad stroked her hair. "How are Markus and Lacy?"

"I haven't seen them yet, but I'll go now and check on them. How does that sound?"

Betje smiled as much as the bandages allowed.

Conrad stood. "You get some rest. I'll come back later to see you."

Betje closed her eyes and Conrad turned to follow Tim's wife to the next room.

Markus lay on the bed. Dr. Kaldenberg stood nearby smoothing white plaster over the right arm.

"Hi, Dad." Markus looked up at him.

"Got a broken arm, I see." Conrad pointed to the doctor's work.

"Yeah. Banged it on the car door when we rolled in the ditch. It hurt a lot, but it's better now." Markus attempted a smile, but it quickly faded.

Conrad tousled his hair. "You were very brave, and I'm glad to see you aren't hurt any worse."

"Can't wait to hear what Earl and Chris say when they see my cast. Burt's been wanting to have one, but I beat him to it." Markus's smile lasted this time.

Dr. Kaldenberg emitted a chuckle.

Conrad sucked in a breath. "Don't worry about Burt. Just get better, all right?"

Markus glanced away and watched the doctor.

"I'll come back to check on you after the doctor has finished." Conrad patted Markus's head.

"You'll find Miss Jones in the room across the hall," Dr. Kaldenberg said.

Conrad's mouth went dry. "How ... how ... is she?"

"Alive." The doctor glanced at him. "But still unconscious. When you go in there, speak to her. Say her name. Maybe now that you are here, she'll start to wake up."

Conrad took the advice with him to Lacy's room. She lay on the sheets limp and frail. A bandage covered her forehead as well as the top of her head. Her golden hair flowed from under it, around her face, and onto the pillow.

He eased into a chair nearby. "Lacy?" His voice trembled. "Lacy, my love, it's me, Conrad."

She mumbled and moved her head to the side.

He reached for her hand and caressed it between both of his. "Talk to me, Lacy. Keep trying."

Another mumble came. She blinked her eyes and then groaned.

He locked his attention onto her face. She knew he was there and wanted to let him know. He watched as he held her hand.

"Car." The word floated from her lips.

"I saw it. You were in an accident. Do you remember?"

Lacy groaned. "So ..." She inhaled a deep breath. "Sorry." A tear trickled from the corner of her eye.

Conrad's heart constricted as he wiped it away. "Don't worry about the car. I'm just glad that you are all right. The car can be replaced. You and Nick like to remind me that I'm wealthy enough to buy any car I want."

She blinked as a smile tugged at her mouth.

His eyes misted. "Come back to me, Lacy, my love. I'm a lonely old man who just bought a huge house. While Markus and Betje were with you, I spent the afternoon moving items from my office out to the orchard."

She pressed his hand and mumbled.

He leaned closer. "I want to fill that house with you. Your photos. My frames and furniture. Our family."

"Me ... me too." She rolled her head to the side and fluttered her lashes over heavy lids.

His heart swelled. "This isn't a fair proposal. You should have the chance to say yes to me when you are feeling well, and your mind has healed. But know that I will ask."

In a clumsy movement, Lacy tugged her hand free of his grasp and brushed her fingers over his lips.

Her request required very little imagination for him to arrive at an accurate interpretation. He moved slow, giving her plenty of time to comprehend what was happening. But she was awake enough to participate in the tender kiss he laid upon her lips.

She probably would have allowed him to stay in that position for quite a long time, but a problem arose. The door opened, and Dr. Kaldenberg, followed by Tim and his wife, Logan, Karen, Nick, and Hannah entered the room.

Heat infused Conrad's face and he pulled away. "She's waking up." He cleared his throat.

Karen came to the side of the bed. "Lacy?"

Lacy's lashes fluttered, but her eyes stayed open.

"We were so worried about you, dear. How are you feeling?" Karen bent over her.

"Headache." The word crossed Lacy's lips.

Dr. Kaldenberg turned to Rebecca. "Get a glass of water."

She nodded and left.

Logan and Nick came over to Conrad while Hannah joined Karen in talking to Lacy. Even though he carried on a conversation with the other men, Conrad heard Lacy's mumbles. The words *cows, Markus,* and *Betje* emerged from the mutters.

Rebecca returned and gave the glass of water to the doctor. He pulled a white tablet from his bag and came to the bed.

"Lift her head and support it with your hand," the doctor said to Conrad.

Conrad stood and followed directions. Lacy swallowed the pill and then Conrad eased her head onto the pillow.

"That should help. I'll give her a second one in the morning if she needs it." Dr. Kaldenberg retrieved his bag. "My work is done here for today. I'll check up on everyone when I come in the morning."

When he left, Conrad glanced at Tim. "How did the accident happen?"

"The best I can tell, our neighbor was moving his herd of cattle from one pasture to another across the road. They must have spooked and gone running. I saw him and a group of helpers rounding them up near the site of Lacy's accident."

Conrad gulped. Lacy must have been so scared in those moments before she left the road. When she woke up, he'd talk with her about it.

"You're welcome to have supper with us and spend the night," Rebecca said to Conrad.

"Thanks. I'll accept that offer." He smiled.

All the visitors went across the hall to see Markus, leaving Conrad alone with Lacy once more.

She turned to him and opened her eyes. "Glad you're … here."

"So am I. I'll eat supper and then come back. Even if you're sleeping, I'll be here."

She smiled, and then her eyes slid shut. The doctor's medication had started to work.

"Good night, Lacy, my love." He bent and placed a kiss on her cheek.

After checking on Markus and Betje once more, he went downstairs to join Tim and Rebecca for the evening meal.

29

Lacy lay on her back, staring at the ceiling. Early rays of sunshine spread over the room. The smell of cooking sausages wafted through the air. Was she dreaming? Had Conrad really been there, calling her Lacy, my love, kissing her, and using the word *proposal?* She turned her head in a slow, careful movement.

Conrad dozed in the chair. His legs stretched out in front of him, one crossed over the other at the ankle. He looked comfortable and relaxed. She turned her head to its original position and watched the sunrise lighten the room.

Had he been there all night? Why didn't she remember? She felt along the side of her face behind her ear. A few tender places remained, but they were much better than they had been last night. Closing her eyes, she allowed her mind to spin back to yesterday. She'd been on a ride in the country with Markus and Betje driving Conrad's car.

The car! Where was it? Had her worst fear of wrecking it happened? Is that why she was in this strange room? And what about the children? What had happened to them? Terror pierced her stomach.

"Conrad." She reached out and touched his arm.

He roused and blinked. Then he smiled at her. "Good morning. You're awake."

"Markus and Betje. Where are they?" She held her breath.

Conrad took her hand and held it between both of his own. "There are here at the Van Kley farm too. Markus has a broken arm and Betje has some cuts on her face, but they will be fine. They'll probably be ready to go home today and back to school tomorrow."

Lacy closed her eyes and exhaled. Such good news.

"How are you feeling?" Conrad leaned forward.

"Better. My headache is nearly gone."

He smoothed a strand of hair from her forehead. "Good to hear. Can you remember anything from yesterday?"

"Cows in the road. I don't know why they were there." Her heart pounded as those last scary moments she spent on the road came to her mind.

"Tim said the neighbor was moving his herd of cattle to another pasture when they got away and took off down the road."

Lacy frowned. Conrad's description made sense, but the name Tim stuck in her mind. She turned to him. "Tim? Do you mean Tim Van Kley?"

Conrad nodded. "That's right. You're staying at his house."

Pieces of her shattered Saturday afternoon fell back into place. "But I still need to interview him. My article is due to the newspaper office Monday morning. Where is Tim? Where are the notes I made on the other farmers?" Lacy pushed against the bed in an effort to sit up.

"Easy." Conrad chuckled and laid his hand on her arm. "Tim's probably out choring. I'll ask if he can talk with you when he comes in for breakfast."

Lacy relaxed, but the article stayed on her mind. How

would she ever get it completed on time if she still lay in a borrowed bed?

Conrad stood and walked to the chest of drawers. "I found these in the ditch. They look like pages of notes for your article." He handed her two sheets of dirty, wrinkled paper.

She scanned them. "Yes, they are. My other notes were in the car. Could you look for them and bring them to me if you find them?" She glanced at Conrad.

"I'll go now." He left the room.

Lacy closed her eyes. Fretting over Markus, Betje, and her unfinished article made her tired.

Conrad returned with Dr. Kaldenberg. He placed a folder on the bed as the doctor held a stethoscope to her chest.

"Pulse is good," he said after listening to her heart. He pressed on various places around her head. "How's the headache this morning?"

"Almost gone."

"Good. The medication helped you." He straightened. "I'll give you another pill to take this afternoon, but you shouldn't be moved until you can sleep without the pain medication. I'll see how your night goes tonight, and maybe you can go back to your own home tomorrow."

Tomorrow! But her article was due at the newspaper office tomorrow.

"Do your best to rest. My wife and I are going to church this morning, and then I'll come later this afternoon to check on you." Dr. Kaldenberg closed his bag. "Have a good day."

When the doctor left, Lacy reached for her folder. Inside, she found her collection of notes. With the pages Conrad had found, her information was complete. If she could get her interview of Mr. Van Kley finished, she'd write up a draft. The article may not get typed if the Van Kleys didn't own a typewriter. But then Jake might not accept it for publication. Her stomach tightened. She had to get this article completed and typed by tomorrow.

Rebecca entered the room with a tray. "Here's some breakfast for you, Lacy. How are you feeling this morning?"

"Better." Lacy eyes the oatmeal, sausage, and cup of coffee sending up tendrils of steam. Her stomach growled, reminding her of the meal she'd missed last night.

Rebecca set the tray down, helped Lacy sit up, and spoke to Conrad. "You're welcome to join us downstairs. The doctor sent the children down. They're looking for you." She settled the tray of food on Lacy's lap.

"I'll be right there." Conrad pressed a kiss to Lacy's forehead. "I'm going to eat breakfast and check on Markus and Betje. Then I'll come back. As soon as you feel ready, we need to talk."

Conrad's words sent little fissures of pain through her midsection. Was he upset about the car? Maybe he was waiting for the right time to express his anger. Or what about that dream she had? Did she dare to hope that the words she'd heard and the kiss she'd felt were real? Maybe Conrad wanted to continue that conversation. She ate her breakfast in the quiet, waiting and thoughtful.

Clatters and thuds from downstairs indicated the family finished their meal and were preparing to leave for church. Soon the house fell silent except for the occasional murmur of voices. Those voices belonged to Conrad and his children. Their footsteps sounded on the stairs, and then they entered the room.

"How are you?" Betje came to the bed.

"I feel well now that I've had a good breakfast." Lacy traced a finger over Betje's bandaged cheek. "Your dad said you have cuts on your face."

The little girl shrugged. "I don't even feel them anymore. Wish I didn't have to wear the bandage."

"Keep it on until the doctor says you can take it off," Conrad said in a stern voice.

"How about you, Markus? Is it true that you have a broken arm?" Lacy asked.

"See my cast?" He proudly held it up.

"He can't wait to show his friends." Conrad tousled Markus's hair.

"I'm so glad both of you weren't injured any worse," Lacy said.

"Why don't the two of you go across the hall and play with those toys we found? I want to talk to Lacy." Conrad pointed at the door. He sat on the edge of the bed as Markus and Betje followed his instruction.

Lacy's stomach tightened. The moment of conflict had arrived. "I'm so sorry about the car. I didn't mean to wreck it. The whole day, I drove as carefully as I possibly could."

Conrad picked up her hand and looked into her eyes. "I'm not worried about the car. Do you remember? I told you last night that I have the money to replace it with any car I want." He smiled at her and then grew serious. "When I received word that you had been in an accident, I got scared. More scared than I'd been since the night ... since the night Angelien died. While you slept, the thought stayed on my mind that I'd lose my wife and another child all over again. I don't want another day to go by without knowing that you're here, and you'll always be with me." His eyes glistened.

Lacy's head spun as another headache pounded in her temples. "What are you saying?"

Conrad pressed her hand. "Marry me, Lacy. I want you to come home with me as my wife, and as the mother of my children. I know the timing of my proposal isn't fair. You deserve to have this happen to you when you are well and whole. I wish I could hold it in and wait, but—"

Lacy had heard enough. She settled her lips on his, cutting

off his words.

Several moments passed before he pulled back. "Is that a yes?"

Lacy nodded. "I love you, Conrad. I have ever since I helped you with your booth at the school carnival. I didn't understand at the time the man of worth that you are, but I know now."

He brushed her cheek with his thumb. "I love you, too, Lacy. I always will."

Tears smarted in her eyes as Conrad leaned in for another kiss. His lips on hers sealed their lives together. He pulled away and looked into her eyes. "I'm going to get Markus and Betje so we can tell them."

He hastened out of the room and soon returned with the children. "Markus and Betje, Lacy and I have something very important to tell you." He settled into the chair and faced them. "I have asked Lacy to marry me, and she has accepted. This means Lacy will be your mother."

Markus's eyes brightened. "She'll cook for me?"

"And she'll read to me?" Betje smiled.

"Yes, and much more, I'm sure." Conrad chuckled. "I'll get us moved to our new house this week. When Lacy and I marry, we'll live there together. How would you like that?"

The children responded with excitement as warmth spread through Lacy. Conrad looked the happiest that she had ever seen him. Markus and Betje came to the bed to share hugs with her. Everyone laughed and talked until the Van Kleys returned. Rebecca called Conrad and his children downstairs for the noon meal.

"I'll be right back." Conrad smiled at Lacy and squeezed her shoulder.

"When you go down, could you please ask Mr. Van Kley if he has time to come to my room? I still need to interview him." Lacy's pulse sped up. So much work must still get done on her article.

Conrad nodded. "I'll ask."

When he left, Lacy leaned against her pillows. She'd close her eyes for a few moments of rest. This morning had been exciting but exhausting. She awoke when Conrad returned. He brought a tray of food and Mr. Van Kley with him.

"Here you go. Rebecca prepared a lunch for you." Conrad sat the tray across Lacy's lap.

"We can talk while you eat." Mr. Van Kley settled into the chair.

Lacy asked him the same questions she'd asked the other farmers and took notes in between bites of food. They finished the interview and then everyone left so that Lacy could rest. She slept far into the afternoon. When she awoke, visitors were waiting to see her.

"Conrad took Markus and Betje home," Mrs. De Witt said. "The doctor has been here, and he gave them permission to go. He also left another dose of pain medication for you. Do you need it?"

Lacy shook her head. "I feel well after my nap. I want to try to sleep tonight without it."

Mrs. De Witt glanced at her husband. "Logan and I have been talking about where you should go, and we'd like for you to come stay with us."

Not return to her apartment? But all of her things were there. It allowed her to live independently, and it gave her a peaceful little corner of the world she could call her own.

"What about my job?" If she couldn't manage living on her own, then maybe the doctor would say she wasn't well enough to work.

"I'm sure you can keep your job. Maybe Eva will work with you to adjust your hours for shorter days until you are recovered." Mrs. De Witt said.

She didn't want shorter days, and she didn't want to leave her apartment. But she'd agreed to marry Conrad. If she lived at the orchard with him, she'd have no use for her apartment. Maybe she'd have to quit working too. She hadn't thought of any of this. How much change would marriage to Conrad mean for her?

"Let me talk it over with Conrad. We are engaged, so I don't want to decide until he's had a chance to hear the plan."

Mrs. De Witt's eyes grew large. "Engaged! Congratulations."

"When did this happen?" Mr. De Witt asked. He looked as excited as his wife.

"Last night after I'd been in the accident. He asked if I would marry him, and I said yes."

"I'm so happy for both of you." Mr. De Witt smiled.

They talked of the accident, of the twins and Sara, and of Markus and Betje. Rebecca served her another meal, and then everyone left so that Lacy could prepare to go to sleep for the night. Her head throbbed, but she didn't take any medicine. The night ahead would be the test to find out if she could leave in the morning or if she had to stay with the neighbors another day.

She awoke twice in the night with a throbbing head but returned to sleep each time. In the morning, her head still pounded. She'd have to tell the doctor, but then he might detain her and make her stay.

He arrived mid-morning and gave her an examination. "If you have assistance at home, you can return to your apartment."

"Mrs. De Witt asked me to stay with her." If moving to someone else's house was a sufficient solution, the doctor might let her go. The article was due today. She had to find a way to type it and turn it in.

"That should work well. You'll only have to stay with them for three or four days, long enough for your headache to completely subside. Then you may go back to your apartment."

Lacy nodded. She could live with that plan, especially since it meant returning to independence within the week.

"What about my job at the dress shop?" She asked.

"Consider taking the same amount of time off. You should nap in the afternoons."

"I'll talk to Eva. I'm sure she'll understand." A call from the De Witt's telephone should take care of the situation, but how she disliked the idea of missing work, even for a day.

"Would you like for me to stop by the parsonage and let them know?" The doctor stood.

"Please tell Conrad too."

Dr. Kaldenberg smiled. "I'll let him know."

By noon, Conrad and the De Witts had Lacy moved into town. She rested comfortable in the parsonage's spare room. Conrad promised to come see her that evening. In the meantime, she had some work to do.

"My article is due at the newspaper office today and it still must be typed. Could I please use your typewriter?" she asked Mr. De Witt.

"I'd bring it over for you, but it's heavy. How about I take your notes with me to my study and type them up for you? I can even deliver it to the newspaper office of you like. I have to make a call out that direction later this afternoon."

Lacy's jaw dropped. She hadn't expected him or anyone else to do so much for her. But what a relief it was to know that her article would be complete and turned in on time. She nodded her consent.

Mr. De Witt gathered up her notes and left the house. The project was now out of her hands. In a few days, the article she'd collected information for and written herself would appear in the newspaper. Official, professional. Hers.

The door closed giving Lacy time alone to rest. But her mind didn't immediately drift to sleep. She lay there thinking, remembering, and deciding. Conrad's words from the day of their picnic whispered in her mind. *Hold the pose.* He'd been talking of her character, and also of the things he loved about her.

Holding the pose meant freedom. She'd already accomplished that by living on her own, holding a job, and learning to drive.

But there were more layers to Conrad's statement than freedom. Holding the pose also meant redefining. Her parents and her brother defined her as the sickly child who needed others to take care of her. The students she'd gone to school with defined her as slow and unintelligent. Boys had teased her. Girls passed her up in spelling bees and test scores.

But here in Oswell City, she'd discovered a new identity. Conrad defined her as loveable, creative, and valuable. Her friends defined her as capable and accomplished. Lacy hadn't been sick the entire time she'd lived here, and she'd discovered success writing for the newspaper. Sickly and stupid no longer described who she was.

Lacy Jones held a new pose. This one was a pose of believing that she was valuable, not only in this new town, but also to God. He'd made her who she was, with the limitations as well as the strengths. Lacy could accomplish anything she wanted, be whomever she wanted to be, and go any direction she chose. She had value and worth. She'd stand on that truth.

For the rest of her life, she'd hold that pose. Reaching a hand to the bookcase near the bed, she picked up her little brown camera and studied it. The small box had led her, shaped her, and brought her into a relationship with Conrad. He was the creator of Angel Frames, and he'd asked her to share her life with him. Memories of times they'd spent together filled her mind, each one its own snapshot, and linked together like pictures in her mind showing to her, and proving to her the good reasons she had for holding the pose.

30

"You have a visitor." Mrs. De Witt came to Lacy's room on Monday afternoon.

Groggy from a recent nap, Lacy rubbed her eyes and scooted to a seated position.

Rose entered. The sight of her brought Lacy fully awake. Other than a quick greeting at church on Sunday mornings, her best friend hadn't spent time with her in several weeks.

"Come in." Lacy pointed to the rocking chair near the bookshelf.

Rose ventured into the room, sat down, and stared at Lacy. "I'm sorry about your accident. Do you still have pain?"

"Not too much. My nap helped." Lacy folded the covers down.

"Will you go back to work tomorrow?" Rose swayed with the rocking of her chair.

"Maybe not. Wednesday I might give it a try."

"How did it happen?"

"I was driving Conrad's car. He let me use it to collect information for my newspaper article. Both of his children were with me. A herd of cattle blocked the road. I tried to get around them but went in the ditch." Lacy rubbed her forehead.

"Were the children hurt?"

"One has a broken arm and the other has cuts on her face. They'll go back to school tomorrow."

"Wow. You were lucky." Rose paused the rocking chair and leaned back.

"Yes, we were." Lacy sat still as the silence grew.

Not her usual, outgoing self, Rose fumbled with her skirt, bunching it up and releasing it again.

"How is college?" Lacy asked.

Rose shrugged. "It's fine, but I don't like it very much. Classes are a lot harder than I thought they would be. Keeping up with all the studying is impossible."

"Don't you want to be a teacher? Remember why you came here," Lacy said.

Rose sighed. "Yeah. If it wasn't for Aunt Helen, I'd drop out. But she's giving me a place to live. If I quit college, I'd lose that."

"But, Rose!" Lacy failed to hide her horror. "This is what you've always wanted. You said coming here was your one big chance. You aren't going to throw it away, are you?"

Shock registered on Rose's face. "No. I'll finish the year, I guess. But it isn't any fun. The only good times I have are with Reggie and Cooper and my other friends."

"Are you still going out with them?" Lacy scowled.

"Yes ... I mean, no. Well, sometimes." Rose's cheeks turned red, and she scowled back at Lacy.

"I thought you said you wouldn't drink anymore." She failed to keep the hurt from her voice.

Rose rolled her eyes. "Why do my visits with you turn into fights? All I wanted to do was tell you how sorry I was about your accident. But you turned it into criticism of my other friends. I should never have come." Rose stood up. "Just get better, all right?"

"Don't leave." Lacy held her hand up. "We can find other things to talk about."

Rose peered at Lacy as if to gauge if she really meant what she said. With slow movements, Rose sat in the chair like danger lurked somewhere in the room.

"Tell me about your aunt. Conrad said she took a job at the hotel." Lacy fluffed her pillow.

"She did, and she likes it."

The tension crept back into the conversation as they fell silent. Maybe Lacy should have let Rose leave. But she didn't want this conflict between her and Rose any longer. If only she could find a way to reconcile with her friend.

Rose shifted her attention away from Lacy, opened her mouth, closed it, and then looked at Lacy again. "How much time do you spend with Conrad?"

There it was, the question that had been hanging between them for many weeks. This wasn't the way Lacy would've chosen to begin reconciliations, but since Rose had asked, Lacy must tell her the truth.

"Conrad asked to court me, and I accepted." Lacy spoke in a quiet voice.

Rose's gaze fell. "He's courting you? Does that mean he's made up his mind to not ... well, I mean, he won't ever ..." A tear slipped down her cheek.

Lacy's heart constricted. She'd never meant to hurt her friend. From the direction her conversation with Conrad took yesterday, there was no longer any chance for Rose to gain his affections. She needed to know this even though the news may hurt her more.

"Rose, there's something you need to know." Lacy exhaled and leaned forward. "Yesterday, when Conrad came to see me, he ... um, he proposed. I'm engaged to marry him."

"Oh." The syllable popped from Rose's mouth like she'd been punched. The tears fell, and then she wept quietly.

Rose should have seen this coming. Why did she hold onto something that could never happen?

Memories tracked through Lacy's mind, one after another. She and Rose had stuck by each other through high school, and through their journey to Oswell City. But their friendship fell apart. Was Conrad the true reason, or was some other intrusion responsible for the breakdown?

Conrad's words, *hold the pose*, came to mind again. Had the redefinition happening in Lacy's life cost her Rose's friendship? Lacy had held the pose of achieving freedom and believing in her own worth. By standing strong, Lacy had caused the world around her to shift.

She handed Rose a handkerchief. Rose accepted it and wiped her eyes. A new thought struck Lacy. Had Rose ever learned how to hold her own pose? Did she know of her own worth, of her great potential, or had she allowed her father's drinking and her college friends to define her?

"Rose." Lacy rested a hand on her shoulder. "You don't need Conrad or anyone else to make you happy. You have value in God's eyes. He will show you what to do about college and the people you should have in your life."

Rose sniffled. "Conrad is different from anyone I've ever met. He's a gentleman. He cares about his family, and he made me feel special whenever I was around him. But I've lost that to you, my best friend." Her voice broke.

At least Rose still called Lacy her best friend. But the hurt of Rose's response outweighed the comfort Lacy found in it. In the moment when she should be receiving well wishes from her friend, Lacy got instead the blame for Rose's hardships. It wasn't fair.

Lacy stiffened. She wanted nothing more than to stomp out of the room and leave Rose alone in her misery. But a display of anger would solve nothing.

A tap came on the door, and it opened. Mrs. De Witt stepped in. "Girls, Eva is here to talk to Lacy."

"I'd better go." Rose sucked in a long draft of air and stood. "Hope you get to feeling better." She offered a tight smile and left the room.

Eva came in. She visited with Lacy about her job, agreeing that waiting two more days for Lacy to return to work was a wise plan.

When she left, Mrs. De Witt served the evening meal. Lacy ventured out of bed and joined the family at the table. A small amount of dizziness accompanied Lacy's movements. After the food was gone and the dishes cleared away, Lacy stayed in the parlor visiting with Mr. and Mrs. De Witt and watching the children play. Another visitor arrived. This one was Conrad. He entered the parlor and took a seat next to Lacy on the sofa.

"I left Markus in charge for a while so that I could check on you," he said.

In a matter of minutes, the room was vacated as Mr. and Mrs. De Witt moved their family upstairs.

Conrad picked up her hand and slipped a smooth band onto one of her fingers. "I bought this today so that you would have an engagement ring to wear."

Lacy held her hand up to watch the sparkly diamond. "It's beautiful. Thank you, Conrad."

THE RING SPARKLED on her finger as Lacy returned to work and went about her daily life. The headaches wore off, and in their place, a renewed supply of energy rushed in.

She reveled in this happy life she lived, working at her job, enjoying evenings with the De Witt family, and preparing to marry Conrad. The sun shone on Lacy until Saturday, when the mail arrived.

"Logan was at the post office and checked your box when he got our mail. He found this letter for you." Mrs. De Witt handed her an envelope postmarked Silver Grove.

Lacy tore it open. The page that spilled out contained a letter from her mother. It read

Dear Lacy.

Your father and I were sad to hear the news of your car accident. We found out from Amelia Harper when she received a call from her daughter Rose. We wish you would have called us, but we understand why you didn't. You probably don't feel well from all your headaches.

Your father and I are coming to Oswell City to get you. Grandma and Grandpa are coming, too, since they are helping us pay for the trip. We want to bring you back home so that I can take care of you and help you recover.

Look for us next weekend. With the Thanksgiving holiday on Thursday, we have to stay around here for our Jones family gathering, but then we are coming straight to Oswell City.

See you soon.
Love,
Mama

Lacy's eyes grew round as a host of emotions swirled through her. Dad and Mama were coming. So were her grandparents. She'd never hold out against such a crew. They'd see her weakened condition and find her living at the parsonage. No time would get wasted removing her possessions from her apartment and loading them, along with Lacy, onto the train bound for Silver Grove.

She must do something about this, but what?

Lacy scrambled to the kitchen in search of Mrs. De Witt. "I have to find Conrad."

"He's moving the rest of his furniture to the orchard. Logan is helping him. Can you wait until supper? Conrad is coming for the meal." Mrs. De Witt's hands fluttered as she wiped them on a towel.

Lacy went to her room. After a moment of deep thinking, she put on her hat and coat. "I'm going to my apartment for a little while."

"Be careful, dear. You still tire easily." Mrs. De Witt's motherly admonishment followed Lacy out the door.

She might tire, but tomorrow was Sunday, giving her plenty of time to rest. Following the sidewalk down Main Street, Lacy walked swiftly. Her apartment had set empty for a week, and she intended to clean it. Polished wood, fluffed pillows, and fresh food in the ice box should send the message that she could still live on her own in complete charge of herself.

By the time she returned to the parsonage, Pastor Logan and Conrad were there. Lacy removed her coat, accepted a kiss on the cheek from Conrad, and helped Mrs. De Witt set the table. She tried her best to conceal her worry during the meal, but it must have shown because Conrad sent questioning glances her direction while they ate.

"What's wrong?" he asked. They shared the parlor while Pastor Logan helped his wife with the dishes.

"Read this." Lacy pulled her mother's letter from the pocket where she'd kept it ever since it had arrived.

Conrad scanned the page. A deep furrow formed on his brow.

"I can't let them take me back with them. But they know I've been staying at the parsonage, and they've heard about the headaches. I'll have to leave. Nothing will work to keep that from happening." Lacy's voice trembled.

"Marry me, Lacy." Conrad dropped the letter and held both of her hands in his.

"I already said I would." Her voice rose in fear.

"What I mean is, marry me next week. You can't leave town if you're married." He grinned.

"Next week?"

"On Sunday. Right after the service. We'll ask everyone to stay so that Logan can perform the ceremony for us."

His words made her head spin. "That saves time sending invitations, but what about my dress? What would I do for a wedding gown?"

"Wear the one you had on the night I took you to the theater and dinner in Clear Brook. You look beautiful in it."

Wear the dress off the rack she'd bought with her first paycheck? That wasn't how a girl went about finding a wedding gown. But Conrad said he liked that dress. She liked it too. Maybe wearing it at her wedding wouldn't be too bad.

"Afterward, we'll have a nice cake from the bakery. I'm sure Mildred will help us out. She's done that for me many times."

"But the flowers. What about flowers?" Lacy's heart raced.

"Let's talk with Logan and Karen. They might have some good ideas." Conrad stood and brought Lacy with him to the kitchen.

"We'd like to get married next Sunday," he announced. "Logan, would you mind having a brief ceremony for us after the morning service?"

"It would be an honor." Pastor Logan smiled and shook Conrad's hand.

"Oh, Lacy. Congratulations! I'm so happy for you." Mrs. De Witt gave her a hug. "Do you have a gown? Next Sunday doesn't leave you much time to find a wedding dress."

"Conrad suggested that I wear the cream dress that I bought at Eva's." Her stomach tightened. Conrad might be the only one who thought that was a good idea.

"You'll look lovely." Mrs. De Witt's hands rested on Lacy's shoulders. "You'll need a veil. Wear mine. It will go nicely with that dress."

"What should I do about the flowers?" Her voice rose as yet another problem needed a solution.

"Hmm." Mrs. De Witt clasped her chin as she thought. "The gardens were finished long ago, so nothing is in season. We'll make a call to the florist in Clear Brook. I'm sure they can help us."

Lacy's heart pounded as Conrad and the De Witts continued to chat about the wedding service and the progress Conrad was making on his move to his new home.

She was getting married. Next week. What about her job, her apartment, and her involvement with the newspaper? She and Conrad still had some things to work out. But the most important matter was staying here in the town she called home. If setting an immediate date for her wedding helped her do that, then the other pieces of her life must adjust. The newspaper editor and the dress shop owner couldn't help her, but Conrad could. If she put her love for him first, everything else would fall into place.

Hiding a smile, Lacy listened to the conversation. Her family thought they were coming to get her and take her home, but they'd actually arrive just in time for a wedding.

31

"Do you have a copy of the newspaper?" Lacy asked Nick. She, along with the De Witt family had been invited to share the Thanksgiving holiday with the Van Drunen family. The doctor and his wife were there, adding to the boisterous warmth and fun of the occasion.

"It's on Nick's desk. Go get it for her." Hannah nudged her husband with her elbow.

"Jake said he planned to publish my article the week of Thanksgiving, so it should be in the paper." Lacy watched Nick leave the table.

"It's a good one. I read it." Nick returned and handed the paper to Lacy.

She unfolded it. "Right on the front page!" She never expected Jake to feature her article above the others, giving it the place of prominence.

"Nicely done. I'm proud of you," Mrs. De Witt said.

Lacy read through the article. All of the percentages and statistics the farmers had given her were accurate. So were the portions of the interviews she'd included. The direct quotes gave the story interest and even made it entertaining. Her chest swelled and her insides glowed.

"Jake will want to give you more assignments now that he knows of your talent." Nick pointed at the paper.

"I would enjoy that if ..." Lacy bit her lip and glanced at Conrad.

He shrugged. "I don't see why you can't keep writing for the paper after we're married. You can even keep your job helping Eva out a couple of days a week. Markus and Betje are both in school during the day. You'll have time to pursue your own interests."

This is why she loved him. Conrad didn't make demands on her. Instead, he championed her.

Her insides relaxed. She could be married while at the same time growing her talents and developing into the person she'd longed to become.

"Tell us all about your wedding plans." Hannah prompted.

Conrad and Lacy took turns sharing the details.

"I can see that Markus and Betje like you. I must confess that I've felt you were too young for Conrad," Hannah said.

"I am a lot younger than him, by at least twelve years."

"You'll fit well into our family, and I'm happy for both of you." Hannah smiled at Lacy and then at Conrad.

"Thanks, Hannah. That means a lot." Conrad's voice turned raspy as though deep feeling and even some tension lay behind this topic.

The children played together, and the men went to Nick's office. The women stayed with Lacy at the table talking about wedding plans. Hannah and Mrs. Kaldenberg helped Lacy solve the problem of flowers. A few fresh ones of Lacy's choice ordered from the florist would be incorporated into centerpieces and bouquets of evergreen boughs from Hannah's yard. Mrs. Kaldenberg would do the arranging.

Lacy felt well enough to return to her apartment, but with

the plans taking shape for the wedding on Sunday, Mrs. De Witt urged Lacy to stay with them.

"What about my apartment? It shouldn't stay empty. Perhaps it should go back to the Gouds," Lacy said as she sat with the De Witts in their parlor one evening.

"Keep paying rent on it until the end of the month and let your family stay in it while they're here," Mr. De Witt suggested.

"Good idea." Lacy nodded. "That will save them money."

On Saturday, Conrad came to the parsonage, picked Lacy up, and drove her to the train station.

"Ready?" He asked as he held her hand.

"No." She turned to him with a rueful smile. As she'd done in choosing the direction of her life and in her friendship with Rose, she'd once more hold the pose. Her past, the years she'd spent in Silver Grove, no longer defined her, and she must make her family understand that. Somehow. Lacy released a sigh.

Conrad glanced at her as he drove. "You'll pull through, Lacy, my love."

She smiled at the use of his nickname for her. Made up in a moment of deception, it spoke truth about her life. Conrad had helped to redefine her existence and give it value.

At the station, they met the train. When Lacy's relatives got off, she and Conrad stood together. Beneath the hugs and welcomes, resistance steeled her frame. Nothing these people could do or say would move her from this place, or from who she was.

"Mama, you've met Conrad." Lacy gestured to him, and he shook Mama's hand.

"Dad, Grandpa and Grandma, meet my fiancé, Conrad Van Drunen," Lacy said.

"Your what?" Mama's brows shot up while Dad frowned.

Grandma murmured, "Oh, my dear," with her fingers on her lips.

"Conrad is my fiancé. We are getting married on Sunday. You've all arrived just in time for the wedding ceremony." Lacy smiled.

"Oh! But ... you ..." Mama sputtered.

"Why didn't you tell us?" Dad scowled.

"There wasn't time. I'm telling you now." Lacy held her head high.

"Lacy!" Dad crossed his arms. "You haven't gone and done something shameful, now, have you?"

"No! It's not like that at all, Dad." Lacy couldn't keep the hurt from her voice. "Conrad has two children, and he is eager for them to have a mother." Her insides heated. Why did Dad have to believe the worst? Was this a tactic to try and separate her from Conrad, pressuring her to go home with him? Lacy drew in a deep breath and stood to her full height. She refused to let that happen.

"Come. You are staying in my apartment." Lacy turned on her heel.

"I brought a car. We can load up your luggage." Conrad's voice reached her ears. He'd borrowed Pastor Logan's car for the day.

"Your apartment? It's small. Will there be enough room for all of us?" Mama caught up to her and walked at her side.

"I'm staying at the parsonage until the wedding," Lacy informed her.

"Are you sure you should get married? You know you're back at the parsonage because of this accident. What if you can't run a household on your own? I'm not sure you're strong enough." Mama's worries poured onto the street as she walked along.

Lacy stopped and turned to Mama. So many words pressed on the back of her throat demanding to be said. She carefully chose the best ones. "Mama, I'm fine. I've fully recovered from the headaches. You don't need to worry about me."

"But—" Mama peered at her.

"No more on the subject. Please." Lacy held her hand up. "I'm glad you're here for our wedding. Don't spoil it with fears about my health."

Conrad drove by with the load of luggage filling the back seat and her father in the front. Grandpa and Grandma joined Lacy and Mama on the sidewalk.

"The apartment is down the street. Follow me." Lacy led the way and got everyone settled in.

Mrs. De Witt had invited the Jones family for supper, so as soon as Conrad had the car unloaded, he drove everyone to the parsonage. She expressed her pleasure at seeing Roy Jones again after all these years that had passed since the days she'd spent teaching school. Her enthusiasm helped ease the tension between Mama and Lacy.

Taking the seat next to Conrad, Lacy relied on his presence at her side for the strength to get through the meal. Grandma enjoyed hearing about the wedding plans, but Mama wore an expression through the evening that spoke of her disapproval and of her unwillingness to accept the fact that Lacy wasn't going back to Silver Grove with her.

Lacy's heart ached. If only Mama could relax. Lacy's health might once have been fragile, but she'd done as well as she ever had during these months in Oswell City. She could live alone, hold a job, and make friends. These questions had been answered. Now the time had come for her to move with new confidence into the reward of taking the risk of asking the questions in the first place. She'd discovered truths about herself that never would have been revealed if she'd stayed in Silver Grove dependent on others, and believing she was the stupid, sickly one without any hope of a future.

THE DAY of the wedding arrived. The Jones family filed into church with Lacy, Conrad, Markus, and Betje. Pastor Logan probably preached a meaningful sermon, but Lacy couldn't concentrate. The special event following this service distracted her.

Pastor Logan prayed to close his sermon and then he made an announcement. "After our last hymn, I invite you to please stay seated. We will be attending the wedding service of Conrad Van Drunen and Lacy Jones." He glanced in their direction. "Conrad, you and your brothers may go ahead to my study. I'll come get you when we're ready."

The organ started to play as Conrad left the pew. Nick and Dan stood to leave. So did Mrs. De Witt. As Lacy's attendant, she gave Lacy the cue to come with her to a room where the veil hung ready to wear.

In a matter of minutes, all was in order.

"They're ready for you." Lacy's brother poked his head in the door.

"Cal?" She couldn't believe her eyes. "You're really here!"

"Grandma sent me a telegram yesterday. I hopped on the fastest train and just now arrived." He gave her a hug. "Congratulations, little sis. I'm happy for you."

Cal had come, and just in time. He brought the perfect touch to her special day.

Mrs. De Witt handed her the bouquet of white roses and evergreen. Cal led her to her father and waited with him for her turn to go down the aisle. At the front of the church, he stepped aside to make room for Conrad.

Pastor Logan guided them through the vows, the exchange of rings, and the prayers that united them together as husband and wife. At the end of the service, Conrad led her to the back of the church where, amidst much celebration, they cut the first slices of cake.

"Picture time!" Jake called out.

Lacy went with Conrad to the corner with a nice background set up. Jake showed each of them where to stand and arranged Lacy's flowers and borrowed veil just right.

"Pictures!" Markus yelled and came running.

"Wait for me." Betje abandoned her plate of cake and followed her brother.

Markus threw his arms around Lacy's waist knocking her off balance and undoing the careful work Jake had done on her veil. "You're really our mother now, aren't you?" He looked up at her.

Betje did too, and her eyes glowed.

Lacy's eyes misted over, and she nodded. This poor, motherless girl and her brother finally had a mother.

"Children shouldn't be in a wedding picture. Get out of here." Conrad tilted his head toward the reception hall.

Lacy laughed. "Let them stay. We're a family now."

Ignoring their father, the children scrambled into place with giggles and quick pats to their clothing.

Jake stood behind the camera ready to click a photo. "Everyone, look this way. On the count of three."

She gave the camera a tiny smile, not allowing her full joy to radiate for the formal picture. This was a pose she'd be happy to hold for the rest of her life. Wife to Conrad. Mother to Markus and Betje. Free to live and serve in who she really was. Valuable to God in her talents, and even in her limitations.

"Now take one with just the two of us." Conrad instructed Jake. He shooed the children back to their cake and stepped closer to Lacy.

Jake took another picture. "For the newspaper," he announced with a happy look on his face.

The time had come to open gifts, so Lacy and Conrad took the seats near the table piled high with wrapped presents. A large package, in gold paper with a showy bow stood in the middle of the table. The tag attached to it bore the names of Gresham and Blaine. Lacy's insides glowed. Their ruse the night these men invited Conrad to dinner and a show must have been worthwhile.

Conrad came up beside her and pointed to the large gift. "I invited them to the wedding, but they had other plans this weekend. Mr. Blaine replied with a promise to come to town for another dinner with us very soon." The pride in his voice spoke to her of his vast sense of accomplishment in the friendship he'd discovered with Gresham and Blaine.

She smiled at him and sat down. Lacy opened the first gift, and Conrad the second. The church doors opened, and Rose walked in carrying a gift. She hadn't been in church that morning, most likely another in a long string of Sundays she'd skipped.

Lacy's heart ached as she watched her friend approach. The skin on Rose's face looked washed out and dark circles sunk the area under eyes. Had Rose been drinking again? Or had she stayed up late, maybe partying, with her college friends? Where was the Rose of their high school days? The cheery, happy-go-lucky girl of the past summer nudging Lacy on an adventure? She missed the girl she'd always known, who'd disappeared behind this sullen, defensive one.

Conrad spotted Rose and stood to shake her hand. "Hi, Miss Harper. Thank you for coming."

"This is for you." She thrust the gift into his grasp. The expression on her face told Lacy she couldn't decide if she should try to ignore the groom or turn on a smile in one last effort to flirt with him.

Lacy tightened her grip on a wad of wrapping paper ready to spring between her new husband and her old friend, should Rose attempt the flirting.

But she refrained. With a quick glance at Lacy, Rose said, "Congratulations," and went to talk to her aunt. Rose said no more to Lacy during the rest of the gift opening. Neither did she look in her direction or even acknowledge Lacy's presence.

Lacy's throat ached as she held back tears. Why did Rose have to come in and spoil a lovely day? She shouldn't think of her longtime friend in that way, but it was true. Sucking in a deep breath, she pushed the troublesome relationship from her mind. She wanted to make new memories today, not wallow in old hurts.

The last of the presents opened, Conrad called his children in preparation to leave. Mama, Dad, Cal, Grandpa and Grandma gathered around Lacy for hugs and to give well wishes.

"Come out to see our house tomorrow if you are still in town. Pastor Logan can give you directions," Lacy invited.

Dad nodded but didn't reply. Grandma was the one who showed enthusiasm. "I'd love to see your new home. We can change our plans and stay another day, can't we, Roy?" She peered at Dad.

He shifted his weight. "I suppose."

Lacy hid her sadness. Why weren't her parents and brother happier for her? If only they'd accept the choices she'd made. But she couldn't change them. All she could do was follow God's leading for her one life. That life was framing up to be a very happy one.

"Lacy." Her groom stood by the door calling her name. She went to meet him.

"We'll have you over for supper again soon." Mrs. De Witt and her husband stood at the front of the crowd of people waving as Conrad and Lacy drove away in Pastor Logan's car.

Markus and Betje had stayed behind at the church to spend the night with their cousins, so Conrad and Lacy traveled to the house in the orchard alone.

Conrad turned off the road and drove down the lane. He parked in front of the house and led her up the porch steps. Swinging the ornate wooden door wide open, he picked her up and carried her over the threshold.

In the stylish foyer of a home well-suited to the man of wealth Conrad was, he set her down. Holding her close, he whispered, "Welcome home, Lacy, my love."

This place of truth, of love, and of freedom attracted her as a destination she could inhabit forever. With Conrad's arms around her and their future glowing before them, Lacy knew that she truly had come home.

ABOUT THE AUTHOR

Michelle De Bruin lives in Iowa with her husband and two young adult sons. She has a bachelor's degree in Religion with a Christian Ministry emphasis, and in Music. Michelle serves as a Chaplain for Pella Regional Health Center. She has been a member of American Christian Fiction Writers (ACFW) since 2015. Michelle writes inspirational historical romance about people who live in rural communities. Characters that bring to life the delights of farm and small-town living, whispers of Dutch heritage, and Christian faith make Michelle's stories distinct. A romantic at heart, Michelle is always on the lookout for glimpses of God's love through the window of a good story.

You can learn more about Michelle by visiting her website: michelledebruin.com.

ALSO BY MICHELLE DE BRUIN

Coming Home to Mercy

Wealthy and sociable Margaret Millerson has always thought of her brother's Chicago mansion as her home. But when she receives the telephone call that her daughter has given birth to twins three weeks ahead of the expected due date, Margaret must leave her comfortable home, her family, and her friends to travel out of state. While she is helping her daughter care for the infants, Margaret becomes reacquainted with the town's doctor, Matthew Kaldenberg.

Dr. Matthew Kaldenberg stays busy caring for the health of the citizens of his small town. His profession offers him daily practice in defeating death, his greatest enemy. During the twenty years since losing his own wife and baby in childbirth, Matthew has saved his money for the purchase of a flying machine. But when Matthew takes Margaret for flights on his biplane, he learns that his dreams of rising above the griefs and losses of his past come with a cost. He doesn't want to lose the trust of the people he cares about most, or the chance at a relationship with Margaret.

Both Matthew and Margaret must make difficult decisions to hold on to the love they have discovered. Will Matthew's heart recover from sorrow? Will Margaret find her true home?

~

Hope for Tomorrow

When Logan De Witt learns of his father's sudden death, he returns home to the family's dairy farm. During his stay, he discovers his mother's struggle with finances and his younger sister's struggle with grief. Concern for his family presses Logan to make the difficult decision to leave his career as a pastor and stay on the farm. As a way to make some extra money, he agrees to board the teacher for their local school.

Karen Millerson arrives from Chicago ready to teach high school but her position is eliminated so she accepts the role of country school teacher. Eager to put her family's ugly past behind her, Karen begins a new career to replace the trust she lost in her own father who had been in ministry when she was a child.

Logan and Karen both sense a call from the Lord to serve him, but neither of them expected that one day they would do it together.

Can Karen learn to trust again? Will Logan lay aside his grief in exchange for God's purpose for his life?

~

Promise for Tomorrow

Living a life of faith isn't going the way Logan and Karen hoped until some special visitors arrive and offer them their future back.

Karen Millerson dreamed of teaching high school but now finds herself boarding with a farm family and teaching country school. She is engaged to marry Logan De Witt and is getting prepared to share in ministry with him. But when she gets blamed for the tragic fire at the school, Karen's future grows uncertain.

Logan De Witt is working to clear his family's name with the bank. But when he breaks his leg, hindering his ability to work the farm, Logan is faced with life-changing decisions. When his best friend can't offer the help he requested, can Logan find a way to care for his family and court Karen at the same time before his love for her destroys all of them?

~

Dreaming of Tomorrow

Popular and eligible, Logan De Witt must convince the women in town that he is engaged to be married. A quiet, simple ceremony is what he has in mind for his wedding day, but when the date and time of his bride's arrival is published in the newspaper, the whole town joins in the celebration proving to Logan and his new wife their sincere friendship and support. Added to the excitement of Logan's marriage is the question of what the congregation should do with the unexpected donation of an orchard.

Karen Millerson is counting the days until her long-distance engagement comes to an end and she may travel to Oswell City to marry Logan. More than anything, she wants to share in his life as a help and support, but keeping a house and finding her place in the community requires much more work than she ever expected.

Learn, laugh, and love with Karen and Logan as they start a new marriage and work together ministering to the citizens of their small town.

MORE HISTORICAL ROMANCE FROM SCRIVENINGS PRESS

Cowboy Cousins: A Novella Collection

by Molly Noble Bull, Kathleen L. Maher, and Kathi Macias

Lucy and the Lawman **by Molly Noble Bull:** While on a business trip to Colorado in 1890, Sheriff Caleb Caldwell stops to inform Miss Lucy Gordan and her widowed mother of property they inherited in Texas, land coveted by a rich and powerful man—willing to do anything to get his hands on what is rightfully theirs, and Caleb feels obligated to protect them. However, he cannot reveal his attraction for Lucy. To do so would mean disaster for all of them.

The Meddlesome Maverick **by Kathleen L. Maher:** A new job as a bronco buster on a Lincoln, Nebraska ranch offers Boyd Hastings a fresh start. Cured of romance after a kiss-and-tell flirt falsely accused him, he must flee his hometown and cousins who have been like brothers. Banjo picking for a music show would lure him to the big city, but an opinionated tomboy with a heart of gold makes grand plans for him. Can he trust a meddlesome maverick to steer him true, or will she lead him into a briar patch of trouble?

***A Panhandle Sunrise* by Kathi Macias:** Thirty-one year old Jake Matthews, newly appointed foreman of the Double Bar-J Ranch, is deeply attracted to the ranch owner's daughter, Anabelle, but he can't work up the nerve to approach her father, Jasper Floyd, and ask for permission to court her. But when tall, handsome, longtime Jasper-family friend, Clint Jordan, gets hired on, it seems Clint doesn't have the same insecurities and begins pursuing Anabelle immediately. Jake now accepts that his dreams of a life with Anabelle are hopeless —until a near life-and-death situation changes everything.

Flight of the Red-winged Blackbird

by Susan R. Lawrence

In 1932, Ruth Russo flees the farm where she arrived as an orphaned teenager and seeks refuge at Sisters of Mercy Home for unwed mothers. When the haven she hopes for becomes a place of tragedy, she flees again, and attempts to support herself in a culture of discrimination and a country burdened by the Great Depression.

Her days brighten when she reconnects with Jack, a friend from high school. But Jack is a budding lawyer, and she is a maid in his cousin's house. Will Ruth be able to lay down her burden of shame and accept love, not only from Jack, but also from God?

Wilderness Wife

by Delores Topliff

Marguerite Wadin MacKay believes her 17-year marriage to explorer Alex MacKay is strong-until his sudden fame destroys it. When he returns from a cross-Canada expedition, he announces their frontier marriage is void in Montréal where he plans to find a society wife-not one with native blood. Taking their son, MacKay sends Marguerite and their three daughters to a trading post where she lived as a child. Deeply shamed, she arrives in time to assist young Doctor John McLoughlin with a medical emergency.

Marguerite now lives only for her girls. When Fort William on Lake Superior opens a school, Marguerite moves there for her daughters' sake and rekindles her friendship with Doctor McLoughlin. When he declares his love, she dissuades him from a match harmful to his career. She's mixed blood and nine years older. But he will have no one else.

After abandonment, can a woman love again and fulfill a key role in North American History?

~

Love's Twisting Trail

by Betty Woods

Stampedes, wild animals, and renegade Comanches make a cattle drive dangerous for any man. The risks multiply when Charlotte Grimes goes up the trail disguised as Charlie, a fourteen year-old boy. She promised her dying father she'd save their ranch after her brother, Tobias, mismanages their money. To keep her vow, she rides the trail with the brother she can't trust.

David Shepherd needs one more successful drive to finish buying the ranch he's prayed for. He partners with Tobias to travel safely through Indian Territory. David detests the hateful way Tobias treats his younger brother, Charlie. He could easily love the boy like the brother he's always wanted. But what does he do when he discovers Charlie's secret? What kind of woman would do what she's done?

The trail takes an unexpected twist when Charlotte falls in love with David. She's afraid to tell him of her deception. Such a God-fearing, honest gentleman is bound to despise the kind of woman who dares to wear a man's trousers and venture on a cattle drive. Since her father left her half the ranch, she intends to continue working the land like any other man after she returns to Texas. David would never accept her as she is.

Choosing between keeping her promise to her father or being with the man she loves may put Charlotte's heart in more danger than any of the hazards on the trail can.

Scrivenings
PRESS
Quench your thirst for story.
www.ScriveningsPress.com

Made in the USA
Middletown, DE
20 June 2022